the RIVER runs ORANGE

A Meg Harris Mystery

R. J. Harlick

RendezVous Crime

Cover design: Vasiliki Lenis

Le Conseil des Arts du Canada Depuis 1957 — The Canada Council for the Arts Since 1957

We acknowledge the support of the Canada Council for the Arts for our publishing program.

We acknowledge the financial support of the Government of Canada through the Book Publishing Industry Development Program (BPIDP) for our publishing activities.

RendezVous Crime
an imprint of Napoleon & Company
Toronto, Ontario, Canada
www.napoleonandcompany.com

Printed in Canada on 100% recycled text stock

12 11 10 09 08   5 4 3 2 1

Library and Archives Canada Cataloguing in Publication

Harlick, R. J., date-
        The river runs orange / R.J. Harlick.

(A Meg Harris mystery)
ISBN 978-1-894917-62-9

        I. Title.   II. Series: Harlick, R. J., date- .   Meg Harris mystery.
PS8615.A74R59 2008   C813'.6   C2008-900030-7

AUTHOR'S NOTE:
The petition on page 102 is adapted from a petition presented by Kitigan Zibi Algonquin to the Canadian Museum of Civilization

For Jim

Acknowledgements

The idea for the plot of this Meg Harris mystery came from the dilemma that occurs, particularly in North America, when ancient human remains are discovered. The archeologists, believing they can help determine our origins, want to study them, whereas the indigenous people, believing they are their ancestors, want to return them to Mother Earth.

I would like to acknowledge the Kitigan Zibi Anishinabeg who petitioned the Canadian Museum of Civilization for the return of such remains and Dr. Jerome Cybulski, Dr. William Moss, Lois King and the Outaouais Historical Society, who provided insight into the archeological, prehistory and legal aspects. I also made use of the research work pertaining to Kennewick Man that James C. Chatters detailed in his book *Ancient Encounters.* Jay Morrison, who has canoed across Canada from the Atlantic to the Arctic Ocean, helped to ensure Meg's canoe got down the river. And of course I must thank Alex Brett, Barbara Fradkin and Judith Nasby and my editor, Allister Thompson, and publisher, Sylvia McConnell, for their critical advice. As always the support I receive from my sisters, Susan McLeod O'Reilly and Sally Miller, is greatly appreciated. And above all, the enduring support from my husband and fellow paddler, Jim, who canoed with me down the sometimes languid but more often swirling waters of the river that spawned this story, the Dumoine River, one of the last great untamed rivers of West Quebec.

The Meg Harris Series:

Death's Golden Whisper
Red Ice for a Shroud
The River Runs Orange

ONE

Our canoe raced towards the rock. "Left! Left!" I shouted above the rapids' roar.

I plunged my paddle deep into the froth and pulled. The canoe veered left and slipped past in a wave of foamy white.

Another rock reared its jagged head. But before I could warn Eric, who was paddling in the stern, he'd already responded and deftly steered us around this last obstacle. I searched downstream for the next set of rapids and thankfully saw nothing but smooth, free-flowing water. We could relax, for the moment.

I loosened my grip on the paddle and let out the breath I'd been holding since spotting the line of approaching white. The map had indicated Class II rapids with the fitting name of "Tight 'Round the Bend", the most difficult we'd encountered since my friend and lover Eric Odjik and I had begun this week-long whitewater venture down the DeMontigny River.

"We did it!" I shouted back to him, as the now familiar rush of adrenaline coursed through my veins.

"Don't celebrate yet, Miz Harris," he called back. "We still have 'Canoe Eater'."

"But you said we'd portage around it."

"That was at the start of this trip. Now I'm thinking after five days of running rapids, we're more than ready."

Eric's eyes twinkled under his floppy white hat as his dimples erupted on either side of the grin. The hot July sun highlighted the grey running through his thick black ponytail. The trip agreed with him. His face had lost the careworn creases that came from the demands of being Chief of the Migiskan Anishinabeg, or Fishhook People, a band of the Algonquin First Nation.

"We'll see," I replied. The knots in my stomach tightened, a feeling I was beginning to think normal, along with the dry mouth. The canoe continued to drift in the fast current. Another hundred metres downstream, the river suddenly ended. Beyond, rising mist.

"Bear Falls," Eric said. "We'll eddy in here and wait for Teht'aa." He steered us toward a patch of still water tucked behind a jumble of rocks. "Then we'll make for the portage."

I could see a yellow sign marking the trail about fifteen metres upriver from the falls.

"There's something special I want to show you on the other side of the portage," he added.

I stabbed the paddle into the liquid mirror as the canoe crossed the eddy line and turned us around to face upstream. Behind me the forest throbbed with the power of the falls.

"I hope it's a nice, soft place to sit. I'm sure I'll be ready for a rest. How long did you say this portage was?"

"Long enough. But what's at the end will be worth it."

"You going to tell me what it is?"

"Nope," he replied, which only served to sharpen my curiosity.

I grabbed onto an overhanging branch to hold us steady while we waited.

It was hard to imagine that less than a month ago I'd known nothing about prys, cross bows and draws. And now I was using these whitewater paddling techniques as if I'd been born to them.

It had started innocently enough. I'd asked Eric to teach me how to paddle whitewater. He'd obliged by taking me down the easy rapids of the Misanzi River that runs through the West Quebec reserve of the Migiskan. On the first trip down the five-kilometre stretch, we'd sideswiped several rocks, leaving behind streaks of red paint and managing to fill the bottom of the canoe with water from two-foot-high standing waves. On the next trip, we'd threaded our way easily between the rocks, avoided the standing waves altogether, and at the bottom of the run were as dry as when we'd started out, with most of the canoe's red paint intact.

After several more clean runs, Eric had declared me ready for real whitewater. Exuberant over my new prowess, I'd confidently agreed. Little did I know that this new challenge was to be filled with kilometre-long portages and Class II rapids that carried names like Keyhole and Snake, and of course the Class III horror, Canoe Eater, whose very name filled me with dread.

We'd flown in five days ago with Eric's canoe tied to a pontoon and our gear weighing down the rear of the floatplane. We'd landed on Lac DeMontigny, a remote lake on the southern edge of Quebec's vast LaVerendrye Park. It was the starting point of our planned seven-day descent down one of the ancient highways of the Algonquins to where it emptied into the Ottawa River. Reputedly named after one of the great eighteenth-century fur trading families, Eric said his people knew it as Wabadjiwan Sibi, meaning River of White Water.

The river also had a more personal connection to Eric. It had once been the traditional territory of his ancestors. For countless generations, the Odjik family had lived and died along its shores, only leaving in summer, when they would head downriver to visit and trade with other Algonquin families at one of the traditional gathering places on the Ottawa River. But his great-grandparents had been the last. Logging had left a wasteland bare of animals and a river too toxic for fish, and when the fish and animals had returned, the Hunting and Fishing Camps had moved in, denying access to all but the wealthy.

Though the exclusive camps had long since been disbanded, hunting and fishing were still highly regulated. Moreover, the Odjiks had moved onto the Migiskan Reserve and lost their nomadic ways. Eric's only link with the river of his ancestors was the occasional canoe trip like this one.

For a day, Eric and I'd had the lake to ourselves. We'd paddled along the edge of its forested shores, floated with a family of loons, skinny-dipped in the invigorating early July water and made love in the glow of the campfire. The next day, his daughter Teht'aa Tootoosis and her boyfriend, Larry Horn, had arrived.

Eric wanted this trip to be a voyage of discovery for his daughter so that she could learn of her ancestral link to the river. He also wanted it to be a journey of peace.

Relations between his daughter and myself, the elder by only ten years, had not warmed beyond half-hearted smiles and innocuous weather observations. Her upbringing on an isolated Dene reserve in the Northwest Territories had left her suspicious of whites. This distrust was further compounded by having to share the father who'd only recently entered her life. Before that, he'd been dead to her. A death invented by a mother whose fear of Eric's off-reserve influence was greater than her love for him.

I knew I hadn't helped the situation. Whenever Teht'aa tossed out one of her snide remarks regarding my spreading middle-aged curves or enhanced red hair, I'd bristle and throw back an equally biting remark.

Her name meant "Lily" in Dene. I sometimes wished the softness I associated with the flower had rubbed off on her. It hadn't. At least, not that I'd discovered.

Eric hoped that seven days alone on the river contending with nature's challenges would bring us closer together. After five days of battling whitewater, bugs and one raging thunderstorm, the best the two of us had accomplished was the task of washing dishes in mutual silence with the occasional noncommittal remark about the trip.

Unfortunately, the boyfriend didn't help. A Mohawk from a reserve near Montreal, he wore similarly-coloured blinkers. Whenever Teht'aa's lips twitched with the hint of a friendly smile, Larry would say in that droning voice of his, "Remember Oka." At which point she'd drop her stone-like mask back into place.

"Where are they?" I asked Eric. "I thought they were right behind us." I craned to see around the bend to the upper section, but the boughs of the overhanging cedar blocked my view.

"Maybe they ran into trouble on that first ledge," he replied. "I'll give them another ten minutes. If they don't come, I'll make my way back up along the shore."

The water shimmered with the intensity of the noonday sun. Sweat dribbled down my face and onto my life-jacket. I soaked my hot arms in a river still cool from the winter snows. Tiny blackflies swarmed around my head. Even though they were at the end of their season, they still packed a stinging bite. I applied insect repellant over my face, arms and legs.

Behind me, a sharp slap, followed by, "Christ, I'm bleeding."

"Sure you don't want to use my DEET?"

Eric growled, "No." Another resounding slap.

"You sure?"

He didn't bother to respond. I figured it was a man thing, braving the elements without sissy interventions like insect repellant, bug hats or even proper clothing. Today he hadn't bothered with his cotton T-shirt and had just put his PFD over his bare chest. At least he'd agreed to wear the life-jacket, but then again it was only after I'd blackmailed him by refusing to come unless he did.

"You don't happen to have any more of that chocolate and peanut butter energy bar, do you?" Eric asked.

As I turned around to pass it to him, I noticed something on the far shore that turned me cold. "Is that what I think it is?" I pointed to a weathered wooden cross that had been jammed into the rocks above the falls.

Eric twisted his body around to see. "Yeah. Probably marking a grave where some poor unlucky logger got caught in a logjam years ago. I'm sure it's not the only death this river has seen over the years. No doubt the odd voyageur lost his life in the upstream battle to get his fur-laden canoe back to Quebec. And of course, the bones of my ancestors are buried along its shores." A mischievous glint appeared in his eye. "And I mustn't forget the odd recreational canoeist."

Although I answered him with a playful splash of my paddle, I couldn't help but wonder if any modern day canoeists like us had indeed succumbed to the force of the turbulent water.

"I'm getting tired of waiting," Eric said. "I'm going to walk back along the shore."

At which point a bright yellow canoe swirled around the bend, sideways, with Larry in the stern and Teht'aa in the bow, frantically paddling. The horizontal plane of its side headed straight for the rock we'd narrowly missed. The canoe struck and held. The river boiled around them. At least they had the smarts to lean downstream to keep the boat from filling up. They jammed their paddles against the rock and pushed off. But they weren't out of danger. The canoe wallowed considerably lower in the water than was safe. Both canoeists balanced precariously, afraid the smallest movement would ship more water into the boat and drown it. They began to paddle gingerly towards the shore, but the current was too strong. It pulled the swamped canoe inexorably towards the falls.

"Hurry!" Eric shouted to them. "Meg, get the throw rope."

Eric shot our canoe through the grip of the eddy line and raced after the floundering boat. They were about ten metres from the drop line of the falls and five from the shore. The cross hovering on the rocks behind them only served to heighten the danger.

"Get ready, Meg. I'll tell you when," Eric shouted above the roar of the falls.

I stopped paddling as we closed in on them and prepared the rope for throwing. When we were about two canoe lengths away, Eric yelled, "Okay, now!"

"Teht'aa, catch!" I yelled.

She glanced up and shook her head. She continued paddling.

"For Chrissakes, catch it!" Eric yelled.

But I could see that his daughter was right. Reaching for the rope might upset the delicate balance of the waterlogged canoe. Besides, they were almost upon a shallow rock garden that would halt their drift to the falls.

Their bow crunched to a stop a little more than a canoe length from the drop-off, but the strong current swung the stern dangerously towards the edge. The boat began to slip backwards. Jumping out, Teht'aa desperately tried to pull the heavy canoe over the rocks towards the shore. Larry's hulking mass, however, remained rooted in the stern, as if paralyzed by fear.

Shouting at him to get out, Eric scrambled over to help his daughter, while I struggled to secure our canoe to the riverbank. I could hear the two of them splashing and cursing as they tried to pull the canoe closer to the shore. At one point, I heard a cry and turned around to see Eric lose his footing on the slippery rocks. His daughter continued to hang on, but the heavy canoe edged backwards towards the chute. Larry still didn't move. As I raced to help her, Eric flung a stone at the man. Its thudding impact was enough to unfreeze his fear. He thrust his paddle into the water and pushed.

TWO

"You bastard!" Teht'aa flung at Larry when we finally had our canoes and ourselves safely on shore. "Why didn't you paddle?"

As if he hadn't heard, Larry pounded his chest in a parody of Tarzan and yelled, "Weeooo! That was sure some ride. Think I'll have myself a beer."

Teht'aa threw down her paddle in disgust and stalked off into the woods.

From the waterlogged canoe, Larry pulled out the large vinyl dry pack that contained what remained of the twenty-four cans of beer he'd brought, despite Eric's warning to keep loads light.

"Better save that until after the portage," Eric said, removing the packs and barrel from our canoe. "We've got a kilometre of sweaty work ahead of us."

"Just need a little fuel, chief." He snapped the lid open and poured the amber liquid down his throat. His trembling hand belied the warrior tattoo on his bicep.

I wondered, not for the first time, what Eric's daughter saw in this lump of lard, with his overhanging beer gut and less than flattering rat's tail that hung limply from the base of his brush cut. Particularly since she was one gorgeous woman. Everything I wasn't. Tall, movie star thin, with the kind of sculpted cheekbones that modelling agencies pay big bucks for. And her hair; a cascade of rippling, ebony silk. If her mother had looked anything like her daughter, no wonder the teenaged Eric had succumbed to her charms.

"Come here, woman," Larry said to Teht'aa as she emerged

from the trees, tucking her T-shirt into her shorts.

She glared at him.

"You done good, girl. Come on, give us a kiss." Larry walked towards her, arms open.

But she ducked under his arms and headed towards their canoe, where she helped herself to a beer. Maybe love wasn't so blind after all. He shrugged as if he didn't mind the brush-off, than took another deep draught of his beer.

She took a similar long drink. "Boy, I needed that." Then turning to Eric, said, "Want one, Dad?" She ignored me, as she usually did. She refused to accept that I was a very real part of her father's life.

Once, when we were still trying the get-to-know-you chats at our local bar, she'd accosted me with the words, "He'll never marry you."

Holding my temper in check, I'd simply replied that time would tell. I hadn't bothered to tell her that marriage was definitely not in my plans. My only experience with marriage had been a disaster. I wasn't about to try it again, no matter how much I loved her father.

Turning my back on her now, I grabbed the dry pack with our clothes, heaved its dead weight onto my back and clambered up the steep embankment to the start of the portage.

Behind me, Eric said, "Don't be all day, Teht'aa. There is something special I want to show you at the end of this portage."

"Relax, old man," said Larry gruffly. "We're just having ourselves a little fun."

Eric's only response was a grunt as he hoisted the heavy canoe upside down over his head and onto his shoulders.

I resettled the heavy load on my back and started along the narrow portage trail, trying not to breathe in the bugs clogging the steamy forest air.

"You okay?" I called back to Eric.

"Yeah," he grunted. "Except for these damn bugs."

With his hands fully occupied with the canoe, he was considerably worse off than I. "Want some repellant?"

"No."

Ah, the pig-headed male species.

I trudged on, my eyes glued to the ground, fearful of tripping on the many exposed tree roots and rocks. The trail meandered up and down granite ledges, through low marshy patches and along dried-up creek beds. Branches brushed my arms and ferns my legs. Sweat coursed off my brow, down my chin, down my arms, down my legs, while the straps of the heavy pack bit further into my shoulders. I tried shifting the weight to ease the pain, but it offered little relief.

Finally, brightness flooded the trail ahead, and an expanse of pink granite came into view. At its edge twinkled the calm waters of the river. I gratefully dropped the bulging pack onto the ground and helped Eric lower the canoe at the water's edge.

"So where's this surprise?" I asked.

"Not until we get the rest of our gear," came the response from up the trail. I hastened after him.

I expected to run into Eric's daughter and her boyfriend, similarly weighed down with their gear, but when we didn't, I figured they were working on another beer. However, when we arrived back at the start of the portage, they were nowhere in sight. Only their canoe, still filled with water, attested to their presence, and of course a couple of empty beer cans.

"Damn them," Eric muttered under his breath and began yelling their names, while I picked up the empty cans, fearful they'd be left behind. After several more shouts, Teht'aa finally replied from further inland, "We'll be there in a second." A few minutes later, she emerged through the trees, her angry scowl replaced by a bright smile. I guessed the boyfriend was no longer in trouble. Then Larry strolled out, making a point of zipping up his fly.

Eric's eyes blazed with anger. "We're not waiting. If you two care to join us, we'll be camping at the Big Steel rapids."

He threw the heavy food barrel onto his back while I hoisted the much lighter dry pack with our tent and sleeping bags onto mine. Without waiting for a reply from his daughter, Eric proceeded down the trail. She remained standing where she'd exited the woods, looking remorseful. For a moment I felt sorry for her.

"We don't need him to get down this pussycat river." Larry opened another can of beer. "Besides, he's just jealous he's not in on the action."

"Shut up," Teht'aa snapped back. "He's my father. I intend to do this trip in his company, with or without you."

I left them to the sound of bailing water and raced after Eric, but so infuriated was he by his daughter's behaviour that I wasn't able to catch up to him until the end of the portage.

"I think we should wait for them," I said, lowering the pack into the canoe. "I don't think they'll delay us again."

"Hmpff," he said as he continued loading the canoe with our gear, but the fact he didn't bite my head off told me he'd walked off his anger. Although he wasn't quite ready to acquiesce, I knew him well enough to know he'd find some excuse that would delay our departure. He was quick to forgive. That was one thing I loved about him.

Soaking with sweat, I plunged gasping, clothes and all, into the cold river and let the swift water wash it away. At this point, the river widened, forming a pool of tranquil water. Still, the current from the falls was strong enough to propel me downriver, so I kept my feet firmly rooted to the rocky bottom.

Eric plunged in beside me and broke through the surface, shouting, "Relief. No bugs, no heat. Nirvana."

"You forgot something," I said, reaching for his hat, which was floating past me.

Laughing, he grabbed it, then tried to shove me under, without too much success, given my PFD's bobbing qualities. I reciprocated with a few well-directed splashes.

"Come on," he said. "I want to show you my surprise."

He drifted with the current along the shore and came to a halt where a mound of greyish-pink granite rose from the riverbed. Together we splashed up its smooth surface to where it abutted a vertical rock wall.

"Look carefully," Eric said, "And you'll discover the river's secret."

While Eric sat back on his heels, almost reverently, I scanned the mottled surface of the wall but failed to discern much beyond lichen-filled cracks and veins of variegated rock.

"Do you mean that?" I pointed to a seam of dirty quartz, which I knew from experience could contain gold.

"Look under the overhang." He pointed to a ledge that jutted out about a foot from the wall. Underneath I could just make out what looked to be faint smudges of red. Then I realized there was a distinct shape to the smudge, and I knew this was no whim of nature but something that had been put there by man.

"A turtle?" I asked.

"Isn't he wonderful? Our people believe he's a symbol of fertility. What do you make of this one?" Eric pointed to a fainter blotch below the turtle.

It was difficult to interpret, so I hazarded a guess. "It looks like a drawing of a stickman."

"Yes, I think so too. Memegwaysiwuk. The Rock People, the spirits of the river. Look, here's their stone canoe."

It looked more like an elongated comb to me. I assumed the teeth were meant to be people sitting in the canoe. I noticed other patches of red, but those were too faint to interpret. "How marvellous. Pictographs." I ran my fingers over the pictures. I felt vague depressions in the stone and of course the heat from the noonday sun. But if they were the voice of the spirits, they remained mute to my touch.

His fingers explored the images too. "Mishòmis, my grand-father, told me that whenever I travel the River of Whitewater, I must pay my respects to Memegwaysiwuk."

"How old do you think they are?"

"No idea, but our people have travelled these rivers for thousands of years. Come and help me gather some cedar. I want to respect the wishes of Mishòmis."

Although red pine was the predominant tree lining this section of shore, we managed to find a clump of cedar in a low-lying area not far inland. Eric also picked up an empty mussel shell, while I, remembering a similar offering once seen at a Migiskan gravesite, picked up a paper-thin piece of silver birch bark.

By the time we returned to the pictographs, Teht'aa and Larry were dropping their loads next to our canoe across the pool from where we stood. Neither said a word, just stared back, uncertain how to react.

Eric shouted across to them. "Come join us in an offering."

Without a word, his daughter slipped into the river, followed by Larry's sweating bulk.

"This is your heritage," Eric said simply when Teht'aa arrived.

Her eyes lit up as she recognized the paintings, and as we had done, she traced their outline with her fingers. She smiled. "I've seen ones like this on the rivers up north. There must be a mine close by, where the ancients found the iron clay to draw these ochre images."

"Probably, but I'm afraid we don't know where it is any more," Eric replied.

He sat cross-legged on the hot stone facing the rock wall while we circled around him. He sprinkled fresh green cedar leaves onto the opened halves of the shell. I placed my offering next to it. Teht'aa added a blue jay's feather and Larry a glittering piece of mica. Then Eric ignited a small mound of dried cedar mixed with some tobacco from his pouch and softly blew on it to create smudge. Its thin tendrils drifted towards the rock wall and caressed the paintings, while he spoke words of homage to the Rock People.

But what should have been a peaceful ceremony was marred by Larry and Teht'aa's restless shifting, almost as if they were bored. Neither tried to stop their constant sniffling. At one point, I even passed Teht'aa a tissue for her to wipe her nose.

No sooner had Eric finished than Teht'aa jumped up and said, "Great, Dad, appreciate it. But we got to get going." And she jumped back into the water with Larry close behind, leaving Eric disappointed and the harmony he'd sought broken.

THREE

By the time we returned to our canoe, the impatient couple were already headed downriver, but with one major change. Eric's daughter now paddled in the stern.

"Good," said Eric. "She's a much better canoeist. This way, if Larry freezes again, Teht'aa should be able to get them out of trouble."

We saw the merits of this change almost immediately when Teht'aa managed a last-second deflection around a rock that Larry's bad cross-draw had driven them into.

For the next several hours, we paddled down the river without incident, with the yellow canoe keeping a good fifty metres or so in front. Whenever we gained on them, they invariably dug their paddles in a little deeper and pulled ahead. It was as if they wanted nothing to do with us. Or was I being unkind? Occasionally, Teht'aa would turn around and give her father a wave. More likely, the couple wanted to enjoy the river in their own way, and that was fine by me. Their way seemed to include a lot of boisterous laughter and loud conversation.

Eric and I, on the other hand, preferred awed silence as the current propelled us forward along an empty shore lined with red pine, past eskers of sand deposited in the ice age and beaches of round river stones. With no rapids and only the occasional swift, we had little to do other than dip our paddles into the smooth water to keep the canoe on course.

The DeMontigny River was said to drop two hundred metres over its hundred-kilometre descent to the Ottawa River.

With rapids and falls, the drop in elevation was obvious, but with flat water, the only indication was the slow realization that the plane of water ahead was several degrees lower than our current position. It was like coasting down a low grade on a bicycle.

There was little evidence of modern man on this empty shore other than the occasional boarded-up hunting cabin. With limited road access, the river was the only way in; so too, the only way out. Nothing remained of the once-flourishing forestry industry that had cleared this land of its giant white pine. Over the intervening hundred or so years, the forest had been renewed by trees of almost equal stature.

At one point a bald eagle floated overhead to land at the top of a nearby pine, from which he watched our passage, almost as if he were making sure we left his world untouched. Then our reverie was over. The roar of rapids broke it. Before I had a chance to get nervous, we were racing through the froth, expertly avoiding the rocks and ledges as we pursued the tongues of smooth rock-free water.

"Wait up, Teht'aa," Eric hollered when we reached the calm water at the rapid's end. But the yellow canoe was disappearing around the next bend, to where the forest reverberated with the might of another rapid.

"Damn, Canoe Eater's just up ahead, and I don't want them going through it. Teht'aa may think she can do it, but with Larry's lack of skill, they're bound to get into trouble. Start paddling, Meg."

We skimmed over the water and rounded the bend in time to see Teht'aa and Larry fast approaching a constricting narrows bounded on either side by steep granite walls, at the entrance a line of rock and spitting white.

"Teht'aa, stop," Eric shouted, but I doubted she could hear above the noise.

Still, the canoe did seem to slow for a few seconds before it shot into the turmoil.

"Christ, I hope she sees the hole," Eric muttered.

And I hope we avoid it too, I thought. I didn't fancy sinking like a stone, canoe and all, into the hole's aerated water, only to be coughed up somewhere further downstream. Or worse, trapped underwater in its sucking, circling current.

"I think I'll pay my respects to the Creator before we head down. Keep us steady, Meg."

While I back-paddled, Eric sprinkled tobacco on the water and murmured a few Algonquin words, the way he'd done at the start of our trip.

Then he dug in his paddle and shot us forward. We headed towards the same imperceptible gap Teht'aa had taken. I watched with trepidation as their yellow canoe slid down a rush of water. For a moment the canoe seemed suspended as if caught on a ledge. Then it broke free and disappeared from sight.

My eyes locked onto the remains of a canoe wedged high up in the rocks. I shivered. Wonder what happened to those poor devils.

"Now you know why it's called Canoe Eater," Eric chuckled, then continued in a more serious tone. "The hole's downriver on the right. We'll stick to the left."

We bumped through this first gap, stuck, then sprang loose and hurtled forward into the mass of boiling white. Rocks were everywhere, with no obvious route, but Eric seemed to know where he was going, for we were slanting towards the left shore. We narrowly missed two lurking demons before we eddied briefly behind another to get into a better position for the slide Teht'aa had gone down. To the right of it, I could see the backward wave of the hole.

But as we reached the top of the slide, I suddenly realized with an icy feeling in the pit of my stomach that we had another obstacle to contend with.

"Strainer!" I shouted as we advanced towards the branches of a fallen pine jutting out into the river.

"Christ!"

The canoe suddenly lurched to a stop on the ledge, swung sideways and held. Eric leapt out onto the flat rock, pushed and shoved and managed to jump back into the stern as the canoe broke loose and plunged down the slide.

Before we reached the bottom, I was already frantically paddling to avoid being sucked into the strainer. Once caught, the river's force would make it impossible to break loose. The only problem was that the sinking water of the hole was close on our right, with almost no room between it and the tree. But Teht'aa and Larry must have made it, for there was no sign of them or their canoe. Unless they'd got trapped by the hole and even now were being held deep underwater by its sucking current.

As our canoe swung to the right, I glanced nervously at the closing gap between the strainer and the hole and said a silent prayer to whatever god cared to listen. Mine or Eric's Kije Manidu. It didn't matter.

The canoe jerked, a branch snapped, and we were through. But we had no time to relax. We were swiftly coming up to Canoe Eater's next challenge, a line of massive rocks with the only opening on the other side of the river.

With both of us paddling as if our lives depended on it, we reached the other side just in time to slip through the gap with only a slight scrape, then we were crashing through several ridges of standing waves, more like a tsunami from this angle. Water poured in, and suddenly we were in the relative calm of fast but flat water, and I could see their yellow canoe pulled onto the shore and Teht'aa and Larry waving at us with huge grins on their faces.

"We did it!" I shouted and laughed as the tension flowed

from my body. I turned around to Eric, whose grin spread from dimple to dimple.

"A piece of cake, eh?" He let out a war whoop.

Then he tossed his hat into the air. But he forgot that our waterlogged canoe hovered a few inches above the water line, and that the swift water was pushing us towards the next set of rapids.

When he reached up to catch it, the canoe wobbled, ever so slightly, but enough to unbalance me, and I toppled over the side. Next thing I knew, I was bobbing like a cork, feet forward on my back, towards the approaching line of white, with my hand still gripping the paddle. I tried to backstroke to the closest shore, but the current proved too strong, and I bounced over the rocks of the next set of rapids.

Fortunately, I remembered the map identified them as an easy Class I. But I also remembered that less than a hundred metres downstream was a chute, not an especially big one, but falls all the same. So when I reached the relative calm of the rapid's end, I released the paddle and swam as hard as I could towards the closest shore. I reached it in time to see our gear float past, followed by the overturned canoe. I raced back into the water and rescued one of the dry packs while I kept my eyes peeled for Eric. I didn't see him, neither in the water nor on shore. With a sickening lurch in my stomach, I watched the other pack and the food barrel, along with the canoe, tumble over the lip of the falls.

Frantic, I raced along the shore, praying Eric would survive. I reached the top of the falls in time to see our gear and the canoe spit out at the bottom, but I didn't see Eric in his bright red lifejacket.

I scrambled down over the slippery rocks lining the side of the cascade and slipped and slid my way to the bottom. The barrel bobbed in an eddy. The packs were disappearing around a bend in the river, along with the canoe.

Still no sign of Eric. I scanned the falls, fearful he'd become caught in the rocks. I looked into the depths below, terrified I'd see his lifeless body.

And then I heard the sweetest music I'd ever heard. "Hey Meg! Over here!"

FOUR

Eric was alive, thank god. He stood on the opposite shore, waving. What looked like blood flowed down the calf of his right leg.

"You okay?" I shouted back, not certain my voice would carry over the thundering falls.

Signalling that he couldn't hear, he motioned me to walk further downstream. He walked with a worrisome limp and seemed to be relying on a support, which I realized with amazement was his paddle. At least we had one paddle. Now all we needed was the canoe and my paddle, then we'd be able to leave these hellish falls behind.

When I reached a point where it seemed quieter, I shouted, "What did you do to your leg?"

"Probably scraped it on a rock. You okay?"

"Only bruises. I'm more worried about you. You took quite a beating."

"Nothing this tough old bod can't take. Look, I've got to go after that damn canoe, otherwise we're screwed."

That was putting it mildly. Without a canoe, the only practical way out was for Eric and most likely Teht'aa to paddle downstream in the remaining canoe in search of rescue, leaving me alone with Larry, for who knew how long, not a prospect I was exactly thrilled with. Still, if I had to, I would.

"Any sign of it?" I asked.

"Nope, not yet. I'm going to walk further along the shore. You do the same."

While I searched for the canoe and the other missing gear, I also watched Eric as he limped over the rocks on the other side. Who was he kidding saying just a few minor scratches? It looked more like some serious bruising or even a pulled tendon.

"See anything yet?" I shouted.

"Nope, but the river widens into a lake up ahead. If we're lucky, the current might have pushed our canoe into the quieter water."

I crossed my fingers.

"Found it!" Eric yelled, his pace quickening, his limp less evident. I heaved a sigh of relief when I too finally saw the thin red line of the overturned hull, a good hundred metres from shore in the quiet water of a lake, but although the canoe still floated, it didn't mean it was undamaged. The flotation tanks would keep it up, no matter how many holes were in it.

"I need the other canoe to get it. While I'm gone, try to find our gear, okay?"

"But what about your leg? Let me get it."

"The portage is on my side of the river. Besides, leg's feeling better. Look." He jumped up and down.

As we both retraced our steps back to the falls, I noticed that his limp was gone, and no blood had reappeared after he'd washed his leg.

Halfway to the falls, Eric ran into his daughter, whose joy at finding him alive almost toppled him over. When Eric pointed in my direction, she made a half-hearted victory sign, almost as if she'd been prompted.

They then appeared to have an argument, for Teht'aa kept shaking her head and trying to get her father to sit down, as if wanting him to stay behind while she went for the canoe, but in the end Eric's obstinacy won, and they both continued to the portage, where they met Larry, just arriving. The three of them then disappeared back into the foliage.

While they were gone, I retrieved the food barrel from below the falls and struggled with it downriver to where the river widened. Then I returned to the falls and scrambled back up to the top to get the rescued dry pack containing our clothes. The only remaining items were the pack with the tent and sleeping bags, and of course my paddle. But I wasn't especially worried about the paddle; I knew the other canoe carried a spare.

On my way back downriver, I chanced upon Eric's battered hat caught in some floating debris but left it to its soggy fate, figuring Eric didn't need a reminder of his ill-timed celebration. I didn't see either of the two missing items. Leaning against the dry pack, I settled myself on a small sandy beach just beyond where the river widened, a spot where I could keep my eye on the canoe as it drifted closer to the other shore. Happily, our other dry pack floated next to it.

For the first time since this ordeal had begun, I realized I was shaking. My nerves, my emotions, not to say my body, had taken a beating. My fingers were trembling so badly, I could barely undo my PFD. My heart pounded. I needed to relax and get a hold of myself if I were to make it down this river. We had at least another day, and I wasn't sure if I had the mental strength to confront any more cataracts.

The late afternoon sun had warmed the beach to a nice baking temperature. I lay down on its soothing warmth, hoping it would calm me. Unfortunately, it wasn't quite sandy enough. Something poked my ribs. I reached under and pulled out what at first I thought was a piece of a branch, until I realized its dark bronze colour wasn't like any stick I'd ever seen, and its pitted denseness didn't have the texture of wood.

It was about eight inches long and shaped like a flattened cylinder, with one end jagged, as if from a break. The other end, bulbous and slightly smooth, finally gave me a clue about what I was looking at. I'd discovered enough of them lying on the forest floor to know this was a bone from a largish animal, probably a deer. The dark colour had confused me. Any animal remains I'd found had been greyish white. I flung it into the woods and settled back down onto the warm sand.

I felt a lump under my leg and pulled up another piece of bone, what looked to be a vertebra. When I noticed several more vertebrae and some flat pieces of what could be ribs, I couldn't help but feel a certain squeamishness. I'd been lying on some poor animal's grave.

"We're here, Meg!" Eric suddenly called from the other shore. He was settling Larry's canoe into the water. Behind him stood his daughter, leaning slightly forward with the weight of the lightest of their two packs. Larry tramped much further behind. Even from this distance, I could see the sweat pouring down his square face as he struggled to remain upright with the pack I knew carried his beer.

After discarding her gear, Teht'aa jumped into their canoe with her father, and they headed out to where ours floated. I assumed they would drag it back to shore, but Eric had other plans. After retrieving the dry pack, he jumped into the water, while Teht'aa positioned herself in the middle of the yellow canoe.

Wanting to get away from the remains, I shifted farther along the small beach. When I leaned back onto a piece of driftwood, my hand touched what felt like fabric buried in the hot sand. I pulled out a filthy NHL cap, complete with the Senators' insignia. While the brim was intact, the cap was ripped at the back. No doubt a casualty from another dump in the rapids. For a moment the bones crossed my mind, but I quickly dismissed the thought.

At the sound of shouts, I turned back to find Eric straddling one end of the overturned canoe, with the other end raised, and pointing to where his daughter sat in the middle of the other canoe. Intrigued, I watched as they maneuvered our canoe onto Teht'aa's then skillfully righted it and thrust it back into the water. Miraculously, it floated.

"Any damage?" I shouted.

Eric shook his head, then, while his daughter held it steady, climbed into the rescued canoe and paddled towards me, while she headed back to Larry.

Taken off-guard by the quickness of the rescue, I hastened to collect the barrel and brought it back to the small beach. When I dropped it against a shallow embankment of eroding sand, the sand collapsed, dislodging some largish rocks, but one didn't look like a rock. It was smooth, round and had the familiar bronze colour.

Curious, I picked it up, but immediately dropped it. Two empty sockets stared back at me. I shuddered. I didn't need to be a zoologist to know this didn't belong to a deer or any other animal. I stepped away, not wanting to be within direct line of sight of those eyeless holes.

"What've you got there?" Eric said, jamming the canoe onto the beach.

"A skull. As in human skull."

"Cool. Maybe another pour soul who had the good fortune to go over those falls." He chuckled.

"Don't joke. It could've been you."

"At least I didn't get my head bashed in." His foot tapped at a jagged hole in the back.

"What should we do about it?"

"Leave it. Probably a logger from the old days."

"I'm not so sure this was an accident. Don't you think a bash against a rock would've crushed the skull, not made a hole like this?"

"Could've been done by one of those heavy chains used to keep the log booms together."

"Maybe, but eventually his body would've floated to shore to be left lying on the ground. I think this guy was buried here. The skull came from this embankment." I tapped it. More sand broke loose, along with another bone.

"Could've been found and buried by another logger."

"Why do I get the impression you don't want to do anything about this skeleton?"

"Well, we could give him another burial. But I can't afford the time. As you're well aware, I've got to be in Winnipeg tomorrow night for that key Assembly of First Nations meeting. I'd just as soon tuck the bones we've found under a rock, give him a quick prayer and be on our way."

"We may not have any choice in the matter. I think this death is much more recent than any nineteenth century logger." I held up the baseball cap. "Probably belongs to him. And as we know, the Senators hockey team has only been in existence since 1992."

I glanced back down at the hole in the skull and placed the tear in the cap over it. They seemed to match. "We have to let the police know."

FIVE

The next afternoon found me regretting my hasty decision. Two hours we'd been waiting for the police. Two thumb-twiddling hours, with Eric relentlessly pacing back and forth in the hot, airless registration office of the ZEC DeMontigny.

We'd spent the night at the Big Steel rapids campsite after having portaged around them, something Eric had suggested, without my having to ask. He'd realized I wasn't up to taking on another rapid. The following morning, after a good night's sleep, I'd steeled myself to paddle down several easy ones and had actually enjoyed them, although I wasn't sure I was ready to take on anything more difficult. Long before we reached the registration office, we passed numerous signs on either side of the river warning that this government-owned land was reserved from the ZEC DeMontigny for the sole use by this and that hunting group.

"Maybe we should just go," I said. "We can leave directions with the guy here."

"The police will want to talk to you. We'll have to stay." Eric's face, one that had seen more of the outdoors than the inside of an office, bore the imprint of the resigned acceptance it often wore when he was dealing with one of my bright ideas.

Sunlight suddenly flooded the dark room, and in strode Teht'aa, her fingers twitching with impatience. Larry's massive frame blocked out the sun as he stepped in behind her. From a back room came the lonely ring of a telephone.

"Larry and I are getting tired of waiting in this heat. We're going to head downriver to a cooler spot and wait for you there."

At that moment, the scrawny kid who was manning the registration booth yelled out, *"Le téléphone pour vous, madame."*

Through the receiver, a guttural male voice spewed out a string of incomprehensible French.

Responding in the same language, I pleaded that he speak more slowly, since my linguistic ability wasn't quite up to his speed. Although my proficiency was much improved from the basic high-school French I'd arrived with in *"la belle province"*, when I'd moved over four years ago from Toronto, I still wasn't able to decipher the fast and often slurred local dialect.

"My apologies, madame," the male voice replied in a much slower and educated French. "I am Sergeant Beauchamp, with the Sûrêté du Québec in Fort Coulange. Sorry for detaining you, madame, but the coroner was not available until this moment. She and I will be departing shortly in a floatplane. Since it is impossible to land at your present location, I ask that you meet us at Lac Orignal. I believe it is about three kilometres downriver."

Imagine, a policeman who actually apologizes. I'd become too used to the arrogance of Sergeant LaFramboise, or Rotten Raspberry as I'd come to call him, whose patronizing sneer had ignited my anger on more than one occasion. "Does this mean that you want me to fly with you to where I found the bones?"

"Yes, madame."

"How long do you think it will take?"

"I don't know."

I glanced at Eric's scowling face. "Are you sure you need me? I can give you their location. It's fairly straightforward."

"Sorry, madame, but it is necessary that you show us."

Eric's scowl had turned to a glower.

"But my friends and I have to be across the Ottawa River by

the end of today. That's at least another twenty kilometres."

"Sorry, madame. It is your duty."

Sergeant Beauchamp's outward tone might be more sympathetic, but inside he was just as overbearing as LaFramboise. After reluctantly agreeing to meet him, I hung up and turned to face Eric.

"Look, I'm sorry. Maybe you can convince the Sergeant they don't need me."

Eric merely grunted and asked the registration clerk for use of the phone. After a brief conversation, in which his face became even more grim, he hung up. "I've told the Grand Chief I'll be a day late to the meeting. But Meg, I can't be any later. There's a key vote on Saturday. I have to be there."

Casting an equally annoyed look in my direction, Teht'aa added, "I've got to get back too. I have a job interview."

"Why don't the two of you continue on down the river then?" I threw out more from a sense of guilt than altruism. "Larry can wait for me, and we'll try to catch up." I didn't dare glance at the boyfriend to see what he thought of the idea.

"We'll see," Eric answered. "Let's meet up with the cops first and decide from there." He started towards the door, then, as if changing his mind, he turned around. "Meg, why couldn't you have just left the bones where they belong, on the land?"

"Yes, why couldn't you?" Teht'aa echoed.

I glanced helplessly at the two faces, Eric's broad and weathered, Teht'aa's sculpted and chic, so different and yet so alike. Both had the high cheekbones people pay plastic surgeons big bucks for, and both stared back at me through silvery grey eyes. Except Eric's revealed a soft tenderness beneath their exasperated arch, whereas Teht'aa's just wore a steely dislike.

"I couldn't. The man has a family, friends, who've probably been worried sick since the day he disappeared. They have a right to know what happened to him. Besides, it looks as if his death might not have been accidental. If so, his killer must be found."

Eric shook his head. "There's nothing but bones. The police may not even be able to identify the man, if it is a man, let alone find his killer. Besides, it's sometimes best not to wake the hibernating bear. His family and friends have gotten on with their lives. Even the killer. Who knows what kind of a hornet's nest you may be stirring up?"

"Eric, you surprise me. Surely you can't believe that a killer should go free, no matter how much time has past since he killed."

"I don't believe it's quite so black and white. Sometimes there are justifiable reasons for a death, ones that a court of law may not necessarily accept. Besides, I have a strange feeling about this. This man, his bones, his spirit have lain there for anywhere up to a dozen years or more. He's returned to where we all come from, Mother Earth. By removing them, we'll disturb his spirit. My people believe that this can unleash sickness, unhappiness."

"And *you* disturbed them," Teht'aa spat, while Larry vigorously nodded his agreement.

"If we're going to get spiritual about this," I said. "I'd say those bones were waiting to be found. You could almost say they made themselves known by falling out of that embankment. I think they want their killer to be found. Now they can have a proper burial in a proper cemetery, complete with the appropriate religious ceremony."

"In the meantime, they get poked and prodded by the police," Teht'aa retorted, "have all sorts of tests conducted on them. Probably not all the bones will be dug up. So what is finally buried won't be the whole man, and some of his spirit will be left to wander."

Before I could come up with a reply, Eric opened the outside door. "Let's leave this discussion for later. I don't want to keep those cops waiting." He walked out into the hot mid-morning sun and headed towards our beached canoes.

*   *   *

The plane was skirting the tree canopy of the distant shore as our two canoes whisked through the last swift and out onto Lac Orignal, or Moose Lake. We waited until it had drifted to a halt on the long, narrow lake not ten metres from us. A young, almost boyish face, peered out at us through the open cockpit door. The young man jumped down nimbly onto the pontoon and waited for our arrival. He was clad in shorts and a T-shirt, and the only indication of his official police status were the words Surête du Québec stamped across the front of his brown cap. And of course the gun belt strapped around his waist.

Through the cockpit windows, I could see several more faces peering out at us. One looked to have the fine features of a woman.

"Bonjour, messieurdames." The cop greeted us with a broad expanse of smiling white. "Sergeant Beauchamp at your service. How I love this river. I envy you your trip."

"Then you can probably appreciate how anxious we are to continue it," Eric answered in a much more fluent French than I could muster. "As Madame Harris said, the location is fairly straightforward. We can give you directions and be on our way."

The cop's grin disappeared. "I will make it as fast as possible, but you must appreciate that in a police matter such as this, it's necessary that we conduct a proper investigation. To do this, we require the presence of the person who found the body. This I believe is Madame Harris."

"Yes, it was me," I reluctantly acknowledged. "How long do you think this will take?"

"One, two hours, I don't know. But I will tell you what I

31

can do. When we're finished with your part of the investigation, I'll have the pilot bring you back to this lake, to your friends. This means you will not have to wait for us to finish our investigation."

I shook my head to clear my ears, not quite sure I was hearing correctly. Imagine, a cop who actually cared. Maybe this guy really could give Sergeant Laframboise a lesson or two.

"Perhaps I should come too," Eric suggested. "I might also be of help."

"Sorry, monsieur, but our small plane has only room for one more person."

I turned to Eric. "This shouldn't take long, but in case it does, why don't you wait for, say an hour. If I'm not back by then, start down the river with Teht'aa. Larry can wait for me, if he doesn't mind."

The boyfriend's unsmiling face reflected my own unvoiced reluctance. "Yeah, chief, I don't mind," he muttered.

"No need, I'll wait. Full moon tonight, guys. Nothing like a moonlight float down a river to make a person at one with the land, eh?"

"That's for sure," Sergeant Beauchamp agreed. "Wish I could join you."

This guy's okay, I thought as I clambered onto the floating plane. I squeezed myself into a makeshift seat between Dr. Langlois, the coroner, and Corporal Fraser, the sergeant's sidekick. Within minutes, we were planing over a forest that stretched from horizon to horizon, its endless green only broken by the shimmers of scattered lakes and the thread of a dirt road winding its way from the ZEC registration office.

We followed the twisting DeMontigny River north until it opened onto the lake where I'd found the bones. After landing on the flat water, we taxied to within thirty metres of the small beach. This time the corporal jumped out onto the pontoon and, working his way to the back of the plane, pulled out from the tail compartment a roll of rubber that quickly expanded into a boat. He unfolded a pair of aluminum oars and snapped them into place. While he held the boat steady, the sergeant, the coroner and I climbed in.

We landed on the far edge of the beach, no doubt to keep from stirring up the spot where I'd found the bones.

"There they are," I said, pointing to the small collection of bronze-coloured vertebrae left on the sand next to the skull and the Senators cap. "I also found this." I reached down to grasp the longer bone but was immediately stopped by Sergeant Beauchamp.

"Please do not touch, madame." The sergeant motioned the corporal to take pictures, during which he stretched a pair of latex gloves over his hands. When the photographing was finished, he reached down to pick up the bone. "What do you think, Dr. Langlois? A partial femur or tibia?"

She inspected the bone through her wire-rimmed glasses. "Most likely. But I find it curious, this dark colour. Most remains of this nature are much lighter and greyer. No doubt the surrounding soil contains a type of mineral easily absorbed by the bone that has darkened it." She placed the bone back on the sand. "Any others?"

I showed her the skull with the gaping hole in the back.

While the corporal photographed it, both the doctor and the sergeant gazed at it wordlessly.

"I don't think that was caused by an accident, do you?" I hazarded. "As I said on the phone, this is one of the reasons why I called you."

"An interesting observation," was Sergeant Beauchamp's comment. He then pointed to the dirty white cap and asked if it belonged to any of us.

"No. I found it in the sand by the bones. Since it's a Senators cap, I figured this person died sometime after 1992, when the team was formed. What do you think?"

This time a noncommittal, "Hmmm…"

"I also find it curious that the ripped part of this hat is in the back, just like the hole in the skull."

The sergeant raised his eyebrows, then placed the hole in the cap over that of the skull.

"This guy was also buried." I pointed to the eroding sand embankment from which the skull had fallen. Dr. Langlois knocked her foot against it, and more bones fell out.

"It looks to me like he was murdered," I said, feeling rather pleased with my deductive skills.

"It is possible," was all Sergeant Beauchamp said, but I could tell from the alertness in his stance that he agreed. He then questioned me on the discovery. As I recounted the story, the corporal continued taking photographs of the beach, the embankment and the surrounding land, while the coroner labelled the various bones and inserted them into plastic bags.

When the sergeant had finished questioning me, he thanked me for my time and asked the corporal to take me back to my friends.

"Before I go, I have one last question," I said. "I'm curious to know how you are going to identify this guy with only an old Senators cap to go on."

"With difficulty, but various tests can be conducted, such as DNA, and of course we check the missing persons lists."

"Won't be easy finding who killed him, will it?"

"No, madame, but I like to think we are like the Mounties. We always get our man." And he laughed heartily at his joke.

I was returned to Eric at Lac Orignal within the promised hour. Having decided that a night paddle would make up for any lost time, he was in a considerably more relaxed mood than when I'd left.

We set out in late afternoon to finish our journey down the DeMontigny river. The difficult rapids were behind us, and what remained were easy sprints through Class I rapids and fun rides along swifts. Under the white brilliance of the full moon, we paddled silently across the black expanse of the Ottawa River to where we'd parked our two vehicles on the Ontario side.

Eric expressed no further interest in the bones. Neither did Teht'aa or Larry, for that matter. But that didn't mean that I would forget about them. My curiosity had been tweaked, and as well, I felt somewhat responsible for them. I would keep tabs on their fate.

SIX

About a week after the discovery of the bones, I came across a small article in the local paper. It talked about the find, even mentioning my name. While the journalist hinted that they might belong to a hunter who'd gone missing in the ZEC DeMontigny in 1995, the police weren't saying. Nor was there any mention of a suspicious death, other than to say that the police were continuing their investigation.

However, a few days later, the same newspaper ruled out the missing hunter. The bones had proven to be that of a female, which made the death even more suspicious, since no female had been reported missing in the area. Needless to say, I conjured up images of a husband bringing his wife to this isolated spot, killing and burying her, then later pretending she'd left him for another man.

A call to Sergeant Beauchamp neither confirmed nor denied my theory. He just said that the bones were currently in the hands of a forensic anthropologist for analysis, a standard procedure for remains of this nature. He suggested I contact him in a couple of weeks' time, when they should know more.

Meanwhile, I continued on with my life. My home, Three Deer Point, and the 1,500 acres of West Quebec wilderness I'd inherited from my great-aunt Agatha were a constant drain on both my attention and my bank account. Even though the six-bedroom Victorian cottage would better serve a family of eight than a single, divorced woman with only a giant poodle to help fill up the rooms, I wouldn't live anywhere else. On my first summer visit as a child, I had fallen in love with its turret and gabled roof, the arched windows that winked in the setting sun, and of course the large verandah, where I used to play endless games of cards with my beloved but eccentric Aunt Aggie.

Isolated on a pine-fringed granite point overlooking Echo Lake, some would think it an unlikely home for a city-bred woman like myself. Particularly since the closest town, Somerset, was a thirty-minute drive away, and the only neighbours were the Forgotten Bay Hunting and Fishing Camp, the Migiskan Reserve and the odd small farm. But it suited me fine, always had.

So when my marriage had disintegrated in a morass of recrimination and betrayal, I'd fled Toronto and all its bitter associations to lick my wounds in the tranquillity of this northern paradise. Gradually, over the course of the changing seasons, my wounded soul had healed with the help of nature's soothing touch and, of course, Eric's. But I'd been wrong to think peace reigned over this endless forest. In the four years since I'd moved here, I'd had more than my fair share of adrenaline-racing excitement. Whoever said country living was boring was dead wrong.

Unfortunately, a hundred-and-twenty-year-old house was never without problems, from leaking roofs to burned-out water pumps, the most recent bank-breaking episode being the replacement of decades-old electrical wiring. The wilderness location added an extra dimension. I was ever on the look out for squirrels nesting where they shouldn't, mice tramping the halls and all other critters that looked upon my home as theirs.

Recently, carpenter ants had decided a section of the verandah was tasty. Terrified they might attack the ancient squared-timbers of the building itself, I'd hastily brought in an exterminator to kill them and a carpenter to replace the ruined wood. But to save money, I'd decided to do the staining myself.

Armed with a brush, a tin of dark brown stain and bug repellant, for the summer heat had not quite chased away the odd blackfly, I started on the replaced section of railing. Despite not being particularly keen on household chores, I didn't mind painting. It required little effort, and the rhythmic back and forth movement of the brush was conducive to daydreaming. Besides, the day was perfect, cloudless and windless, if not bugless.

My faithful companion, Sergei, although not exactly in a working mood, joined me. His black curly body lay doormat style, stretched out on the wooden verandah floor. Being no dumb poodle, he'd removed himself as a target for skin-twitching bugs and retreated to the protection of the screened porch. Occasionally he'd lift an eyelid to glance in my direction, then shut it again and return to whatever canine dreams he was pursuing.

Although peace might be reigning on the verandah, above my head war raged yet again. A finger-sized spitfire of electric green and ruby red zeroed in on interlopers, his needle-like beak ready to do damage. A hummingbird, the ruby-throated male to be exact, was intent on protecting the feeder he'd deemed his from all and sundry, including his spouse, who was slightly larger and less colourful. Usually, she made a fast getaway, with him in hot pursuit, but occasionally his beak would connect with an ominous slap of feathers.

Once I'd had to intervene, when the poor female had become entangled in one of the red flower-shaped feeder ports and her partner, now that he had his quarry firmly under his control, wouldn't let up on his attack.

It was a situation that too closely mirrored many a relationship in the human world, including my own bad marriage. But at least I'd managed to escape that with only a broken arm and a battered psyche. Although the arm had quickly healed, it had taken Eric's unflinching trust to wean me out of the alcoholic haze into which I'd escaped. These days I rarely drank, and when I did, I was satisfied with a glass or two of wine.

The bird hovered at my side, no doubt attracted to my shocking pink halter-top, a colour I'd been brought up to avoid because of its clashing brilliance with my own flaming hair. But now that my mother's influence was six hundred kilometres away and my hair wasn't quite as carrot red as it once had been, I rather liked the combination's jarring effect.

The bird buzzed me again. When I turned to face him, he retreated to the safety of his feeder. I figured the amount of energy he consumed on his lightning attacks was more than compensated for by the quantities of sugared water I added to the feeder almost daily. At least he allowed me to do that in relative peace. I think he recognized me as the necessary source. But no sooner would the refilled feeder be back on its hook than the feisty bird would zoom down to reestablish his authority over it.

So as war raged, the bugs buzzed, the dog snored and I slapped on the dark chestnut-coloured stain. Unfortunately, this rich new coat was making the older sections of the railing look dowdy, something I was trying not to notice. If I dwelled on it too much, I might convince myself to re-stain the entire verandah, one of those massive Victorian structures that wrapped itself around three sides of the house. It was a job my idle inclination did not want to take on.

I'd finished about half the new railing when the ringing of my phone provided an excuse for a break. Robbie Kohoko's raspy voice greeted me. "Meg, I got a couple of buyers. Yanks. Think you can help me out?"

He should be used to dealing with outsiders, since his father, Albert Kohoko, the esteemed Migiskan elder, called Grandfather Albert by many, regularly entertained spiritual seekers from all

Nations. But Robbie's friendly manner shut down in front of strangers. Fortunately, he recognized that this wasn't good for business. When a key buyer approached him, particularly one wanting to be involved in the making of a canoe, he involved me. He figured I could talk their language because of my city roots.

"What are you building this time?"

"A sixteen-footer. Damn sight better than makin' those little barkies."

"But I thought there weren't any more birch trees large enough to provide the length of bark needed to build a canoe that big?"

"Got one I been saving. So, you on?"

"You bet, any excuse to stop painting."

A short while later, his silver Ford pick-up, a considerably newer and larger model than my own rusted out rattletrap, rounded the last curve of my road. Two muddy all-terrain-vehicles were crammed into the back, while a small trailer with a ladder hanging out its end bumped behind. Behind this loomed a tank-like Lincoln Navigator, its glossy black coat dusty from the gravel roads. I could just make out a couple of large heads behind the tinted windows.

Behind this drove another SUV, one I recognized, the champagne-coloured Grand Cherokee belonging to Eric. It hauled a trailer containing Eric's red ATV. I frowned, for I knew who'd be driving it. Not Eric. He was away at another AFN meeting, a continuation of the contentious one he'd managed to attend despite the delays in our canoe trip.

I waved a half-hearted greeting to Teht'aa in the passenger seat and Larry, the driver, and was returned a similar lukewarm hello. I'd not run into either since watching the red taillights of Larry's truck disappear at the end of our canoe trip, leaving a fuming Eric and me to deal not only with our own gear and canoe but the common stuff, including the garbage.

The convoy rolled to a stop beside the front verandah stairs. I watched Robbie's slight, wiry frame jump down from his truck and stride towards me. A nervous smile twitched under his moustache. He grunted in greeting.

"I see you brought some additional company," I said more as a question than a statement. Normally, Robbie liked to keep the number of people involved to a discreet few, in case someone inadvertently did something to upset the deal. Exactly the kind of thing Larry and his big mouth might do.

Robbie's bony shoulders raised imperceptibly beneath his white T-shirt. "Came as we was leavin'. Chief's daughter. Can't say no, eh?"

While the sun sculpted the fullness of his black braids, making them appear thicker than they perhaps were, it was no friend to his face. The deeply pitted scars from teenage acne were revealed in all their cruelty. But his almond-shaped brown eyes twinkled with affability, serving to direct your eyes away from the scars.

The heavy doors of the Lincoln closed with a well-oiled click. A tall, elderly man, lean and tanned, dressed in cowboy chic complete with an over-bearing black Stetson, tooled-leather boots and silver-tipped collar points, gripped my hand firmly. It was all I could do to keep from smiling at this parody of a man from the "Big Country". When he spoke with the languorous drawl of a Texan, I wasn't the least surprised.

"Ed Payne at your service, ma'am. Y'all sure got some mighty pretty country up here." His face creased with benevolence. "I'd appreciate y'all meetin' my wife, Billie. She's the collector in the family. Likes this here Indian stuff."

A small, grandmotherly woman, her grey hair neatly tucked under a white Stetson and her softly rounded figure similarly attired in Texan clothes, clasped my hand. I felt the coldness of metal against my wrist and glanced down to see the twinkling array of diamond-encrusted charms dangling from a heavy gold-linked bracelet. I had to extricate one, a flamingo coated in pink diamonds with a ruby for an eye, that had become tangled in my beaded bracelet.

"Why, honey, is this place all yours?" she drawled. "I ain't seen better in Bah Ha'bah."

It took me a second to realize she was talking about Bar Harbour, Maine, once the seaside home of many a monster Gilded Age cottage before a raging fire consumed many of them.

"My great-grandfather Joe Harris had it built in the late 1800s. In fact, I think he used an architect he met while visiting friends at that Maine resort. If you like, I could show you around after we finish up today."

"If it ain't too much bother, Ed and I would surely appreciate it."

At that point, a small head popped up beside Billie, and I saw Jid, the young boy who'd become my friend.

"Noshenj," he called out to me, the Algonquin word for auntie, a term children used to address favoured older women. "Did ya see the monster car? It's got leather seats and a DVD player. They let me ride in it. I wanna buy one just like it when I grow up." Jid's brown eyes mirrored his excitement.

The cowgirl ruffled the boy's short black hair. "Ain't he a darling? All squirmy, just like a puppy."

"And like his namesake. His full name is Ajidàmo, which means squirrel. We call him Jid for short."

From the screened porch, Sergei whined with equal excitement. The two of them had become great buddies after I'd discovered the boy together with other kids on a sub-zero day last winter lying passed out from a drug overdose. The dog had kept Jid warm while I'd gone for help.

"Can I go get Sergei?" he pleaded.

"Just don't let him jump all over everyone, okay?"

With a quick nod, he was off and running. Although small for his nine years, he looked sturdier and healthier than when I'd first laid eyes on him.

As we watched the two friends express their friendship, a muddy green Civic drove in and stopped behind Eric's Jeep. A man, blond, in his late thirties, with the build of a football player and a slight limp, walked towards us.

"Excuse me," he said, "is one of you Meg Harris?"

I indicated as much.

"I'd like to talk with you." He handed me a business card.

Dr. George W. Schmidt Ph.D., Fossil Finds Inc., Specialists in Archeological Digs. Remembering Sergeant Beauchamp's words, I asked, "Are you the anthropologist?"

"Yes, I'm hoping you could spare me a moment of your time."

Out of the corner of my eye, I noticed Teht'aa step behind Larry, but not before seeing an expression of surprise on her face that was immediately replaced by annoyance.

As if sensing her animosity, George motioned me to follow him a short distance from the group. "I don't mean to interrupt, but perhaps you could let me know when you will be free. I'd like to find out more about the bones you discovered."

"Surely the police have told you everything."

"It's always best to learn firsthand from the person who found them."

Since I didn't know how long I'd be tied up that day, I suggested the following afternoon.

As I watched him back up his car, Teht'aa said, "Don't trust him. They're all thieves wanting to rob us of our heritage."

"I doubt it. But in this case you won't have to worry. These bones likely have more to do with my heritage than yours." Little did I know how wrong I would be.

SEVEN

R obbie's truck lurched over a narrow rocky track that had more twists and turns than a game of snakes and ladders.

As the track looped back upon itself for the umpteenth time and headed up yet another impossibly steep hill, I asked, "You sure this is going somewhere?"

"Big birch would be long gone if it was easy to get to, eh?" replied Robbie in his slow, measured way of speaking.

I glanced behind to ensure his clients were still following and received cheery waves from both of them, while Jid beamed from the back seat. Unfortunately, Eric's dusty Jeep was also in view. I'd been hoping we'd lose it on one of the switch-back turns.

"Sure want to thank you for helpin' me out," Robbie continued. "Nice people, but can't always tell what they're sayin'."

"Yeah, the accent is a bit thick. How'd they end up so far from home?"

"Ya know that computer thing the kids at the school done for me? Wife seen it way off in Texas. Imagine that. Says they have a Chippewa and a Seneca canoe. Just needs an Algonquin one."

"Is she buying for a museum?"

"Nope, says it's for their own collection. Something about the grandkids."

"Guess you can charge a little more, eh?"

"Gotta pay off my truck somehow." He grinned.

Although I'd traveled with Eric to various parts of the nine thousand hectare reserve, I'd never been in this northern section. "How much further?"

"A ways. My grandfather saved these trees. Stopped the loggers from cuttin' 'em like they done on the rest of the rez."

Clear-cut logging, initially by outsiders, then by the band members themselves, had been extensive. Since Eric had become chief eight years ago, he'd persuaded the band council to adopt a more sustainable approach to logging, so that the land would eventually return to the forest of their ancestors.

The track came to an abrupt halt at the edge of a river. On the other side towered the canopy of a mature forest of an age to harbour big birch. After hitching the trailer to the back of the ATV, we climbed onto the rugged four-wheeler and splashed through the rocky shallows to the other side. Behind us on Robbie's other ATV came Billie and Ed with Jid sandwiched in between. All three wore ear to ear grins. And bringing up the rear bounced Teht'aa and Larry. Neither wore grins.

We ascended yet another steep slope, following the rough outline of a trail through the thick trunks of a hemlock forest, past several granite outcroppings until we reached the top of the hill. With little regard for the steep descent, Robbie aimed the ATV straight down. We careened around trees, boulders and deadfall. I hazarded a glance backwards to see how the Paynes were faring. Their broad smiles told me they were having fun.

As we descended the hill, the colour of the trunks gradually changed from black to grey-streaked white. When we were surrounded by giant birch, we stopped. Slender limbs of silvery white arched high overhead, the bark made brighter by the backdrop of summer green.

"Beauties, eh?" Robbie's bronzed face creased into a smile. Although he would never be called handsome, some women would find his sombre, no-nonsense demeanour attractive.

He tore off a paper-thin piece of bark. *"Wìgwàs,* the Creator's gift. Our people have been using it to make stuff since the Creator gave it to us. Canoes, baskets, even wigwams." He turned it over to reveal the coppery-pink underside. "Don't rot. Don't leak. Good for startin' fires."

"Yeah, great stuff," Larry piped up. "Mohawks use it too."

Billie, her once neat hair a windblown halo beneath the Stetson's brim, turned an inquiring gaze towards Larry. "Y'all a Mohawk, sir? I ain't familiar with your people."

"Iroquois Confederacy."

"Like the Seneca and Onondaga?"

"Yeah, warriors." He flexed the warrior tattoo on his arm. "In the good old days, we used to fight these Algonquins. Mind you, we took the pretty ones for our wives." He squeezed Teht'aa's buttock through the taut fabric of her shorts.

She slapped his wrist away. "And we'd follow the teachings of our grandmothers and put a curse on your manhood."

Noticing the frown on Billie's face, I hastened to intervene. "Let's follow Robbie. He's looking for the perfect tree for your canoe."

I steered her towards Robbie's back as it disappeared behind the trunk of one particularly large specimen. Dead leaves and withered underbrush crunched underfoot, while dried-out saplings snapped with the passage of legs. The forest floor was dry, almost too dry.

As if reading my own thoughts, Ed said, "These here conditions might be fine for Texas, but I reckon y'all could do with a touch of rain."

I couldn't remember the last time we'd had rain. Certainly not since our return from the canoe trip two weeks ago and probably not for a week or two before that.

We found Robbie beside a birch about a foot and a half in diameter, not quite as large as its neighbours. It, however, had one key requirement the others didn't: its trunk was straight for a good ten metres, without a single bump or branch to mar the smoothness of the bark. With a sharp knife Robbie sliced off a section of the white bark and held it out to Ed.

The Texan ran his hand over the bark's smooth inner surface and squeezed it. "Feels kinda rubbery."

"That's the way you want it," I answered, about to begin my spiel for Robbie.

But with a toss of her ebony hair, Teht'aa interjected, "Fabulous, eh? That rubbery stuff makes a birchbark canoe float and keeps it from breaking up when it hits something. As my dad says, with bark as good as this, a canoe can last forever. He even has an old one that used to belong to grandfather. I could show it to you, if you like. A real museum piece."

Unsure what Teht'aa was trying to do, I hastened to intervene. "Do you mean that old thing with the big hole, hanging in the back shed? I thought it was some manufactured copy Eric picked up at the Somerset flea market."

Teht'aa's eyes flashed anger.

I continued my spiel. "This is also the perfect time of year to gather the bark. It comes away easily from the trunk. In the fall and winter, it's too difficult to remove because of the lack of sap."

"But, honey, don't y'all want to use that there winter bark? It makes such pretty designs," Billie said, displaying her own knowledge of aboriginal canoes.

"As you'll discover, the traditional Algonquin method is to keep the canoe simple. Even when they do use winter bark, they rarely etch designs into its thick coppery layer."

Teht'aa picked up on the hint of disappointment in Billie's blue eyes. "I know what you mean. I've seen some gorgeous canoes with pictures of moose and other animals on the sides. I'm sure Robbie would be happy to make you one like that, or if not, I could—"

Still not liking where she was heading, I cut in. "Billie, when you become the owner of a Robbie Kohoko canoe, you will be among the privileged few. He is one of a handful of true masters. He learned the techniques from his father, who in turn learned them from his father and so on, back through countless generations."

While the Paynes continued to explore the texture of the bark sample, Jid ripped off a piece from another tree and folded it several times, with the copper-side out. Teht'aa did likewise. Soon the two of them were biting into their folded piece of bark, their smiling eyes focussed on each other, almost as if they'd entered into a friendly competition. I knew the boy was quite skilled at producing intricate designs by this traditional method of biting. Teht'aa's focussed biting suggested she might be equally as good.

Robbie began chanting in Algonquin as he walked slowly around the chosen tree, sprinkling bits of tobacco.

"Oh, my," Billie whispered, adopting a reverent pose. Ed joined her. And surprisingly, Teht'aa. She ceased working on her piece of bark and joined Robbie in his chanting. Larry, on the other hand, stood with his arms crossed against his broad chest, casting a puzzled glance at Teht'aa.

When Robbie finished, Billie gushed, "Such a nice touch, thanking the Creator for his bounty. I do love these native ceremonies."

Robbie responded by firing up his chainsaw. But rather than tackling the birch, he headed off to a clump of spruce trees.

"What's he at?" Billie asked.

His saw bit into one of the thin trunks, and the spruce's thick foliage landed with a bouncing lightness on the ground. He started in on another young spruce.

"He uses them as a soft landing bed so that when the birch

hits the ground, the bark isn't damaged. Come on, let's help him drag them over."

When the two spruce were properly placed, Robbie began cutting wedges on either side of the birch's trunk, about knee high from the ground. His lithe body arched with an effortless grace as he drove the saw deeper into the wood. I noticed Teht'aa watching him intently, while Larry's hungry eyes were focussed solely on her.

"Get of the way!" Robbie shouted as the tree began to waver. He'd angled the cuts so that the tree would fall between other giants. But the tree seemed reluctant to give up on life as it continued to balance on what remained of the hewn trunk. Robbie gave it a strong push. The tree wavered then stopped. In a slow but determined motion, it began leaning over, away from us and from Robbie. As the angle increased, so did the speed. Suddenly from above came a loud snap.

As the tree thundered to the ground, Teht'aa abruptly cried, "Watch out!" and lunged forward, knocking Robbie to one side, just as a large branch hit the ground where he'd been standing. Twigs lashed against Teht'aa's bare legs, but the large piece missed her, burying its pointed end in the ground beside her.

We all froze, too shocked to do or say anything, then as one we leapt forward. "Y'all okay? You were lucky, that's damn sure." Ed helped Teht'aa to her feet, while Billie brushed the dirt from Robbie's back.

I picked up his saw. "That was close, too close."

Robbie smiled sheepishly. "I shoulda knowed better. I seen that dead branch hanging up there." He turned his gaze to the chief's daughter. *"Migwech.* I thank you for my life."

For once, Teht'aa was at a loss for words. She even seemed to be blushing under her dark tan.

Jid unfolded his piece of bark to reveal an intricate whirled design of tiny perforations. He handed it to Teht'aa. "This is for you. Yours got squashed." And he pointed to the ripped piece lying on the ground at her feet.

"*Migwech,* Jid." She kneeled and hugged him tightly.

Throughout this time, Larry had remained silent. Now he stepped forward. "Ya stupid broad, what in the hell do you think you're doing trying to get yourself killed like that? Come on, we're gettin' outta here."

Teht'aa, still somewhat shaken by her ordeal, straightened her shoulders and said, "You go. I'm staying."

"Christ, girl. Ain't nothing for us here. Besides, we got all the business we can handle."

My antenna went up. "Oh? Do you make—"

I was abruptly cut off by Teht'aa yelling, "Shut up, Larry. Just get out of here."

His angry glare was enough to tell me that he made canoes too, and it helped to explain Teht'aa's cryptic interference. She'd been hoping to take the Texans' money away from Robbie.

But it now looked as if she'd changed her mind. I wondered why.

EIGHT

A s the sound of Eric's ATV faded, Teht'aa offered no explanation for Larry's abrupt departure or her sudden about-face. She merely apologized for her boyfriend's bad behaviour and set about helping with the removal of the bark. But as Billie sympathized with Teht'aa's woes, I began to wonder if it wasn't due more to a change in tactics than giving up on getting the Texans' business. Compassion could work wonders on a potential buyer.

With the birch lying on its spruce supports, Robbie trimmed it to about a six-metre length, then continuing with his chainsaw, he made a deep cut from one end of the log to the other. Next he took his axe and began carefully peeling the thick bark from the trunk. Usually, I helped Robbie with this, but after Teht'aa asked very politely if she could do it, I found myself watching on the sidelines. Needless to say, this sudden politeness didn't quell my suspicions.

It was slow, patient work and a bit boring to watch, but finally, after about an hour, a canoe-length of prime birch bark lay on the ground. Robbie rolled it into one very large jelly roll, with the white outer bark inside and the tawny interior on the outside. Not wanting to waste the remaining wood, he sawed it into lengths for later milling.

After securely stowing the logs and the bark into the trailer, we headed back the way we'd come, with one exception. Because Larry had taken off in Eric's ATV, I found myself at the back end of Robbie's ATV, with Teht'aa sandwiched in between.

It was all I could do to remain on the seat as the machine lurched over the uneven terrain. Thankfully, Robbie, more concerned about protecting his cargo than going fast, kept the bouncing to a minimum.

When we reached the trucks, Teht'aa surprised me yet again. Not only wasn't she the least upset by Larry taking off in her father's SUV, but she also showed no inclination to take advantage of furthering her business concerns by travelling with the Paynes. Instead, she suggested it would make more sense for me to go with the Texans, since they were staying next to my property at the Forgotten Bay Fishing Camp. She and Jid would return to the Migiskan village with Robbie. Seeing Robbie's willing smile, I had no choice but to agree.

Once we reached the main road, I watched Robbie peel down the road in the opposite direction, with Teht'aa's head a hand-width away from his. Curious.

A white van stood in my drive, while a bald, plump man watched us from the front porch. Neither the vehicle nor the man was familiar.

Ed must've felt me tense, for he said, "Y'all expectin' company?"

"No."

"If it's all right by you, I'll wait here until you're finish with him. These here woods are kinda lonely."

"Thanks, I appreciate it, but don't forget I invited you both for a tour of my house."

As we climbed out of the Lincoln, another man appeared from around the back of the house. His well-groomed brown hair and earnest hazel eyes reminded me of someone. I glanced back at the van and noticed for the first time the distinctive red CBC logo with blue lettering. Of course. I saw this guy nightly on TV announcing the latest news story.

"*Bonjour.* You are called Margaret Harris?" He asked in

French as he approached. "Pierre Bourke with Radio-Canada. I would like to ask you about the bones you discovered."

"Oh? Have the police finally identified the individual?" I replied, also in French.

"In a manner of speaking. Come, we'll do the interview over here." He motioned me to a place that showed off my Victorian house to advantage. "This will provide a nice backdrop. Just give my cameraman a few minutes to set up."

"I don't think my French is good enough."

"Sounds pretty good to me." He broke into his signature smile.

I turned to the Texans to suggest they wait for me on the verandah and noticed their perplexed frowns. "Of course, no French, sorry," I said and explained about the interview and my role in the discovery of the bones.

"Honey, that must've been a scare, finding a dead person like that," Billie replied, as she attempted to shove loose strands of hair under her hat. "No need to worry about us. But, child, y'all sure do have lovely red hair. Shame not to have it looking pretty for the TV."

My hand leapt to my head, and I felt a mass of tangled curls. Then I noticed the dirt and bits of bark covering my shorts and T-shirt. I raced into the house, and by the time I returned with my hair neatly combed, make-up applied and clean clothes, the TV men were ready.

Pierre brought a furry microphone up to his mouth. "Tell me how it feels to discover an eleven thousand-year-old woman."

He shoved the microphone under my nose.

"It was a bit—" I stopped. "What did you say?" I sputtered in English.

"I asked you what it felt like to be the discoverer of a woman who died more than eleven thousand years ago."

I blinked. The camera lens homed in on my confusion.

"I guess the police haven't told you yet."

"No. Are you saying the bones I discovered are not recent?" I asked, recovering my French.

"That's right. The radiocarbon tests indicate that these bones are… Let me see." He took a sheet of paper from his pocket. "11,245 years old, the oldest human remains ever to be found in Quebec, in fact in eastern North America."

"Wow." I felt like some starry-eyed kid seeing his first roller coaster, or whatever kids get starry-eyed over these days.

"So perhaps you could start by telling us where you found them."

"On a sandy beach on one of the river's many lakes. I have no idea what its name is."

"And the name of the river?" His face had taken on a hopeful look.

"Oh, I thought you knew."

"No, the police haven't yet revealed it."

"Well, I think I'd better not give out the name either. They probably don't want people going there until the archeologists have extracted all they can from the site."

Shrugging off his disappointment, he continued, "Then perhaps you can tell us how you came to find them."

Still feeling as if I'd been plunged into some kind of never-never land, I proceeded to explain about the canoe trip, being dumped and ending up on the beach where I discovered the bones.

He asked me a few more questions about their appearance and number. When he finished, he thanked me and told me it would be aired on that evening's news.

"I have a question. Did the police say anything about this ancient woman being murdered?"

"No. Why do you ask?"

I described the hole in the skull and my theory.

Now it was his turn to be wowed. As he turned his microphone off, I knew what his story's lead-in would be. "Remains of oldest murder found in Quebec."

Ed and Billie were suitably impressed and spent more time talking about ancient bones and other artifacts than my great-grandpa Joe's lovingly built cottage. Turned out, Ed loved nothing better than to go off on an archeological dig. And although they oohed and aahed over the expansive front room with its floor-to-ceiling stone fireplace and wall of windows overlooking Echo lake, I could see that their minds were more focussed on the eleven-thousand-year-old bones, exactly where my mind was too. I was itching to call Dr. George Schmidt, PhD. However, when Billie spied Aunt Aggie's antique mahogany secretary, her eyes lit up, and for the next hour I found myself showing her all the treasured pieces I'd inherited from my great-aunt.

"Y'all so blessed, honey, to have such an old respected family to pass these here wonderful things on to you. Why, mine were nothing but a hassle of cow wrestlers, ain't that right, Ed?" She winked at him. "Only thing they left me were a few acres of dried-out scrub. Ain't nothing nobody could do with it till my honey here found the oil." And she reached up on her tiptoes to give him a big kiss.

It was all I could do to keep from laughing out loud. Of course, oil, where else would a couple of Texans get their millions from.

After sipping tea and munching on shortbreads—I felt I had to offer them some real Canadian hospitality—they were gone with a promise to meet again tomorrow at Robbie's when construction of their canoe would begin. The door had no sooner closed behind them than I was dialing the number of the archeologist.

NINE

"National Museum of Canada," the crisp female voice answered at the other end of the phone.

Confused, I looked at the card again. Fossil Finds Inc. was definitely the company name. "Sorry, I must have the wrong number. I'm looking for Dr. George Schmidt."

"Just a moment, I'll connect you with him."

"Schmidt here," said the brusque male voice.

"Dr. Schmidt? It's Meg Harris calling."

"Who?"

I repeated my name.

"Right. Of course, the Quebec bones. How'd you find me here?"

"Called the number on the card you gave me."

"Right. Guess I forgot to remove the forward. In case you're wondering, Fossil Finds is my consultancy business. Hope you're not cancelling tomorrow's meeting?"

"Still on, but I couldn't wait. I gather these bones are considerably older than I thought."

He laughed. "You better believe it. Your discovery is going to set the history of this country on its nose, and its anthropologists too."

"How so?"

"It all has to do with the answer to the question: who were the first inhabitants of Eastern Canada, and where did they come from?"

"I thought that was answered long ago. They're the ancestors of today's aboriginals, aren't they? Supposed to have come from Asia during the last Ice Age."

"Maybe, maybe not."

"What do you mean?"

"I'm afraid it's rather complicated. I'd rather explain it in person. Now, about tomorrow, something's come up. Would it be possible for you to come to Ottawa instead?"

"Not possible. I'm tied up."

At that moment, my doorbell rang. Through the front window I could see another van. This one had CJOR News written along its side.

"The media sure think this discovery's big news," I said to the archeologist. "Here's another one banging on my door."

"Look, can you hold off talking to them, until you talk to me?"

"Why?"

"There's something I'd like to discuss with you."

"Okay, talk."

"No, I'd rather not do it over the phone. Look, if I leave now, I can be there by six o'clock, okay?"

Although I was surprised by this sudden change of plan, I was curious to know what he had to say. "All right, I'll be waiting. Must be important if you want to drive all the way back here again on the same day."

"Right. It is. Though I'd appreciate you not mentioning anything to the media. In fact, it's best if you don't talk to them at all until after my visit."

"You still haven't given me a good reason not to."

"Let's just say it might not be in your best interests. See you in two hours." And he hung up, leaving me wondering.

The knocking was now being answered by Sergei's warning

yelps. Surely there was no harm in talking about this discovery. Besides, they already knew I had found them. Why else would they be here? So I answered the door and found myself providing the same information as in the previous interview. Once again, I refused to reveal the name of the river.

My phone rang just as I closed the door on the journalist. I heard Sergeant Beauchamp's fluid French on the other end. "Madame Harris, I am calling to inform you that the analysis of the bones you discovered has been completed, and we are satisfied that they are not the remains of a recent death."

"So I've been told by the media. Quite a find, eh?

"Yes, very exciting. I have never investigated human remains of such age."

"What happens to them now?"

"I don't know. I have no experience with such things. It is for my superiors to decide."

"Not that I really want them, but don't I as the finder get them, or at least have some say in their disposition?"

"I don't know. But I can find out for you. The forensic anthropologist who did the analysis will know."

"No need, I'm seeing Dr. Schmidt this evening."

"Dr. Schmidt? I'm not familiar with this name. I have been working with Dr. Claude Meilleur at our forensics laboratory in Montreal. Perhaps this Dr. Schmidt is a colleague."

It was a possibility. There couldn't be many anthropologists with the appropriate forensic credentials. Maybe Dr. Meilleur had contracted with Fossil Finds Inc. to do the actual analysis. Still, from what little I knew of Quebec's xenophobic politics, it seemed unlikely that a Quebec government lab would seek out an Ontario-based archeologist, especially one with associations to the federally-based National Museum.

"But you can have the Senators cap," the policeman suggested.

"Obviously, it doesn't belong to the remains."

"You never know. It seems as if hockey has been played in Canada forever. Maybe they played it back then."

"And it was a girl's hockey team too," Sergeant Beauchamp added.

I laughed. This cop had a sense of humour. "Thank you. I would like the cap. It'll make a nice souvenir. Strange how the rip in the cap seemed to match the hole in the skull. Is it possible this cap belongs to an as yet undiscovered murder victim?"

"Madam Harris, you have a wild imagination. No, I'm certain the rip was accidental, and the hat was lost by someone who left the area alive."

"What about the remains? Are the archeologists saying whether they think she was murdered?"

"You'll have to ask them."

True to his word, Dr. Schmidt arrived just as Aunt Aggie's grandfather clock started bonging six o'clock. Although bursting with questions, I refrained and showed him onto the screened porch. As he lowered his muscular frame into the wicker chair, I tried to reconcile his football player image with my image of a nerd-like archeologist and failed.

He seemed tense, keyed up, so I rather apologetically offered him lemonade, and not the stiff drink he was no doubt thirsting for. Since giving up drinking, I no longer kept alcohol in the house.

After listening to him wax eloquent on my gorgeous home, the fabulous lake view, my wonderful dog and of course my luck in living in such an unspoiled wilderness, I finally managed to get a word in. "Before we begin, Dr. Schmidt..."

"Please, call me George."

"Okay, George. I'd like to understand your involvement with these ancient bones and with Dr. Claude Meilleur."

"I see you've been talking to Claude."

I winced at his English pronunciation of the name, making it sound like "clod" instead of the more elegant "clode". "I understand Dr. Meilleur was asked by the police to conduct the analysis. I'm just not sure where you fit into this."

"Easy. Claude needed my expertise. Couldn't find it amongst his French-Canadian colleagues." His wicker chair creaked as he guffawed smugly. His leg began twitching in an annoyingly nervous manner. "I specialize in the skeletal remains of paleo-Indians or paleo-Americans, as they call them south of the border. Not too many of us around."

He must've noticed my puzzled look, for he added, "In case you don't know, that's anything older than 8500 years. Did my post-doc at Washington State U, close to the site of one of the oldest discoveries on this continent. Kennewick Man. You may have heard of him."

I shook my head.

"This guy you found—sorry, I should really say gal—she has him beat by almost two thousand years. And this gal, she's going to be my ticket to the Clovis Chair at Cornell. But hell, I'm losing you, so let me explain."

He pulled out a folder from his backpack and spread a series of photographs across the wicker coffee table. In several I recognized the skull I'd found. Then he pulled out a number of maps and diagrams.

"I could've talked you through this stuff. But you know what they say about pictures. Thought it would be easier to show you what a monumental discovery your find is."

He pointed to a number of dots on an outline map of North America. "These indicate the sites of thirty-nine people who died more than nine thousand years ago. Notice any pattern to their location?"

It wasn't difficult to discern. "Yeah. They're located mostly in the western and south-western parts of the U.S."

"See any in Canada?"

I answered, "Only one. Looks to be in B.C. Does this mean no one is bothering to look for these remains in Canada?"

"Yes and no, but for a very good reason. Take a look at this map."

He spread out another map of North America. On this one most of Canada was shaded in with the words "Ice Cap". "Twelve thousand years ago, much of this country was covered by a thick glacier, some places over a mile in thickness. What we call the Late Wisconsinan glacial period."

"Considering the heat we've been having lately," I said, "I wouldn't mind being on top of one right now."

George laughed. "Cold it may be, but you wouldn't last long in such inhospitable conditions, not only because of the extreme cold but also because of a lack of the necessities of life, like plants, animals and fish. As this ice sheet melted, it created great bodies of water, equally incompatible to human life. But as these drained and dried up, the vegetation began to grow, the animals moved in, mammoths, sabre-toothed tigers and the like, soon followed by their predators, humans.

"It melted earlier on the western and southern parts of the continent than it did on the eastern half. Until your find, anthropologists had only theorized that life might be possible on the margins of the melting Laurentian Ice Sheet covering eastern Canada. A few stone implements dating from 9000 BP have been found. But no human remains of that age have been. Until now." He grinned broadly.

"Is this what you call a 'missing link'?" I asked.

"Yes, you could call it that." For a moment, the twitching in his leg stopped, then resumed.

Wow. And I had actually found it. Held it in my hands.

"But let me continue. Because this part of Eastern Canada was either covered by ice or a large glacial sea, called the Champlain Sea, until about 10,000 years ago, it was believed that humans didn't inhabit this area until about 9,000 to 8,500 years ago. To date, the earliest skeletal remains, pegged at about 7,000 years-old, were found at the Côteau du Lac site near Valleyfield, which as you know is considerably south of here, along the north shore of the St. Lawrence River."

He stopped to take a sip of the lemonade and pat the dog lying between us. The flat waters of Echo Lake reflected the orange brilliance of the setting sun. It was hard to image that eleven thousand years ago it would've been buried under hundreds of feet of ice or the frigid salt water of the Champlain Sea. Either way, I doubted my "missing link" or her relatives would've been anywhere near here. So how had she ended up on the shores of the DeMontigny River, little more than a hundred and fifty kilometres west of here?

As if reading my mind, George continued, "I can only theorize how this paleo-female ended up where you found her. Maybe she was part of a hunting party that had roamed onto the melting ice sheet in search of mammoth. Or maybe she came by boat. We believe the people of that time were capable of building watercraft. Regardless, she lived and died on what is today known as the—" He stopped to take another sip of lemonade.

I finished his sentence for him. "The shores of the De-Montigny River."

He turned his blue gaze towards me and nodded. "Yes, the DeMontigny River, which happens to flow along the margin of the Laurentian Highlands. Another possible explanation for her presence. This height of land would've been above the water level of the Champlain Sea."

He paused again for another drink "DeMontigny. Yes, I think we should call her the DeMontigny Gal."

"I prefer Lady. Sounds more dignified."

"DeMontigny Lady it is." And he settled back in his chair. The tension I'd noticed on his arrival seemed to have disappeared. His leg no longer shook.

Pointing to the photo that showed the large hole in the skull, I asked, "Do you think she could've been murdered?"

"I've been wondering about that myself. I believe it was caused before her death, but whether as the result of an accident, or intentional, we can only surmise."

He stood up and rubbed the leg with the limp. "Old football injury. Gets a little stiff. All that sitting I've been doing today." His smile flashed white. "I hope I've managed to show you just how valuable the DeMontigny Lady is to anthropologists and to the history of Canada and North America. But, and this is a big but..." He paused to ensure I was paying attention. "This pales in significance to the real import of your find, the one that's going to get me that Cornell Chair."

Before I could ask how, Sergei leapt to his feet. His barking almost drowned out the ringing of the front door bell.

TEN

"Probably more media," I said, getting up to answer the door. "Want to come with me? You can certainly tell them more than I can."

George's knee began twitching again. "No, I'll stay here. Look, I'd rather you didn't mention anything about what we've been discussing, okay? Or the fact that I'm here."

"Why, my dear George," came a man's deep voice from around the corner of the verandah. "What has happened to the pre-eminent paleoanthropologist Dr. George W. Schmidt that he is afraid to show his face to his favourite audience?"

The baritone voice had prepared me for a large man. What I saw instead was a rotund elf, the top of his bald head a shiny pink, his round nose a perch for his Ben Franklin glasses. He waddled towards us, completely oblivious to Sergei nipping at his heels. While his brow dripped with sweat from the heat, his brown eyes reminded me of a Cheshire cat, inscrutable and smugly amused.

"Why should I not be surprised that you are here with this charming lady, eh, George?" For the first time I noticed the slight intonation of a French accent. So when he finally introduced himself, I wasn't totally taken by surprise.

"Dr. Claude Meilleur, at your service, Madame Harris." He gave my outstretched hand a firm but sweaty shake. "I do not mean to interrupt this quaint *tête-à-tête,* but the purpose of my visit is no doubt the same as the good Dr. Schmidt's, *n'est-ce pas?*" He smacked his lips gleefully.

I could feel George's guarded stillness beside me. He'd said not a word. His only movement the now violent shaking of his leg. Other than responding to Dr. Meilleur's greeting, I decided not to say anything. Clearly there was something going on between the elf and the football player. It would be more interesting to let them hash it out without my intrusion.

"I see you have found your way to Madame Harris's house. Curious. I do not remember giving you this small detail," said Claude Meilleur.

I turned towards George in time to see him turn a brilliant red, which, unlike his colleague, I doubted was caused by the heat. Then I watched him squirm. "How ya doing, Claude, little buddy? Long time no see. Knew you were busy with that Gaspé dig, so thought I'd start the ball rolling on this one. Can't afford to keep the, ah…" he paused. "DeMontigny Lady waiting, can we?"

"DeMontigny Lady?" Claude pursed his lips in consternation.

"Yeah, that's right." George straightened back into his chair and crossed his arms, as if to say "so there". "Meg named her, which is only fitting. After all, she found this ancient lady…" he looked squarely at Claude "…on the shores of the DeMontigny River."

As I watched the anger spread across the francophone archeologist's face, I had an inkling about George's real reason for visiting me. He'd wanted the location. Apparently, Claude hadn't passed this crucial bit of information on to his anglophone colleague. Why not? Competitive rivalry between two archeologists?

"*Eh bien, mon ami,* you are too impatient. I was planning on inviting you to join me on my next trip to the site. Quebec has need of your assistance."

And while the elf's flushed face broke into the kind of smile not even a mother would trust, I knew I'd just heard the answer to my question. Though professional rivalry was no doubt involved, Quebec nationalism was more likely its root cause.

Couldn't have an anglo, especially one that worked for the federal government, getting top billing for such an important history-making discovery. Still, it did make me pause to consider Claude's initial question. One sure way of ensuring one's name was tagged with the find would be via the media. So why had George been so reluctant to face them?

"Mais, mon cher collègue," George replied, revealing a truly atrocious accent, "now that I know where more bones can be found, I don't need you."

Claude smiled sweetly. "One small matter you overlook. The site is on Quebec government land, and, as you well know, only a Quebec-registered archeologist has authority to work the site. And I of course am that archeologist. Also, I have the DeMontigny Lady's skull and other important bones. I doubt a few ribs or metatarsi would get you the Clovis Chair. So please, I propose we make this a collaborative project."

"You turned me down first time around, Claude. What's forcing you to change your mind now?"

"Let us just say, we can be mutually beneficial to each other."

George gave him a hard once-over, almost as if he were trying to see beyond the Quebec archeologist's cherub face to his underlying motivation. Finally, he said, "You're on, but I get first authorship on this."

"You know that is not possible. Since my government is funding this initiative, my name must come first." He removed the glasses from his nose and began cleaning them with the less-than-clean edge of his cotton shirt. After a second or two, he glanced back at George. "That is, unless…"

A smirk spread across George's face. "Your government hasn't coughed up enough, has it? You need my link to federal money," he crowed.

Claude's left eye twitched.

George continued, "I don't know. Money's tight these days, what with the current freeze on spending. I'd need to offer them something good in return. Like top billing on this project. You know how the feds are. On any joint venture with Quebec, Canada's name's gotta be up front and centre. So what do you say, little buddy? Top billing for me, and I'll get us the cash."

"On the English version only. My name will need to be first on the French version, otherwise my government will not even give me the authority to go ahead with this dig, let alone provide funding."

The anglophone clamped his large hand onto the francophone's small fist and shook vigorously. "You're on. Now let me go back to what I was telling Ms Harris about the real significance of this find. In fact, *mon cher ami,* you may want to listen in on this, too. It's something that I hadn't gotten around to mentioning. Something that's going to secure me that Chair."

His broad grin was joined by Claude's ironic smile as the francophone realized he hadn't been the only one holding back.

On the table in front of us, George placed two photographs; one of a frontal view of the skull I'd found, and another a side view, showing the jagged hole. Next to each he placed frontal and side views of two other skulls.

"Notice any similarities or differences between these three skulls?" George asked.

I shook my head. They were just cracked old bones to me. The only differences I could discern were the variations in damage and colour. Claude, on the other hand, studied them carefully. He pulled out a tape measure, a pen and notepad and began taking measurements of various aspects of each of the three different skulls.

After several minutes of numerous measurements and calculations, he turned a querying eye to George. "These two skulls have many similar characteristics." He placed the photos of the DeMontigny Lady beside those of one of the other skulls and moved the third set further away. "These two have similar characteristics, such as the forward placement of the face, with the braincase angling further back and a considerably narrower jaw. Not sure what you are trying to tell me here, George."

George smiled enigmatically.

Claude continued, "It is evident that the DeMontigny Lady and this second one have the same origin, Amerindian. But I'm not sure of your reason for including the third skull, whose structural characteristics suggest a different race."

"Come on, Claude, put those anthropological skills to work." George pulled out a fourth set of skull photographs. "Compare this to the other three."

Claude picked it up. "This is mine. Taken from the St. Louis de Ha-Ha cemetery site. Seventeenth century European female. Whereas DeMontigny Lady is an eleven-thousand-year-old paleo-Indian female. There is no relation between the two."

"Compare." George still wore that strange enigmatic smile.

This time Claude didn't bother to use his measuring tape. He simply gazed intently at the four sets of photographs. When finished, he placed his seventeenth century female skull beside DeMontigny Lady. "If I didn't know better, I'd say many of the features of this Caucasian female are also present in the paleo-female skull. But it can't be. Where is this other similar skull from?"

George turned the photo over to reveal the words *"Kennewick Man—solar calendar age 9,500—discovered near Kennewick, Wash."*

Claude's jaw dropped. *"Mon dieu,* I forgot about this Kennewick Man."

"That's why you need me, eh, Claude?"

"But I thought the research was suggesting that he cannot be an ancestor to modern day Amerindians because his physical characteristics are closer to the Caucasian features of Polynesians and Europeans than the Asian characteristics of Amerindians. Surely you're not suggesting that the same applies to this DeMontigny Lady?"

"Tell you the truth, at this point I don't know what to think, but I do know that this DeMontigny Lady has the same skull structure as Kennewick Man. Shit, you picked it out yourself."

He flipped over the third set of photos, the ones of the dissimilar skull, to reveal the tags. "As you can see, this set comes from your own forensics lab. They're of a murdered Mohawk that was found a few years back. I've also compared the DeMontigny Lady skull to other Amerindian skulls. Same result. More differences than similarities."

George leaned back into his chair and continued, "I'm afraid you'd have a tough time convincing me there's a link between the 11,245 year old DeMontigny Lady and today's Amerindians."

Dr. Meilleur's eyes glowed. *"Mon dieu!* Can it be true? Such a momentous discovery. *C'est incroyable."*

Feeling a little like a moron, I asked a question that had been nagging me for some time, "So what's the big deal?"

They both cast surprised looks in my direction, as if suddenly remembering I was there.

George was the one to answer. "As you probably know, the long held theory is that this continent was originally populated by Northeast Asians crossing the Bering Strait land bridge during the last ice age, about thirteen thousand years ago." He held up the photo of the DeMontigny Lady. "This little lady refutes all that. The only way her Caucasian ancestors could've arrived on this shore was by water, probably followed along the edge of land and ice, either from southern Asia or even Europe."

Claude beamed. "Something I've always dreamed of. To be involved in such a history-making find."

"Yeah, maybe we'll even have a university chair named after us." George let out a loud guffaw.

The Frenchman cast him an exasperated glance. "I do not care for such honours. For me the real honour is to be able to hold and analyze such unique and rare artifacts. But, *mon ami,* we must not be too impatient. We must carefully study all the artifacts from the DeMontigny site before we announce our findings. Now I understand your reason for not speaking with the media."

"Why not?" I asked. "Surely you've got enough info now. Looks pretty obvious to me. Besides, wouldn't it help in getting the money you need to continue the research?"

Both archeologists looked at each other. Finally, Claude answered, "There is a complication."

But before he could tell me what it was, I heard footsteps on the gravel walkway and looked over the railing to see Eric's dimpled grin shining up through the twilight. He'd plaited his thick heavy mane into two long braids, no doubt to provide some relief from the heat.

I rushed to welcome him back from his trip. By the time I returned to the archeologists with Eric in tow, the photographs had disappeared from the table, and both men were sitting upright with polite smiles planted on their faces.

I had no sooner introduced them to the chief of the Migiskan than the two men hastily offered their excuses and departed, but not before reminding me to keep our topic of conversation a secret until I heard from them.

"What was that all about?" Eric asked as we watched the two cars disappear into the growing twilight.

Believing he had a right to know, I told him about the momentous significance of the bones we'd found, and in so doing discovered Claude's complication.

ELEVEN

At first Eric was equally excited by the ancient age of the bones, but then his brow creased with concern. "She's got to be an ancestor of our people, which might cause problems."

"What do you mean?"

"Our people believe a person's remains must be returned to the land, otherwise their spirit can't rest."

"But the bones could be reburied after they've been studied," I replied.

"Might not be as simple as that."

"But they say she can't be one of your ancestors because her bone structure is more like a Caucasian. So there shouldn't be a problem."

"That so?" His brows arched in interest.

"So the two archeologists say."

"This distinction could be crucial. I'd better follow up." His dimples erupted. "I've missed you."

He opened his arms, and I folded into his warmth as the heat of his kiss raced through me. Yes, it was very good to have him back.

When we finally broke apart, the sun had sunk behind the far hills, leaving us bathed in the translucent twilight of a hot evening in July, or as Eric would poetically say, *miskomini-kìzis,* the month of the raspberry. A loon's haunting wail rose from the lake, while the twinkling lights of fireflies flitted in the deepening darkness.

Eric bent down to a plastic bucket by his feet. "Hungry?" He held up a fat lake trout. "Caught it on the way over. Thought I'd use some of those chanterelles you picked last week and some sorrel from your garden to make one of my famous stuffings." He grinned unabashedly. Since his culinary skills were considerably better developed than mine, I readily agreed.

*   *   *

The DeMontigny Lady remained in the background until a couple of days later, when Teht'aa pounced on me at Robbie's outdoor work area. While I was trying to keep the level of wood chips littering the dirt floor to a minimal depth, Ed was helping the master canoe builder form the canoe's structural pieces. Yesterday we'd both helped Robbie split a cedar log into sixteen equal pieces. Today Ed was holding the cedar lengths steady, while Robbie planed them into gunwales, outwales, ribs and other canoe sections. To do this, he used a homemade knife called a "crooked knife", considered by traditionalists to be the most essential tool for canoe building. The handle bent away from the carver, while the blade curved up on the end.

Billie and Jid had been tasked with splitting spruce roots into the thin strips needed for binding the bark to the frame. Each, however, tackled the job differently.

Billie, her white Stetson shoved forward to block the hot sun, focussed all her attention on her work. Her jewel-encrusted wrist blazed as she used a stick to pull out a long thin spruce root soaking in a bucket of boiling water. After removing the bark, she split the root into narrower lengths and rolled them into small bundles before placing them into a bucket of cold water to keep them pliable until needed. She started on the next root.

Jid treated his root more like a toy. After rubbing off the

bark, he whipped the long slippery strand through the air like a rodeo cowboy, which prompted a chuckle from Ed and a "Be still, child," from Billie. Grinning, he resumed his seat on a log and continued with the next stage of the preparation.

We were well into our working rhythm when Teht'aa burst in. "Meg, it's all your fault," she cried without any pretense of a greeting.

I felt my anger rise. "What are you accusing me of now?"

"I told you not to move those bones."

I gritted my teeth. "As I told you at the time, I brought in the police because I believed those bones belonged to someone whose family had every right to know what had happened to their relative."

"Yeah, well, I guess you can say we're her closest relative. So you have to give them back to us."

"What are you talking about?" Robbie broke in.

"The bones Meg found belong to our ancestors."

"No, they don't," I said and explained the theory of the two archeologists.

Teht'aa sneered. "Shoulda known you'd believe that shit. Ancestor robbers would say anything to keep what doesn't belong to them."

I was about to fling back a fitting retort, when Ed intervened. "Don't y'all have a law up here like we have back home? This here law says Indian remains must be returned to their people for reburial."

"Nope, this government don't respect the ways of our people," Robbie answered, with more volubility than usual. "Museums got some kind of understanding. But a lotta good that does. They return some remains, keep others. A sister rez is in a big fight with a museum right now over some bones that was found in an ancient burial site. Damn museum says it needs to study 'em to figure out how we come to this land."

"That's exactly what these archeologists want to do with the DeMontigny bones," I interjected. "In fact, they are so old and so unique, they might lead to new theories on how North America was populated."

"So what?"

"But wouldn't you like to know your origins?"

"We already do. Our legends tell us."

I was all set to tell him that they were just nice stories made up to explain the unexplainable but saw from his scowl that it wouldn't be well-received. Instead I said, "Don't you think it would be nice to have two versions, traditional legends and modern science?"

"Our people only need the legends. Passed down from elder to elder since our beginnings. Science is for your people. You can do what you want with the remains of your own ancestors, but leave ours alone."

"But this eleven-thousand-year-old woman is probably not your ancestor."

"She was found on our ancestral land. She's our ancestor." And he crossed his arms, as if to say "end of discussion". But after a few seconds, his face softened. "Meg, you're a good woman. Please understand, her bones are sacred to us. Her spirit won't rest until she's returned to Mother Earth. Could you please try and get them back for us?"

"I doubt there is anything I can do at this point," I replied, not wanting to agree to his request. Although I respected his desire to follow the traditional ways, I felt this was one time when modern ways should take precedence.

Ed, on the other hand, lent his sympathy to Robbie. "Know what you mean, boy. Can't say as I'd want the bones of my ancestors being mucked about by strangers. Best bury 'em. That's what I'd do."

While Robbie nodded his head in solemn agreement, Teht'aa shot me a "so there" look.

Billie gave her husband a long, thoughtful gaze, then she spoke up, "That's right, kids. Bury them in a deep hole with a few prayers. And don't tell nobody where that hole is. Else someone'll come along and dig them back up again." As she said these last words, she directed her gaze straight at me.

"Hey, wait a minute. Hope you're not accusing me. No way," I said, feeling I had to defend myself. "I will certainly respect whatever decision is made about these bones."

And while Robbie gave me a supporting grunt, Teht'aa muttered, "Yeah, sure."

I didn't bother to respond and merely returned to sweeping some more wood chips into the corner. And although the sun continued to beat down with a penetrating heat, a chill had descended over our little group.

*   *   *

When I reached Dr. Schmidt on the phone later that day to warn him of this latest development, his response was more philosophical than I'd expected. After all, if he couldn't study the bones, he had a lot to lose.

"I was expecting something like this," he said. "Had a long talk with your friend Eric. Although he's prepared to accept our position, he isn't sure about other band members."

"What happens now? Will you have to give the bones to the Algonquin for re-burial?"

"Afraid it's not my problem. It's Claude's. He's got the bones. Quebec has a special law that says no one can own human remains. So even though they don't belong to us, they don't belong to the Algonquin either."

"And I suppose, as the finder, I don't own them either?"

"Right."

"If I understand correctly, Dr. Meilleur isn't obliged to give them the bones?"

"No, but Quebec has adopted a policy that says human remains should go to the closest cultural or religious affiliation."

"But in this case, if as you say these remains are closer to Caucasian than Amerindian in physical structure, couldn't it be argued that the closer affiliation would be with those of European descent rather than aboriginal?"

"That's what Claude and I are counting on."

"I must admit I feel caught in the middle. The Migiskan are my friends. But although I sympathize with their desire to leave the dead alone, in this case I feel science should take precedence. It's not as if these bones had been taken from a sacred burial ground."

"Never can tell. Won't know if this is a one-off until we start digging at the site. Should get our permit to go ahead any day now from the Quebec Ministry. That is if these guys don't gum up the works."

"Can they do that?"

"Yup, by making a real ruckus, going to the media, that kind of thing. Although they don't have the legal right to stop us, they could make the bureaucrats think twice about giving us that permit, and, worse, insist on Claude giving them the bones we already have."

"I don't think you need to worry about that. The Migiskan are pretty level-headed. They may get upset, but they aren't the type to block roads or make a three-ring media circus out of something."

"Your friend, Eric, he sounds like a reasonable guy. Think you can convince him to let us keep the bones?"

I promised to do what I could.

TWELVE

Sated and mellow after another of Eric's scrumptious dinners, we paddled my canoe to the middle of the lake, hoping to escape the night's heat, one of the hottest yet in this unrelenting heat wave. When far enough from shore to capture a faint breeze, we stowed our paddles and floated in relaxed silence under the Milky Way, or "the spirits' road to the stars", as the Algonquin would call it. For an eye-blink, a shooting star blazed across the black sky, then vanished as if it had never been. A fish jumped and returned to the water with a dull plop.

Although my intention had been to mention the DeMontigny Lady once dinner was over, I found myself reluctant to disturb this peaceful calm. Eric, however, had no qualms.

"Meg?" he said from the stern. "Will you be terribly upset if my people insist that these ancient bones be returned to us for burial?"

"But Eric, how can they? They will be destroying a part of our history, yours, mine and theirs. The fact these remains have survived over eleven thousand years is a miracle. You can't just toss them back into the ground. Surely you understand that."

The canoe tipped as he shifted his position. "I do, but many of our people don't."

"Can't you persuade them? They have a great deal of respect for you, surely they'll listen."

"I'll certainly try, but it won't be easy. In spiritual matters, the elders hold sway, and most of them, including Grandfather

Albert, sincerely believe that the removal of ancestor bones from Mother Earth is a violation against the Creator."

"But they aren't even the remains of your people's ancestors."

"I've already tried that argument. But as far as they're concerned, physical characteristics have nothing to do with it. What matters is that these bones have been found on land that the Algonquin consider traditional territory. Don't forget the rock paintings."

"Yes, but say these Caucasian bones were only two hundred years old. I'm sure no one would be calling them ancestral bones."

"No, they wouldn't. But only because Europeans were a part of the landscape in the 1800s. Eleven thousand years ago they weren't."

"I beg to differ. These bones say they were."

"Yes, you have a point. And I'm not going to give up, not yet. But it's not going to be easy persuading the elders and the Band Council that they are not the bones of our ancestors. In fact, Grandfather Albert has begun calling them 'The Ancient One'."

"And if you can't convince them, what will you do?"

"I'm their chief. I have no choice but to follow their wishes." The canoe shifted again as Eric resumed paddling. "Don't forget, I've spent more years in your world than living amongst my own people. For this very reason, it is important that I represent their views, ones that may not necessarily be my own. It took at least five years for me to gain acceptance after my return. Even today, after six years as chief, there are some that still call me an 'apple' behind my back."

He didn't need to explain the insult to me. Teht'aa had already told me, "red on the outside and white inside".

During one of our initial get-togethers, when I was still trying to become friends with his daughter, she'd told me one of the reasons her pregnant teenage mother had fled back to her isolated northern reserve was out of fear that the child would grow up to be an "apple", like Eric. As much as Teht'aa's mother had loved the young man, she'd hated his white man's hockey playing world. When Eric had refused to give up his burgeoning hockey career, she'd severed all connection. A year after giving birth to their daughter, the young Dene woman had died in a car accident.

Growing up believing her father dead, Teht'aa had been in her late teens when she'd discovered the truth. But even so, it had taken her another five years to seek out the father her mother's family believed had betrayed his heritage by adopting the white man's way of life.

Her history had not come as a surprise to me. Eric had already told me some of it. What surprised me was the extent of her distrust of things not Indian. It was at this point that I realized the size of the challenge facing me, and it had left me saddened, not knowing what I could do to change it.

So I knew what Eric was up against. If he pushed too hard, he would be viewed once again as an outsider, with the risk that many of the modern improvements he'd brought to his community would be viewed with distrust and tossed out.

"But regardless," Eric continued, "I'll do all I can to convince them. I don't want them destroyed either."

He chuckled. "How about a swim, Miskowàbigonens?" He used his Algonquin name for me, meaning "Little Red Flower".

He started paddling vigorously towards the black hump of Whispers Island. Tucked into the far side of the uninhabited island was a small cove with the best sandy beach on Echo Lake. It also had another mark in its favour. The guides of the Forgotten Bay Hunting and Fishing camp had deemed it a poor fishing spot. With little chance of being surprised by an enterprising fisherman, it had become our favourite beach for skinny-dipping and other *en plein air* pleasures. I dug my paddle into the water, too.

* * *

Three days later, the Migiskan Band Council met to discuss the DeMontigny Lady. Although I wasn't allowed to attend, I heard the verdict when Eric finally arrived at my place hours after the meeting would've normally ended.

Despite his face being drawn with exhaustion, I could detect a barely contained anger.

"I was that close," he said, using his finger and thumb to indicate the narrow distance. "I had more than half the council ready to agree they were not our ancestors' bones, when my daughter and her damn Mohawk boyfriend burst in, shouting that sickness would come to our people if we didn't immediately return the bones to the land. She even had the nerve to say that a fishing accident last week was caused by the spirit's anger." He stopped to drink his coffee. "Still, I thought I was going to be able to swing it. I could see the distrust in my fellow councilmen's eyes. After all, Mohawks and Algonquins were enemies before they were friends. But I could also see that they weren't completely convinced the remains weren't those of our ancestors, so I offered them a compromise. To be on the safe side, we would rebury the bones, but only after the archeologists had learned all they could from them.

"And then Robbie arrived along with his father, and in true Kohoko fashion, rather than shouting and carrying on, the two of them said nothing, merely sat cross-legged on the floor, lit smudge and let it do the talking. Before long, the council, one after another, joined them on the floor. I had no choice but to become a part of the circle." He turned towards me. "I'm sorry, Meg."

I put my arms around him. "I'm sorry too. But the key thing is you tried. Your people's wishes are what matter, not mine, not the anthropologists. Still, I don't understand why they wouldn't accept your compromise."

"Our people believe that the handling of the remains is a desecration. Grandfather Albert insisted that they must be returned to the land immediately."

He straightened up. "Tomorrow, I'll make a formal request to the Quebec authorities for the return of the bones. But you know bureaucrats. Haven't met one yet who could make a quick decision. So in the meantime," he paused, "well, in the meantime, I leave it up to you."

He didn't have to say more. I knew he was telling me to warn Dr. Schmidt to fast-track their analysis in order to complete as much as possible before they had to give up the DeMontigny Lady's bones.

*　　*　　*

For a week we carried on with our lives, expecting any day to hear from the government. Eric pursued the affairs of his people, while I helped with the construction of the birchbark canoe.

Although neither Robbie nor Teht'aa made any comment when I turned up at his workshop the day after the council meeting, the smug smile on Teht'aa's lips told me she was gloating. To make matters worse, Larry had decided to join us. He didn't even bother to acknowledge my presence.

The Paynes were taking a break. Billie, appearing quieter than usual, cited the need to take a spell from the hard work, so they were going to drive the hundred and fifty kilometres to Ottawa for a few days of touring the national sites. They would also take Jid. A nice gesture, I thought, since this was probably the first time the boy would have visited Canada's capital city. Mind you, Teht'aa and her militant boyfriend would probably dispute that the city represented the nation of this young Indian boy.

Ignoring the smug couple, I pretended nothing had happened and focussed my attention on the job at hand, which today happened to be one of the most crucial and most delicate, forming the birch bark into the shape of a canoe, without ripping it. But Teht'aa decided my usual job more rightly belonged to her. Giving Robbie a come-hither smile, she brushed me aside as she rushed to help him pull the roll of birch bark from the iron bathtub in which it had been soaking to keep it pliant. Beaming, Robbie didn't even try to pretend he'd rather have my help. I contented myself with making sure the materials for shaping the canoe were handy, while she and Robbie started rolling out the length of birch bark along a raised wooden platform.

Larry, with arms crossed against his expansive chest, sneered. "Hey, canoe man. Some master builder, eh? What happened to the old ways?"

Robbie blinked at him in confusion.

"Yeah, man, where're the stakes, eh? Everyone knows the only way to shape the bark is between stakes hammered into the ground."

Robbie took up a two-foot stake from a nearby pile and deftly inserted it into one of a series of holes bored into the platform. He shrugged. "New ways sometimes better."

Teht'aa looked at her boyfriend with annoyance. "See, only you would be dumb enough to waste your time hammering stakes into the ground."

Larry glowered back then stomped over to a table where some cedar strips lay. Declaring himself as good a canoe builder, if not better, he removed his own crooked knife from his pocket and proceeded to plane the cedar into what looked to be ribs. Still, despite his challenge, I could see much of his bluster had gone. He must really love Teht'aa, I thought.

Once the sheet of bark, white bark facing upwards, was fully extended along the length of the platform, Robbie trimmed it to a few inches beyond the canoe's planned sixteen-foot length. Because I held it in my hand, I helped him centre over the bark a piece of plywood in the size and shape of a canoe. Teht'aa, not to be outdone, quickly commandeered a pile of round boulders, which she handed to Robbie as fast as he could place them on top of the plywood.

Once the bark was firmly weighted down, Robbie cut five evenly spaced slits on either side of the exposed width. Figuring it wasn't worth the hassle, I stepped back and let Teht'aa help him with the positioning of the inner gunwales and outwales. Although Larry continued to plane the ribs, I caught him casting mournful glances in the direction of Teht'aa and Robbie. I couldn't help but feel a bit sorry for him. It was not easy watching the person you love turn their attention towards another. I should know. It had happened to me.

The placing of the stakes was best done with three people, so Eric's daughter and I stood stiffly side-by-side, holding up first one side of the bark with its five slits then the other, while Robbie began inserting the stakes into the platform holes.

But before he could finish, Larry intervened with a sudden loud and ominous snap.

"What the hell ya doin'?" Robbie shouted.

In one hand, Larry held his crooked knife, in the other a broken section of cedar. The other end lay on the ground.

"Get away from that!" Robbie shouted and lunged towards the bigger man.

Larry raised his knife, but before he could strike Robbie, Teht'aa grasped his arm. "Stop it! No fighting!"

For a second, I thought Larry would turn on her, but then he shook his arm from her grasp and stalked off, muttering, "Stupid thing won't float anyways."

While Teht'aa glowered at his disappearing back, Robbie returned to the stakes as if nothing had happened. Me, I just let out a deep sigh of relief and resumed my position holding up the bark. Poor Larry. It looked as if he'd lost her. But then again, he didn't exactly have the most winning of ways.

By the end of the day, we had the rough shape of a canoe, with the inner and outer gunwales firmly bound in place by the spruce roots, a triumph of good teamwork.

*   *   *

About a week after Eric had sent off his letter requesting the return of the DeMontigny Lady, he slapped the response on my kitchen table. He watched with a wry smile as I read it.

The first thing I noticed was the language, French. Eric had sent his request in English. Although equally conversant in Canada's other official language, he'd written in English to make a point. Many years ago, his band had adopted English as its operating language in addition to Algonquin. He had every right to correspond with the Quebec government in that language. It looked as if the Ministry of Cultural Affairs also wanted to make a point: communicate to us in English at your peril.

The government official acknowledged receipt of the Migiskan Band Chief's letter and appreciated the council's position with respect to repatriation of ancestral remains. However, before they could proceed further, the attached form must be completed.

I fluttered the five-page form, in French only, in front of Eric, who rolled his eyes and shrugged. "What did I tell you. Bureaucrats. Can't do anything quickly. Since you know more about the bones than I do, I'm hoping you can help me fill it out."

I agreed, albeit reluctantly. What else could I do? I loved

Eric. Still, the form didn't need to be completed immediately. I slipped it under some magazines on the kitchen table and propelled a very tired Eric upstairs to bed. Maybe by morning it would be lost in the clutter of all the other priorities demanding his attention.

THIRTEEN

The next day, the Paynes arrived back from their Ottawa trip. In the trunk of their SUV, they carried gifts for friends they'd made in the community, including a pretty turquoise silk top for me, which left me feeling somewhat embarrassed. Not only because I didn't think I deserved it, but also because I felt it was a comment on my rather unfeminine way of dressing. Since most of my time was spent outdoors, I didn't see the need to wear anything other than utilitarian outdoor wear.

In the back seat slumped a sick Jid, flush with fever and complaining of a painfully sore throat. He was whisked immediately off to the Migiskan Health Centre, where he was diagnosed with strep throat. Armed with a bottle of antibiotics and strict instructions to stay quiet until his temperature dropped, he was sent home to be nursed by his grandmother.

A few hours later, when I stepped through the open door of the old woman's vinyl-clad bungalow, the first thing I noticed was the sweet pungent aroma of smudge, and the second thing, a shiny new kettle sitting next to a bag I recognized belonged to an Ottawa store. The Paynes had gotten this one right. Jid's grandmother loved her cup of tea.

The boy lay on a threadbare sofa shoved against the far wall of the tiny bungalow's main room. Although his eyes still glistened with fever, he managed a mischievous grin. Next to him sat his grandmother, Kòkomis, as everyone affectionately called her. And on a nearby table burned the sweetgrass.

When I identified myself, her time-ravaged face relaxed for a second in greeting, then returned as quickly to the tightness of worry. The arthritic fingers of one hand clenched what looked to be a piece of red cloth. The other gripped her grandson's hand.

"How are you feeling today?" I asked him as a bead of sweat trickled down my cheek. Even though the door and front windows were open wide, they did little to alleviate the cloying heat of the narrow room.

"My throat still hurts, but I'm feeling way better. Just Kòkomis, you know, making a fuss."

At the sound of her grandson's voice, the old woman turned her cataract-shrouded eyes towards his face. Wisps of grey hair clung to her damp brow.

Although many, including myself, had tried to convince her to undergo the simple operation for removal of her clouded lens, she had refused, insisting it was the Creator's way. I'd since learned from the nurse at the Health Centre that the operation would probably not improve her sight. Doctors suspected that her diabetes of many years had damaged her retina.

Her face crinkled in a broad grin. She said something in Algonquin.

Since neither of us spoke more than a few simple words of the other's language, Jid translated, "Kòkomis says I'll get better now that my good luck auntie with the red hair is here."

"Tell her it's a loving grandmother's touch that will make you better."

Despite the handicaps of blindness and age, the old woman seemed to be doing a good job of raising her energetic grandson. Apart from the usual mischief young boys get into and, of course, his one-time bout with drugs, Jid had stayed out of serious trouble. On the whole, he seemed a well-adjusted nine-year-old who loved his *kòkomis* dearly. I knew little about his parents other than the fact that his mother was dead and his father was locked-up in the Kingston Pen for killing a man in a drunken brawl.

"Adjidamò good boy," Kòkomis said in her limited English as she patted his hair.

She waved her other hand above the dish of burning sweetgrass in an attempt to brush the smudge towards her grandson. "Mishkikìwininì come. He make better."

Unfamiliar with the name, I asked, "Is he a friend?"

The boy answered, "Nope. Medicine man."

He squinched his face in disgust while his grandmother beamed. "Medicine man good guy. Make better."

She extracted what looked to be Jid's bottle of antibiotics from a pocket in her flowered cotton dress and held it up. "Bad." She unclenched her other hand to reveal a knot of red cloth. "Good," she said and finished the sentence in Algonquin.

"What did she say, Jid?"

"It's old people's stuff. She thinks it's going to make me better." He spoke quickly as if afraid his grandmother might understand, but she nodded in agreement, obviously assuming he was conveying her words.

"Tell me anyway."

"The red thing's a tobacco tie. Inside is some tobacco that the medicine man is supposed to smoke. It's supposed to tell him what's wrong with me. Then he'll know what to give me to make me better. It's stupid. The nurse has already told me what's wrong. Stripe throat."

"You mean strep throat."

"Yeah, that's it, and she gave me pills to make it better."

"True, but all the same, you must respect your elders. And who knows, maybe the medicine man's medicine will help too."

Jid squinched up his face again. "He smells and…he's scary."

A soft patter on the outside steps punctuated his last words. I turned around to see a small, dark figure standing in the open doorway. A halo of sun-fired hair framed the head. A strong odour of wood smoke and something spicy mingled with the humid air of the small room. While the smell was not unpleasant, I could understand why a small boy might not like its sharp tanginess.

"Kwey kàdìdàdj, Kòkomis," sounded a frail but steady male voice.

I knew enough Algonquin to know this was a respectful greeting.

The old woman replied and motioned for him to enter. In stepped a man I immediately recognized: Robbie's father, Grandfather Albert. He stared at me through horn-rimmed glasses, his face a wrinkled mirror of Kòkomis's. Although stooped, he held his old man's body with a confident dignity. A beaded deerskin headband kept his long but skimpy grey hair in place. He was dressed simply in a clean white T-shirt and worn blue jeans, while his feet were clad in a priceless pair of intricately-beaded moccasins. A leather pouch dangled at his side with what looked to be the end of a pipe protruding from the opening. In his right hand he held an eagle feather.

He turned his gaze towards the sick boy and smiled. *"Kwey Adjidamò."*

Then he turned back to me. His smile gone. "Go. You are no friend."

"Of course I am. I've known Jid and his grandmother for a couple of years," I hastily replied.

The boy chimed in with "She's my auntie", while his grandmother let out a string of Algonquin.

But the medicine man was adamant. "Go. You make Adjidamò sick."

"Me? I'm healthy. He picked up the bug in Ottawa."

"You make spirits angry."

At first I didn't realize what he was referring to, then it hit me. "The bones, right?"

"Enhenh!" he spat out, refusing to say "yes" in English.

I sought support from the old lady and her grandson, but their now-closed expressions told me they wouldn't go against their elder.

I had no choice but to leave. Before I stepped out into the hot sun, I turned around for one last look. The three faces directed towards me were a study in contrasts. While the expression on Kòkomis's face remained impassive, Albert Kohoko's stoniness was broken by a hint of smugness. Jid, on the other hand, had raised the shutter to reveal doubt tinged with fear.

"Everything'll be okay," I said. "Just don't forget to take your pills."

Jid nodded imperceptibly and opened his hand to reveal the bottle.

*   *   *

Two days later found me again at Robbie's workshop. Teht'aa was pouring boiling water over a strip of planed cedar, while Robbie was bending another, already softened, into the shape of a rib. Both acknowledged my greeting with a brief "Hi" and continued without interrupting their work.

"No Larry today?" I asked.

"That jerk," Teht'aa said with a finality that told me the romance was over. Her glance towards Robbie confirmed another was on the rise. She handed him another rib, which he in turn began to bend into shape with his knee. I noticed the unfamiliar line of a gold chain encircling her neck and wondered if this was her present from the Paynes.

"Where are Billie and Ed?" I asked.

"Over here, ma'am," came Ed's drawl from behind a stack of wood. The top of his black Stetson loomed into view, soon followed by his smiling face. "Billie's home restin'."

"Oh dear, I hope she didn't catch Jid's strep throat?"

"No, just feeling a might tired." He emerged carrying a couple of planks. "Robbie asked me to find cedar to make ends for the bow and stern. Do y'all think these'll do?"

"Yes, they look about the right size."

Just then Jid wandered into the workshop sporting a new Stetson just large enough for his small head. "Hi, guys," he said, not quite with his usual exuberance.

Ed playfully pushed the boy's hat over his face. "How's the cowboy? Feeling better?"

"Yeah, I'm okay." Jid carefully replaced his hat.

"Glad to see you took your medicine," I said.

He nodded faintly, then glanced towards Robbie. "Medicine man make me better."

Robbie grunted in acknowledgement.

Then the boy said, "Kòkomis is sick," and began to cry.

FOURTEEN

Three days later, Kòkomis died at the Somerset Hospital with her distraught grandson by her side and a chanting Grandfather Albert speeding her spirit onwards. On her death certificate, the doctor wrote "heart failure brought on by complications resulting from a streptococcal infection". What had been a mild infection in her otherwise healthy grandchild proved to be a killer for her. But the doctor cautioned us not to lay blame. With her history of diabetes and high blood pressure, it was only a matter of time before she succumbed to either a stroke or a coronary complication. The infection had just brought it on a little sooner.

But the medicine man wasn't buying any of it. "The spirits are angry," the old man exclaimed at her funeral. "We must return the Ancient One to Mother Earth."

He reiterated the same words to Kòkomis's family and other band members as they sat around the sacred circle of the smudging ceremony held afterwards to commemorate her memory. Many sombrely nodded their agreement.

"We should get an answer from the government soon," Eric said.

Then I saw his eyes flash with the memory of the application form and knew my ruse of hiding it was about to backfire.

"Too late," countered Grandfather Albert. "We bury the bones now. If not, we get sicker." He fanned the smudge with his sacred eagle feather, sending its purifying smoke swirling around the circle.

"I'll call them tomorrow," Eric said in an attempt to placate the elder.

I tried to avoid the suspicious glance he shot in my direction but knew I'd been wrong to hide the forms. The plight of these bones was too important to Eric.

"Hrumph," came the response. The old man closed his rheumy eyes and chanted softly.

Jid sat silently on the floor between Eric and me. He held his small body firmly upright, as if afraid to reveal the depth of his grief. Only the redness in his eyes betrayed the crying I'd heard coming from his room these past few nights. For the moment he was staying at my place. His aunt's crowded bungalow couldn't squeeze in another child, and no one else on the reserve had offered to take him.

"You know my Joey's sick," said a woman across the circle from us. "Came down with the same thing Jid got."

"My boy, too," added a man in a baseball cap.

"My girl's got it too," offered another.

Another, her face twisted in anger, pointed her finger at Jid. "What's he doing here? He'll make us sick."

The boy tensed beside me as he tried to hold in his tears. I put my arm around his thin shoulders and felt his trembling. Last thing he needed was to be cast as the band's pariah.

"Look, these things happen," I said. "Strep throat is a common infection. Usually harmless. But with Kòkomis it wasn't. She was old. She was sick. Any one of you could've passed on an infection that would've killed her. So please, don't blame her grandson. He has enough to deal with."

"We don't blame the boy." Albert's piercing black eyes locked with mine. "We blame you. You found the Ancient One. You got to return her."

Eighty-odd pairs of eyes turned towards me. Some heads

nodded. Some people grunted. Others said, "Yes."

"I don't have them." Why couldn't he just keep quiet? Saying the bones were making people sick. What nonsense.

"You find a way." The old man continued to hold my gaze. I stared back with equal determination. Then he closed his eyes and returned to his chanting. He fanned the rising smudge with his feather. People shuffled and fidgeted and grew quiet.

What was I going to do? He'd backed me into a very difficult corner. Many of these people were my friends, and I didn't want them to turn against me, but I couldn't let their superstitious beliefs prevent the DeMontigny Lady from telling her story.

After the ceremony and the potluck feast that followed, I returned with Jid to Three Deer Point. Eric stayed behind to speak with Robbie, who'd approached him as we were leaving.

While we waited for Eric, I talked briefly to George on the phone to forewarn him of the direction opinion was taking and to seek his advice. He could offer little help other than to say that it was always tricky with situations of this nature, and the course he usually followed was to keep plugging away at the research and let others do the talking.

Afterward, Jid and I cooled off in the lake. The sun had sunk behind the far hills, leaving the pregnant stillness of a crimson sunset. As I sliced through the red-reflected water, I couldn't help but worry about the bones.

I assumed Grandfather Albert was the key. Perhaps if he could be convinced these were not the bones of an Algonquin ancestor, others would follow. But how to convince him? Maybe if George or Claude sat down with him, they might be able to persuade him.

Upon reaching my destination, the exposed end of a massive log wedged in the lake's rocky bottom, I clung to its slippery end while I caught my breath. I watched Adjìdamo and Sergei play on the dock at the base of the Three Deer Point cliff. High above them the cottage windows glimmered through the giant pines covering the top of the point.

The boy was trying to convince Sergei, who hated water, to go for a swim. The boy would try to sneak up on his buddy, but the dog, no stranger to being pushed in, always kept just beyond arms' length. Finally Jid outwitted him with a dog biscuit, grabbed onto the collar and tried to drag the struggling animal to the dock's edge. Suddenly, the collar slipped off the dog's head, and the boy fell back into the water, amidst a gale of splashing laughter. Sergei stood at the edge and barked in triumph, but not for long. Jid reached up, grabbed the dog's two front legs and pulled. Sergei slid into the water with a yelp. Now it was Jid's turn to crow.

As he laughed and played with the dog, I couldn't help but reflect on the resilience of youth. For the moment, his grief was all but forgotten, and so it should be. He had a full life ahead of him. His grandmother's was behind her, and although he would no doubt miss her, he did have his aunt, uncle, cousins and a community that embraced children.

I headed back to the dock. By the time I was climbing the ladder onto the slippery wood, Eric's heavy but firm body was striding down the steep stairs that clung to the side of the cliff. He ruffled Jid's wet locks. Me he honoured with a peck on the cheek before diving arrow-straight into the lake.

"Man, did I need that," he said as his head burst through the surface. "Race you," he challenged, and he headed out towards the big log.

Jid and I dove in after him, while the annoyed Sergei remained firmly rooted to the dock, yelping at our retreating backs. Like a small dolphin, Jid slipped through the water after Eric, while I just glided along with my usual breast stroke. I turned back when they passed me on their return trip.

"So what did Robbie want?" I asked as we sat drying out on the dock.

"He thinks we should get the media on our side. If we can create a big enough uproar, it might convince the authorities to release the remains to us sooner than later."

"How?"

"Hold a ceremony to honour the Ancient One's spirit at the lab in Montreal where the remains are and invite the media."

Oh, dear, this just might work. "Look Eric, is it possible that if Grandfather Albert could be convinced the bones aren't that of the Ancient One, he would stop insisting they be reburied?"

"I've already gone through the archeologists' findings with him. He doesn't care. Insists that the Ancient One is an ancestor because she was found on traditional lands. Besides, all ancestor robbers are liars. His words, not mine."

"So I guess it wouldn't help if one of the archeologists spoke to him?"

Eric shook his head. "I want them to be studied as badly as you do, but Grandfather Albert won't budge. He's adamant that they should be returned to us immediately and without any further work being done on them."

"What about the other elders? Surely you could persuade some of them."

He shook his head. "Grandfather is our most revered elder. Now that he has made his views public, it would be impossible for me to go against him, nor is it practical. He's got the same authority as a priest has over the spiritual life of his flock.

"And to doubly reinforce his position, several more people have come down with strep throat. The Health Centre says we have an epidemic on our hands. So I'm sorry, Meg, but there's nothing I can do."

"But surely you don't believe that these bones are causing this sickness?"

"What I believe isn't important. What our people believe is."

"Look Eric, I want to respect your traditional ways, but this time I'm finding it very difficult. Don't you think that as the years pass and the influence of the modern ways becomes stronger, that your people will one day deeply regret the knowledge that will be lost by burying the Ancient One now? Is there nothing that can be done?"

He sighed. "I suppose I could give it another try."

"Dr. Schmidt has told me they need another two and half months to finish their analysis, after which the bones could be buried. That's all the time that is needed."

"Something you should keep in mind, Meg. I'm not sure we have to convince Grandfather Albert to gain what you want. Even if we do raise a lot of public support for our cause through this proposed ceremony, I doubt the government will move any faster than is necessary. And if they feel the study of these bones is more important, I'm sure they'll wait until the analysis is finished before releasing them to us."

He held out his arms. "Let's not argue. I believe whatever will come of this will prove to be the right thing for all of us."

FIFTEEN

Two days later, the TV cameras greeted our convoy of trucks, SUVs and compact cars as we drove into the parking lot of Montreal's Forensic Science Laboratory. While Eric and Robbie went inside to announce our presence, the rest collected in a ceremonial circle on the front lawn of the modern glass building.

Throughout the long four-hour trip from the reserve, I'd waffled back and forth on whether I should participate in the demonstration or not. The Migiskan decided for me. Their closed expressions and shifting eye contact were enough to tell me I wasn't wanted. So I found myself a discreet spot by a statue of some Quebec dignitary from which I could observe.

Before leaving the reserve, Eric had decreed, "No confront-ations. This is a peaceful demonstration. I want to show the world the solemnity of our purpose. I want them to recognize and respect our spirituality and in so doing grant us our petition."

So the twenty band members chose a location that would not interfere with traffic. It also lent itself to the import of their purpose, honouring Mother Earth, for over their circle stretched the branches of a maple, albeit a rather environ-mentally-challenged one.

At the sight of Ed and Billie nestled in amongst friends, I felt like an outcast. These were my friends too, more so. Still, the Paynes were entirely sympathetic to the Migiskan demands. I hoped my friends would come to understand why I couldn't be.

Their Texan outfits blended in with the western-style clothing of many of the band members. Only their Stetsons jutting above the myriad baseball caps and headbands betrayed their origins.

Teht'aa, making a concerted effort to avoid eye contact with me, sat directly in my line of sight on the far side of the circle. Looking like the poster girl for an Indian Princess, she wore the white, silky deerskin dress that had once belonged to her great-grandmother. She was certainly beautiful, I'd give her that.

To honour the occasion, Grandfather Albert wore a fringed deerskin vest over his usual white T-shirt. With studied solemnity, he spread the wolf skin of his medicine bundle over the sparse grass at the circle's centre. Next he placed four flags, white, red, yellow and black, one in each of its four corners. Meant to show the connections of nature and man to creation, they represented many things, including the four directions: north, the direction of cold and wisdom; east, dawn and new beginnings; south, warmth and growth; and west, night and unknown mysteries.

As the elder continued to lay out the objects of his medicine bundle, a handful of tiny shells, a jagged green rock, a small carved bear and other items sacred to him, another band member tapped a soft beat on a drum. It lent a timeless sound to the occasion.

Cameras flashed. Broadcasters' voices murmured. People began collecting.

Jid sat next to the old man. The youngest, he'd been given the privilege of holding the petition, a tanned beaver pelt stretched across a round frame made from a birch branch. The day before, Robbie had spent the entire day making it. His father had dictated the words, written in Algonquin on the pelt. Teht'aa had drawn the fish with a fishhook dangling above its head to represent the Migiskan, the Fishhook people.

Out of the corner of my eye, I caught sight of the red and blue flashing lights of police cruisers. I then noticed the flat caps of several policemen standing well back of the crowd.

Suddenly the wall of people parted and through it walked Eric and Robbie, accompanied by a lean, bespectacled man in a lab coat and a woman clad in designer chic, her hair perfectly coiffed, with the no-nonsense demeanour of a woman clearly in charge. Behind them bobbed the bald head of Dr. Claude Meilleur, his face a mask of impending doom. At the sight of me, he raised his eyebrows in surprise, then nodded in greeting. I ran my eyes over the crowd, searching for George, but didn't see him.

Albert lit the smudge. Fanning the smoke with his eagle feather, the elder offered it first to Eric and Robbie then to the Lab people for the ritual purification. Akin to the burning of incense, it was intended to cleanse the mind, body and spirit in order to set the tone of balance and harmony.

The boss lady pursed her lips in distaste, but obviously realizing her reluctance would only serve to exacerbate the situation, she went through the motions of washing herself with the smoke. She then entered the circle, following the direction indicated by Albert. When she reached the opening made for her, she couldn't quite keep the horror from her face as she looked from the ground to her white silk skirt. An elder sitting nearby passed her a shawl to sit on, which she took with a brusque *"merci"*.

After Claude and his colleague had been cleansed, the old man went around the circle, stopping at each participant to allow them to do likewise. He was halfway around when the circle was disturbed yet again. Larry, his warrior tattoo bulging on his upper arm, burst in, followed by five of his fellow Warriors.

"What are you doing here?" Eric cried out, then realizing

he'd broken the harmony of the circle, immediately apologized to the elder.

Grandfather Albert motioned them to enter. "My friends, you welcome, but you gotta respect peace of circle, okay?"

"Yeah, sure, man," Larry said, then turned towards Eric. "What'sa matter, chief? Afraid we're going to do an Oka on ya?"

At the mention of the word "Oka", the faces of the Lab people twisted in apprehension. No doubt the standoff at the nearby Kanasetake Mohawk reserve over a decade ago was still vivid in their minds. The dispute over land ownership had resulted in the death of a policeman. It had required the intervention of the army to bring an uneasy armistice between the reserve and its neighbours.

"We've just come to show our brothers a little solidarity." His eyes passed hopefully around the circle, but when they reached his former girlfriend sitting beside her new boyfriend, they hardened before abruptly turning away. I thought I saw him mouth the word "bitch" before he turned back to the elder. After the six men had washed themselves, Larry led them to a place in the circle that was as far from the loving couple as possible.

Under an arch of extended microphones, Eric began his appeal. He spoke French to respect the language of the laboratory. "Madame Doctor LaForge and esteemed colleagues, we, the Migiskan Anishinabeg, have come today to present you with this petition for the return of our ancestor's bones to the land where she once lay, on the shores of the river we call Wabadjiwan Sibi, River of White Water. Our people have hunted along its shores and fished on its waters since our beginnings, when the Creator put this land into our care."

Motioning the nervous Jid to step forward with the beaver pelt, he then read out the inscribed petition, first in Algonquin, then translated into French and English.

"If my bones could speak, would you listen? No, you would say, bones do not speak. But we, the distant voices, will be heard.

"We are born of Mother Earth. When we die, we go back to Mother Earth. It has always been that way.

"Listen to us, the distant voices. Put the clay back into the earth."

Silence greeted his last word. As cameras flashed and whirred, Jid walked stiffly towards Doctor LaForge with the large pelt slanted to one side so he could see around it. He stopped when he reached her seated form and offered it to her.

But her hands remained clenched in her lap, a frozen smile on her face.

"Please, you're supposed to take it," he whispered in English. She remained stonily still.

Jid glanced back at Eric, as if asking what he should do.

But before Eric could respond, Dr. Meilleur stood up and took the petition. Smiling, he mouthed a *merci* to the boy.

Her face a mask of marble, the lab director responded in French. "A unique approach. I am directed by the Ministry to tell you that your request will be given due consideration according to the policies of Quebec."

"But there is nothing to consider," Eric said, "The province's stated policy says that human remains must be returned to their closest cultural community. We, the Migiskan Anishinabeg, are the Ancient One's descendants. We insist that her bones be returned *today,* not ten years or a hundred years from now." He proceeded to tell her about the spreading epidemic.

"I am sorry to learn of this, monsieur. But I cannot help you."

"Of course you can. The bones are in your laboratory. With your forensic work now completed, you no longer need them. You can simply go inside and retrieve them."

"I sympathize with your request." She paused. Her eyes

shifted briefly to Claude, then back to Eric. "But the remains are no longer in our possession."

"Who has them now?" Eric shot back.

Maybe George had them, I thought. Still, the brief exchange with Claude suggested this was a strategic lie.

Ignoring his question, she replied, "I will pass your petition on to the appropriate officials."

She strode towards the circle's entrance, with Claude, their colleague and the petition not far behind. Larry and his buddies made a move to intercept her, but a sharp command from Eric stopped them. She swept out of the circle into the glare of camera lights and waving microphones.

While Claude's colleague disappeared with the petition after their boss, Claude detoured towards me. "A lovely ceremony, but I don't think it will achieve the desired result."

"Why do you say that?"

"I'm afraid my boss is somewhat biased. Her parents owned land involved in the Oka land squabble. Of course, the decision isn't hers, but I think she'll do what she can to influence it."

"What about you? Are you sympathetic?"

"I would be if I thought the Demontigny Lady really was a direct ancestor, but I don't. The more I study the bones, the more convinced I become. It is very possible that her forebears came by boat from Europe and not across the Bering Strait from Asia, as the ancestors of the modern Amerindian did. What happened to these people is a mystery. Perhaps they died out."

"Or maybe they interbred with the Asians that came across the Bering Strait?"

"True, but even if this were the case, they cannot be considered the direct ancestor to the Algonquin. It is much like saying Neanderthal man is a direct ancestor to modern day homo sapiens."

"But you know the Migiskan won't accept this."

"I know, and it pains me, because I do like to respect the cultural ways of other peoples."

"Is there anything you might be able to do to persuade them?"

"I will give it some thought. But there is something you might be interested in. I have discovered a most curious thing about this prehistoric lady. I think she could be the ancient equivalent of a battered wife."

I felt myself go cold at these words.

"Yes, apart from the hole in her skull, which I believe probably caused her death, I've discovered healed breaks in one of her femurs, in a couple of ribs and in her ulna. Forensic analysis suggests these injuries didn't happen at the same time. So I think either she was accident-prone, or she was being repeatedly beaten."

"Poor woman. But if wife-beating is considered an inherited trait, then I think all of us can claim a link to the DeMontigny Lady." I thought of my own abusive marriage.

Before Claude could respond, we were interrupted by a journalist intent on asking him questions. With a quick *adieu*, the tiny archeologist turned around and began his interview.

Not long afterwards I noticed him in a heated discussion with Larry and wondered what it was about.

*   *   *

Seven hours later Eric, Jid and I arrived back at Three Deer Point feeling tired. Surprisingly, Eric was in an upbeat mood. He hadn't expected the Lab people to turn over the bones. He knew they didn't have authority. He and the other organizers were counting on the TV images of the ceremony and their interviews to engender public support and thus push the government into making the decision in their favour.

Unfortunately, we didn't arrive in time for the six o'clock TV news. Despite our exhaustion, we forced ourselves to stay awake for the ten o'clock *National*. At least Eric and I did. Jid, his eyelids drooping, was carried up to bed, where he snuggled into sleep the minute his body sank into the bed covers. I felt like joining him.

Just as well I didn't. The Migiskan petition opened the news. No, not quite. It was the second story. The first announced the death of Dr. Claude Meilleur.

SIXTEEN

Both now fully awake, we sat up and fixed our eyes on the TV screen.

"Damn," Eric said, voicing my feelings exactly.

The camera panned across the front of the Montreal lab to a long shot of the ceremonial circle on the front lawn. Then it zoomed in to capture the worry on Claude's cherub face.

"Less than four hours after receiving a petition from the Migiskan Algonquin for the repatriation of the eleven-thousand-year-old remains of the DeMontigny Lady," the announcer said, "Dr. Claude Meilleur, lead archeologist on this project, was found dead of a stabbing in the parking lot behind the Montreal Forensic Science Laboratory."

"Oh dear, I'm so sorry. He seemed like a nice guy. Certainly a lot nicer than Dr. Schmidt."

"It's gotta have something to do with the damn bones. Christ, if one of our people did it, I'll kill them." Eric slammed his fist down onto the fragile veneer of one of my aunt's antique end tables.

I winced. "Calm down. You don't know if his death is related. It could just be a coincidence," I said, not really believing it myself. The timing was too close.

"The police have also discovered," the announcer continued, "that the ancient bones sought by the Algonquin are missing. Apparently Dr. Meilleur was about to transport them to the Ministry of Culture and Communications in Quebec City."

Shit.

The story ended with a close-up of Eric coldly facing down the petite and sweetly smiling Dr. LaForge.

"They're already accusing us."

"Eric, for what it's worth, Dr. LaForge lied to you. She told you she no longer had the bones, but it looks as if they were still there. Maybe she's lied about other things, too."

"What are you saying? She did it?"

"No, of course not. I'm just pointing out an inconsistency. Perhaps there are others."

Eric reached for the phone.

"Who are you calling?"

"I want to find out when everyone got back. At best, it's a three and a half hour drive from Montreal. If we can establish that everyone was back at the rez within that time period after the guy was killed, we can prove we're not involved."

"Sounds like a good idea, but don't forget that after the ceremony, several stayed to see some of the sights in Montreal."

"Yeah, I know. I'm just hoping they all got back here within that window."

"And if not?"

"We'll at least know where everyone was, so when the police come calling, we're prepared. Nothing like a bit of boy scout training, eh?" he said with a wry smile.

"Anything I can do?"

"Yeah, could you track down Tommy Whiteduck? I think we'll need a lawyer on this."

"Will do once you're off the phone."

He looked at my only phone in his hand. "Sorry, wasn't thinking. I'll make a few quick calls. Then the phone's all yours. Any I don't reach, I'll go look for. I also need to call the police chief to give him a heads up."

"Better yet, why don't you get him to do the checking? That way, if there do turn out to be problems, it won't look as if you're interfering."

"Good thinking. I always knew you had more going for you than just a pretty face." He chuckled as I planted a gentle punch on his chest.

Eric called Will Decontie, chief of the Migiskan First Nation's Police force. After he explained the situation, they agreed to meet in fifteen minutes at the police station.

"I'll come with you." I turned off the TV.

"Good. I'll need help remembering who all went to Montreal." Eric started towards the door, then stopped. "What about Jid? Should we be leaving him alone?"

"Whoops. Forgot. Not used to having kids around. I guess I'd better stay."

"Before I go, help me put together a list to give to Decontie."

Using the various vehicles as reference points, we managed to come up with a list of twenty. When we reviewed it, we realized we'd forgotten the big Lincoln, so we added the Paynes' three passengers to the list, giving a total of twenty-three Migiskan who'd driven to Montreal to deliver the petition.

As the door clicked shut behind Eric, I dialed Tommy Whiteduck's home number. Son of a friend of mine who'd come to a tragic end, he was an obvious choice for a lawyer. Although it was many years since he'd lived on the reserve, he hadn't forgotten his roots. He had a small legal practice in Ottawa, which specialized in native cases. A year before he'd proved invaluable in helping out on a murder case involving one of the band's misguided youths. I had no doubt that he would help his friends out now.

Except when I asked him, he said, "No."

"Why not?"

"A little matter involving conflict of interest."

"Over what?"

"I see Eric hasn't told you."

"What are you talking about?"

"Let's just say I'm working for the other side. I'll let Eric tell you the rest."

"But he's your chief."

"Sometimes you have go with whoever is paying the bills."

"I'm disappointed in you, Tommy. I didn't think you were that crass."

"Yeah, well, we aren't all rich. With all your millions, you can afford to get them a fancy lawyer."

Before I could come back with a fitting reply, he hung up, leaving me feeling disheartened. I thought he'd buried his resentment over the symbiotic relationship our two families had had for over a hundred years. But even if it had been an employer-employee relation, friendship had been at the root. Also, his family had benefited from the money the Harrises had given them, over and above their wages. Tommy himself had been the last recipient of this largesse which, combined with his government funding, had enabled him to become a lawyer.

As for millions? Hardly. My great-aunt Aggie had left me enough to generate an income that covered the ongoing costs of Three Deer Point, with enough left over to live on without working, as long as my expenses remained within the bounds of country living. Nothing more. My only other source of income was the settlement I'd received from my divorce. And given slippery Gareth, who'd managed to hide most of his money offshore, it wasn't much.

Nonetheless, I did take Tommy's advice and left a message at the office of an Ottawa lawyer with whom I'd had dealings in the past, hoping he would know of a Quebec-based lawyer who would be able to help us. Thinking the Paynes might know who had returned, I next called the Forgotten Bay Hunting and Fishing Camp, where they were staying, only to discover they'd not yet arrived back themselves. It looked as if proving whereabouts at the time of the murder was going to be a lot more difficult than either of us had thought.

How difficult I discovered when Eric came back two hours later.

"Of the twenty-three on the list, only twelve arrived back here within the three and half hour window," Eric said, not bothering to hide his discouragement. "Another six came later. Decontie's collecting their statements now. That leaves five who are still not back. Probably spending the night in Montreal."

"The Smiths and their son Gilbert were with the Paynes. Who else?"

"Robbie and my daughter."

Not good news. Two of the most vocal opponents. They were bound to be prime suspects. "What about Robbie's father?"

"No problem there. He came back with the McGregors' immediately after the ceremony."

"Any idea where Robbie and Teht'aa could be?"

Eric shook his head. "Montreal's a big city. They could be anywhere."

Worried about what the morning might bring, we headed upstairs to bed.

At three o'clock, the phone's ring woke me out of a fitful sleep.

"Can I speak to my dad?" a female voice said without so much as a "Sorry to bother you."

"It's Teht'aa." I passed the phone to Eric.

"Where are you?" he demanded. His grip on the receiver tightened as he listened. "I'll get you one." He hung up and turned towards me, his shoulders slumped with defeat. "She's been arrested."

SEVENTEEN

Teht'aa needs a lawyer." Eric picked up the phone again. "What's Tommy's home number?"

"You'd better get another one. Tommy says he can't work for you because of some problem with conflict of interest."

"Christ, this has nothing to do with that mess."

"What mess?"

"The problem I'm dealing with at the AFN. I'll tell you about it later. Probably faster anyway if I get a Montreal lawyer."

"I might be able to help you there."

Not caring that it was the middle of the night, I called the emergency number of the Ottawa lawyer, who gave me the name a colleague in their Montreal office. Ten minutes later, Eric had the lawyer on the way to the police station where his daughter was being held. But rather than returning to bed, he started dressing.

"What're you doing?" I asked.

"Going to Montreal. I wasn't there for my daughter when she was growing up. I need to be there for her now."

"I wish I could come with you, but Jid makes it impossible. Besides, you don't need me getting in the way. This is between you and her."

"Yeah, you're right." He held me tightly. "If only she would accept you."

"Do you think she did it?"

"I don't know what to think. She has a lot of anger inside

her, I know that much. Enough to make her kill? I'd like to think not. But regardless, I'm not going to judge her. I'm going to do what I can to help her."

Worried over what awaited Eric, I watched the headlights of his Jeep flash through the trees lining the Three Deer Point road. When their glow vanished into the black night, I returned to bed. But sleep came only in fits and starts, and as dawn's grey light washed over me, I got up. The night's heat had chilled enough to make me want to put on a terrycloth bathrobe over my bare skin.

From down the hall came the echo of the boy's intermittent coughs—a holdover from his bout with strep throat—mingled with the dog's heavy breathing. Last night Sergei had crawled onto the double bed and nestled beside his buddy. When I'd looked in later, the dog had become the boy's pillow. Passing them now, I smiled to see that the two friends were still a tangle of black fur and orange Senators pajamas.

Downstairs, I flipped on the kitchen radio to catch the six a.m. news. Although Dr. Meilleur's murder headlined the report, there was no mention yet of an arrest.

I put on the coffee, then headed outside. The air was thick and still. My nostrils twitched at what at first seemed to be smoke from a woodstove, but given the summer temperatures, it was more likely someone burning brush.

As I descended the stairs to the lake for a brisk sunrise swim, the thickness of the mist became more apparent, so too the smell of smoke. I figured the most likely source was the Migiskan-owned Fishing Camp at the end of Forgotten Bay about a half mile north of Three Deer Point.

I dove in, expecting a refreshing coolness, and found it less than exhilarating. The heat wave had warmed the water to such a degree that it was the temperature of a tepid bath. Still, it was sufficiently refreshing to prompt several forays to the log and back.

By the time I was drying myself on the dock, the rising sun had transformed the hazy greyness into an eerie orange glow. The smell of burning seemed more pronounced. I hoped this didn't mean one of the Camp buildings was on fire. Just what Eric needed, another disaster. I headed back up the cliff to the cottage to find out.

Sergei rushed out the minute I opened the back door, and he sped off to the nearest tree. The silence he left behind told me his buddy was still asleep. Just as well.

After pouring myself a mug of strong coffee, I called the Camp.

"Hello," answered the groggy voice of Pete Smith, one of Eric's guides.

"Little early for you, eh?"

"Big date last night," he laughed. "Surprised you're up at this hour. Look, is the old man there? I need to talk to him."

"No, he isn't." I explained about Montreal.

"Holy shit. Do you think she done it?"

"I've no idea, but that's not why I called. There's a strong smell of smoke this morning, and I was wondering if you were burning brush."

"Nope, not us. I noticed it coming into work. Some crazy fog, eh?"

"Yeah. Reminds me more of Southern Ontario smog. But can't be. We're too far from any industrial areas. Maybe a building's on fire somewhere on the reserve."

"Jeez, hope not. These damn woods're so dry, a spark from somethin' like that could torch the whole damn area."

"Yikes, I hadn't thought of that."

I hung up and dialed the Migiskan police station.

"You're about the hundredth person to call this morning about the smoke," Will Decontie said. "I've had my men out checking around the reserve but haven't found anything yet."

"What about a forest fire?"

"Yeah, that's my biggest worry. I've got calls into SOPFEU, the forest fire people. Hell, we're surrounded by hundreds of square miles of tinder dry bush. Could be coming from anywhere. But I tell you, Meg, with this amount of smoke, it's got to be big."

"Thanks for lessening my worry. Anything I should be doing?"

"It's too soon to be thinking about evacuating. I'll let you know the minute I hear from the forestry people."

I hung up with the word "evacuating" ringing in my ear. I hadn't thought that far ahead. If I had to leave, what would I take? There were four generations of family history in art, furniture and mementos, and my home—the squared timbers, which had had over a hundred years to dry out, would no doubt burn to the ground, leaving only the stone chimney to indicate where my family had once laughed, loved and wept. Not to mention the magnificent old growth pines. They'd be nothing but scorched, blackened spires, as well as the sugar bush and all the other trees on my land.

I shook my head. No, I didn't want to think about it. Not yet. I poured myself another coffee and went out to the screen porch to console myself on Aunt Aggie's old bentwood rocker. It was one item I wouldn't be able to leave behind, not after the many hours I'd spent rocking away my fears, my uncertainties, my loneliness.

Despite the orange glow that continued to cast a surreal sheen over the lake scene before me, I tried to tell myself that the smell of smoke had lessened. Even the density of the haze seemed to be thinning. I could now see the distinctive porcupine outline of Whispers Island on the other side of Echo Lake, even the yawning gap where some of the ancient pines had been felled before the loggers had been stopped.

Eric should know about this, but I would wait until I heard from the police chief before I overloaded him with more trouble. Besides, he would still be on the road and unreachable unless his cell phone was turned on, which was rare.

I switched on the radio for the seven o'clock news. Nothing about a fire and nothing yet about an arrest in the archeologist's murder. The announcer, however, did add, "We have learned that the murder weapon is very unusual. Although our sources would not divulge its exact nature, we understand that it has considerably narrowed the search for the killer."

I started at the words "search for". Did this mean that they were still looking? If so, what about Teht'aa? Unless the police believed she had an accomplice and were keeping her arrest quiet. And if this were the case, I didn't need to be a homicide cop to come up with a suspect. Robbie, who was even more committed to getting those bones reburied than she was.

I fed the dog, checked up on the still sleeping Jid, poured myself another coffee and returned to the porch. A rising breeze was dispersing the fog.

Fifteen minutes later, Will Decontie called. "Not to worry," he said. "SOPFEU officials say this is coming from several major forest fires near James Bay, about six hundred kilometers north of here."

"Thank God. You had me loading up my truck."

"It doesn't mean we're out of danger. Until we get a good rain, I suggest you be careful. I'm issuing an advisory for the reserve. No fires, no smoking in the bush, no barbecuing. Any little spark could set off an inferno."

"Do you know about Teht'aa's arrest?"

"Yes."

"Anything you can tell me about it?"

"Meg, you know better than to ask."

I did, but I persisted. "They looking for anyone else?"

"Sorry, I can't discuss an open case."

"Just thought I'd ask. I'm worried what this will do to Eric."

"Tricky, but hell, most of us got our skeletons," he answered with little sympathy, which made me wonder about his own skeletons. But then again, who was I to talk?

As the morning progressed, the smoke gradually dissipated, leaving the dull blue sky of another hot summer day. Jid woke about ten, full of energy and chatter, more than my tiredness could handle, so I drove him over to his young cousins to let them wear him out, and I left Sergei with them too.

I expected a voice message from Eric by the time I returned and was disappointed to discover none. I tried dialing his cell but got only the "not currently in service" message. With eyes drooping and spirits equally low, I crawled back into bed.

I was frantically beating back the flames that threatened to engulf my house when a shrill ringing broke through, and I found myself waking to the cleansing smell of pine drifting through the open bedroom window.

The ringing persisted. I scrambled to answer the phone and caught it before the voice mail clicked in. "Good, you're home," came Eric's deep, resonant voice.

"Where are you?"

"Still in Montreal. Just wanted to let you know I'm leaving now."

"How'd it go?"

"Okay. Better than I thought."

"How's Teht'aa?"

"Okay, though a bit shaken."

"I'm sure. What happens now?"

"That's for the lawyers to decide. Look, that guy you got us turned out to be one hell of a lawyer."

"Good." I glanced at the alarm clock. "It's three fifteen now. Don't bother to eat on the road, I'll have dinner waiting, and you can tell me all about it when you get here."

He paused. "Look, if it's okay by you, I think I'll go straight to my place. After all she's been through, I think Teht'aa will want to forget dinner and go to bed."

"Teht'aa?"

"Yeah, she's out on bail. I'm bringing her back with me."

EIGHTEEN

After spending the rest of the afternoon and into the evening worrying about Eric, I decided, despite his daughter's presence, that I would go to his place. If ever there was a time he needed moral support, this was it. And when I saw the worry and fatigue etched on his face, I knew I'd been right to come.

"I think you need some TLC." I hugged him while the tension slowly eased from his body.

After a few minutes, he relaxed his grip. "Thanks, I needed that. It's been a tough day."

I followed him into the front room of his government-issue bungalow. Although Teht'aa wasn't there, evidence of her presence was. The deerskin dress she'd worn at the ceremony in Montreal was draped over the back of Eric's favourite chair, a bedraggled tweed-covered lazy-boy that had seen better days. I'd once offered to buy him a replacement, but he had refused, saying that this chair had stuck by him through thick and thin, and he wasn't about to get rid of it just because it was old.

The three-seater leather sofa, however, was reasonably intact, with only a few scratches on the brown cowhide and no stains to speak of. Housekeeping wasn't exactly one of his strong suits. Nor was it mine, for that matter.

At least he tried to keep the dirt at bay. Still, I wasn't surprised to see a couple of empty beer bottles, a half-eaten plate of food and a cup of cold coffee cluttering the pine coffee table. Since his daughter had moved in a couple of months before after losing her job, his bungalow had taken on a considerably more lived-in look.

Her presence also meant that Eric ended up spending more time at my home than I did at his. Her animosity towards me made any stay at his place all but impossible. I hoped she'd find a job soon, and we could get back to our peaceful life together.

I joined Eric on the sofa. "Teht'aa in bed?"

"Yeah, she was exhausted." He yawned.

"You should be in bed, too."

"Shortly. I'd like you to stay."

"What about Teht'aa?"

"I'll handle her. But wait a minute, I forgot about Jid."

"No problem. I have him strategically placed at his cousins. Sergei's there too."

"Good." He reached for the dirty plate. "Guess I'd better clean up this mess."

I took it from him. "You rest. I'll do it, but later. First, I want to know what happened at the police station."

"Not much to tell, really. She did a very foolish thing, and she'll have to pay for it."

"I'd hardly call killing a man foolish!"

"Sorry, I thought I'd told you. Guess I really am tired. Police didn't arrest her for Dr. Meilleur's murder. They nabbed her for stealing some of the bones."

"Why not the murder? I thought the two were related."

"No evidence, thank God." He tried to stifle a yawn.

"So that's why the news said they're still searching for the killer."

Eric nodded.

"Besides, I had an alibi." Teht'aa spoke from the entrance to the hallway leading to the bedrooms. Even though her hair was tousled and her face puffed with sleep, she still looked as if she'd stepped off the page of a glamour magazine. A cinched-in bathrobe only served to emphasize her curves.

"That's good. What were you doing?" I asked, feeling not only glad for Eric but also for her. Even though I didn't like her, I didn't want to see her guilty of murder.

"Was with Ed and Billie."

"Was Robbie with you?"

"Yeah, of course."

"Good, that means he's in the clear too."

She nodded.

"So when did you steal the bones?"

"I didn't steal them."

Eric cast a stern look in her direction. "Teht'aa."

"Okay, okay, so I pinched them. But I didn't set out to take them, okay?" She moved the deerskin dress aside as she slumped into Eric's chair. "The opportunity just sort of presented itself."

"How?" I noticed her nose was running. In fact, she always seemed to have a runny nose.

"The spirit thief showed them to me." Extracting a tissue from her pocket, she wiped her nose.

"Why would Dr. Meilleur do that?"

"No, not him. Another one. George."

"But why you? It's not as if you're friendly to his cause."

"Probably wanted to get me in bed." She laughed, just a little too harshly.

"When was this?"

"After the ceremony. I was walking back to the car when he came up to me."

"You sure? I didn't think he was there."

"You don't believe me?"

I tried to read deceit behind her challenge and couldn't see beyond the jutting chin and blazing eyes. "Okay. Go on." There had been quite a crowd. I could easily have missed George.

"Anyways, he wanted to buy my great-grandmother's deerskin. Said he'd never seen such a well-preserved example of late nineteenth century workmanship."

Eric's eyes opened wide in shock. "You didn't tell me this part. Of course you said no."

"Of course. What do you take me for? No way would I betray our heritage to those spirit thieves. Told him as much. He said he was sorry about the Ancient's remains. If he had his way, he'd give them to us."

Yeah, sure, I thought to myself.

"I asked him if I could say a few prayers over the Ancient One. So he took me into the lab and showed them to me. When he wasn't looking I grabbed a couple of small ones, vertebrae I think, and stuck them into my purse. Figured he wouldn't miss them. Then I—"

"I thought all the bones were missing," I interjected.

"If they are, I didn't take them. You gonna listen to my story or not?"

"Okay, sorry," I said, wondering if this would further confirm her innocence.

"I chanted a few prayers to the Creator. It sure gave me a thrill to see the Ancient One again. Then the spirit thief shows his true colours, says she's too important to be returned to the land, and he'll make sure it never happens."

For very good reason, I thought to myself. They were his ticket to fame. "If you didn't take the rest of the bones, any idea who did?"

She shrugged and wiped her nose again. "The killer, I guess. After I said my prayer, George put them back in the cabinet. I never saw them again."

"How did the police discover you had these few bones?"

"They nabbed Robbie and me as we were driving out of town. It was after they found that dead spirit thief. Served the guy right, if you ask me."

"Teht'aa," Eric cut in, "I thought we'd agreed to tone down the rhetoric."

"Yeah, yeah."

"Sounds as if the police were looking for you. Why?" I asked.

"We've got red skin. What other reason do they need?"

Eric emitted an exasperated sigh. "Teht'aa, because of our petition, the police had very good reason to suspect any one of us. I wouldn't be at all surprise if they didn't take down our licence plate numbers while we were performing the ceremony."

"And what happened to Robbie?" I continued.

"He took off after the police let him go," Eric growled. "Didn't even bother to call me about my own daughter."

"Is he home?"

"Not last time I checked. Wanted to give him a piece of my mind." Eric's eyes watered as he tried to suppress another yawn.

"Well, nothing more we can do now." I stood up. "I propose we worry about him in the morning. You two go to bed while I clean up here."

Teht'aa's eyes narrowed. "If you're staying, I'm leaving."

"You're both staying," Eric replied in a quiet but commanding tone. "Teht'aa, you forget yourself. You forget that it is a tradition of our people to welcome all visitors, to show them respect by offering them food, drink, a place to sleep, whatever they require. Please apologize."

For a second, I wasn't sure if she would hit me or spit on me, but her father's command held sway. She mumbled a few incomprehensible words, turned on her heels and stomped down the hall to her room.

"I'm so sorry, Meg." He took me in his arms. "I don't know what I'm going to do with her. I can only hope that over time, she'll come to accept that you are very much a part of my life."

Dreamer, I thought. But as long as we carried on as we were, friends, lovers with no binding commitments, which suited me just fine, she couldn't cause any real problems.

NINETEEN

Next morning, I was enjoying the sun streaming through Eric's bedroom window when I thought I heard a knock on the front door. I looked over to see if Eric had heard it too, but he remained blissfully asleep. The knock echoed again, this time with more force. I threw on the rumpled shorts and T-shirt from the day before.

I checked his daughter's room, but she was equally comatose, so I headed to the front. The sight of what looked to be a policeman's hat through the door's frosted window made me hesitate. Should I pretend that no one was home?

"Come on, Eric, wake up," boomed Chief Decontie's gruff voice through the door. He knocked again.

I opened it.

"Eric in?" Will asked, without so much as a raised eyebrow at my presence.

Behind the Migiskan First Nations cop stood two from the Sûreté du Quebec. One I recognized.

"*Bonjour,* Sergeant Beauchamp. Little far from your Fort Coulange Territory, aren't you?" I said in French, remembering his unexpected Gallic gallantry at our first encounter at the time of the bones discovery. Perhaps this sudden call wasn't as threatening as I thought.

The slim young man with the eager boyish face smiled. "A transfer to the Somerset detachment, madame. I am replacing Sergeant LaFramboise. Perhaps you knew him?"

Rotten Raspberry, my nemesis. "Yes, our paths may have crossed once or twice."

Will Decontie tried to hide his own satisfaction but failed. He'd also had his run-ins with the arrogant and bigoted policeman.

"This is Detective Frazer from Montreal." Speaking in English, Decontie pointed to the other SQ officer, a short, plump woman, whose brown suit strained to cover her buxom chest. "She'd like to speak with Teht'aa."

I had cause to worry, after all. "I thought you'd finished with her."

Detective Frazer answered in a thick French accent, "I have more questions, *madame*. Mademoiselle Tootoosis, she is at home, *non?*"

"Yes, but she's sound asleep. Can you come back later?"

"It is not possible, madame. Wake her, please." Much like the HMS *Queen Mary*, the Montreal detective plowed through the open door, with the two men following in her wake.

I hated to rouse Teht'aa. She'd had a rough night, and she looked so peaceful. For once, her features weren't knotted up in anger and distrust. I watched the shadows of a dreamcatcher play on her cheek. I had fond memories of this charm with its delicate web and slender wood duck feathers. Eric had hung it in this guest bedroom window when he'd offered me sanctuary what seemed a lifetime ago.

I shook his daughter. "Teht'aa, wake up."

She groaned and fluttered her eyelids. "Jeez, what time is it?"

"Ten fifteen. You'd better get up. A detective from Montreal is here to speak to you."

She sat up. "What for?"

"No idea. I suggest you put something decent on." I left her to wake up Eric.

Despite Eric's entreaties, Detective Frazer refused to let him sit in on Teht'aa's questioning. He and I retreated outside to the rough patch of grass that served as his outdoor terrace. Although there was still a hint of smoke in the morning breeze, it was nowhere near as strong as yesterday.

With a glint in his eye and a motion to keep quiet, Eric silently carried a green plastic chair to within a foot of the bungalow's clapboard wall and pointed to an open window above his head. I could hear the murmur of voices. When I placed my chair next to his, I could make out words. He grinned, but not for long.

"Mademoiselle Tootoosis," rapped Detective Frazer's brusque voice. "We wish to question you about your relationship with Dr. George Schmidt."

"Relationship?" She couldn't quite keep the hint of panic from her voice. "What do you mean? I don't have relationships with spirit thieves."

Eric groaned.

"Mlle Tootoosis, you told us that this was the first time that you meet Dr. Schmidt."

"No, I didn't."

I heard paper shuffling.

"Last night at ten hour twenty, you answered 'no' to the question 'Have you had previous dealings with Dr. Schmidt?' Do you wish to change this answer?"

Silence. A chair squeaked. "Yeah, I guess I met him a couple of times a few years back. So I forgot. So what?"

"Our information tells us that he was your lover for more than two years. Why do you lie to us?"

Eric gripped the arm of his chair.

Silence.

"Answer the question, *s'il vous plaît.*"

The chair squeaked. "I was going through a bad spell in my

life. Something I'd rather forget about."

"Last night you told us also that you did not see him after he showed you the remains of this, ah, DeMontigny Lady. Do you want to change your statement?"

Silence.

"A witness saw you with him on the street near Le Vieux Chat Café on Parthenais St., close to the forensics laboratory."

"Okay, so I saw him. What's the big deal?"

"He is missing. You are one of the last persons seen with him."

At this point Eric jumped up. Not caring that he was betraying our eavesdropping, he shouted, "That's it. Teht'aa, don't answer any more questions."

He raced inside, with me close on his heels. A strained silence greeted us in the living room. Chief Decontie sat upright on a kitchen chair he'd pulled into the front room, his worry plain beneath his official demeanour. His pen tapped out a nervous staccato on the spiral notepad resting on his knee.

On the leather sofa across the room from Decontie sat Sergeant Beauchamp, his face devoid of emotion. He too had an open notepad, its pages likewise filled with writing. Sitting on another kitchen chair with her knees almost touching her victim's loomed the threatening bulk of the detective.

Eric's daughter sat hunched over in his lazy-boy chair, her usual haughtiness replaced by outright fear. She glanced up with relief when her father entered.

"I believe it is within our rights to have a lawyer present when being questioned by the police." Eric held the portable phone in his hand. "So if you don't mind, I request that no further questioning take place until our lawyer arrives."

From the corner of my eye, I caught Decontie's faint nod.

Detective Frazer leaned back in her chair and gave Eric a long, thoughtful once-over. "Yes, *monsieur,* you are correct."

She glanced at her watch. "Sergeant, make note that this interview is terminated at ten hour thirty-eight." She stood up. "It is possible I bring your daughter back to Montreal to continue this questioning. But we are finished for the moment. *Merci. Bonjour.*" And she strode back outside with the other two cops once more in her wake.

The door had no sooner closed on their heels than Eric yelled, "Christ, Teht'aa, what in the hell was that all about?"

"Shush!" I said. I could see the two cop vehicles still parked in Eric's drive. The three of them were huddled around the open door of the SQ marked car. Then the two Quebec police officers climbed into their vehicle and drove off. Chief Decontie lumbered back up the walkway to Eric's door.

Eric flung it open before he could knock. "Will, what's going on? Surely they can't suspect my daughter had anything to do with this guy's disappearance."

Will slumped down on the sofa and removed his cap. "I shouldn't be telling you this, but it looks like this Dr. Schmidt has taken a runner. Apparently he missed an important meeting in Ottawa yesterday. His office doesn't know where he is. He's not answering his cell, and neither the Ottawa police nor Montreal police have been able to locate him."

"Does Montreal think he killed his colleague?"

"I guess they'd like to. It'd make things neat and tidy, particularly since there is a clear motive. Apparently the Ministry of Culture had decided to exclude him from any further research on the remains. Wanted to keep it 'in-house', if you get my meaning."

I most assuredly did. Quebec versus the "Rest of Canada" politics interfering yet again.

"But it seems he was giving a lecture at McGill University at the time of Dr. Meilleur's death."

Eric's impassive face revealed none of his inner thoughts, but I knew he'd probably connected the dots in the same way I had. "Surely, they're not suggesting…" Eric let the unspoken words hang in the close air of the room.

Decontie shrugged.

"Thank God Teht'aa has an alibi." Eric ran his hand through his hair. "So what happens now?"

"Perhaps if Teht'aa can tell me a little about her last meeting with Dr. Schmidt, it might help direct the search for him."

Eric eyed his friend's seemingly relaxed slouch, no doubt noting the tense line to his shoulders. "Good cop, bad cop, eh?"

Will nodded imperceptibly. "It'd be best for her. Clear up any suspicion. And Eric, there's something else you should know. The weapon used to kill Dr. Meilleur clearly points to one of our people."

TWENTY

None of us spoke. A bee buzzed at an open window. Eric's feet shuffled on the pine floor under his chair. A resigned, almost apologetic mien had settled on Chief Decontie's broad features. Teht'aa continued to hunch in her father's lazy-boy.

"Will, I heard something on the news about an unusual weapon. Is that what you're referring to?" I asked.

"Yeah. What we call a crooked knife. One of the tools used in making birchbark canoes."

My heart sank at the memory of where I'd last seen one. "Surely they don't think Robbie could've had anything to do with it? Besides, he has an alibi, doesn't he?"

"That's something else I want to talk to Teht'aa about."

She sank back even further into her father's chair and turned imploring eyes in his direction.

Eric's jaw firmed. "I think it's best you tell Will what you know."

"But before you begin, there's something else you should know," I interjected. "Larry Horn also owns a crooked knife. And just after the ceremony, I saw him arguing with Dr. Meilleur. Maybe you should talk to him, too." For a second I thought I saw something like gratitude appear on Teht'aa's face.

"Good. I'll pass this info onto Detective Frazer," the police chief replied, jotting something into his notepad. "But right now I want to talk with Teht'aa."

For a second her back stiffened, as if she were going to refuse, then, much as her father would, she firmed her jaw in resolve. "Okay, what do you want to know?"

"Let's start at the beginning. How long have you known Dr. George Schmidt?"

"I guess about five years now. Met him at the Black Horns Pow Wow in Calgary. Gets his kicks by hanging out with natives. Didn't know that at the time, though. He really came on to me."

I could see Decontie trying not to eye her partially revealed cleavage and thought, here's another dupe who'd go after her if given half the chance.

"I guess you'd say I was flattered by this big blond hunk paying attention to a no-name Indian like me. So I fell for his line: sorry my forefathers stole your culture and all that shit."

Will cleared his throat. "You said you went out with him for about two years, that right?"

"Yeah, took me that long to figure out I was just a chest medal for him. He could flaunt me to all his archeologist buddies to show them what a true Indian lover he was." Her laugh rang out hollowly. "Yeah, in more ways than one."

"A twinkie?" Decontie suggested.

"You got that one right." She flashed her gaze to me, then back to the policeman. "But the minute I figured that out, I took off."

I shifted uneasily in my chair. Was that her reason for hating me? Did she think I was using her father for some kind of ego trip? Surely she must've realized by now that ours was a straightforward love between a man and a woman. Nothing more, nothing less.

"Did you have any further encounters with him?"

"Oh, he'd call me from time to time, but I refused to have anything more to do with him. Last time I saw him, he had another squaw in tow."

I winced at the hated word and wondered about the resentment that must lie behind it.

"So why did he approach you in Montreal?"

"Like I already told you. He wanted to buy the deerskin dress of my *ànikekòkomis.*"

"And later on the street?"

She fiddled with the ties to her bathrobe, glanced out the window, then back at Decontie. We waited.

Finally, she said, "He wanted me to use my influence to get my father to take back our people's request for the return of the Ancient One."

Eric winced in disgust at this latest disclosure.

"What did you tell him?" Will asked.

"What do you take me for? Of course, I said no."

"How did he react?"

"Oh, he was mad, real mad. Brought up all the old shit between us. Said I owed him."

"What did you owe him?"

"Way back when, he got me a job. A good one at his museum. 'Course it went when I split."

"Yes, I can see that would make you feel you had to help him. What did you say after that?"

She glanced at her father and mumbled, "I said I'd see what I could do."

"That was it, nothing more?"

"What do you mean? Of course, there was nothing more." She clamped her lips into a line of stubborn refusal.

"You sure? I understand Dr. Schmidt gave you something."

"Jeez. Who's your fucking spy? Robbie?"

The policeman remained silent.

"Okay, okay. So he did. What's the big goddamn deal?"

"What did he give you?"

"You tell me, if you know so goddamn much."

"What was the money for?"

Her shoulders dropped. Her back slumped into the chair in defeat, her bluster gone. "It was a downpayment," she whispered.

"For what?"

She stole a glance at her father. "For the dress."

Eric's eyes flew to his family's rare white deerskin dress. No longer able to keep his control, he yelled, "You sold our heritage?"

She nodded.

"How dare you!"

"I needed the money."

"For what? All you had to do was ask me."

"It...it was for drugs." Her voice was so low I could hardly hear.

"Drugs?"

She sank even further into the worn fabric of the chair. "Yeah, cocaine."

"Christ. You saying you need it? That you're an addict?"

"No. I can stop any time I want," she said defiantly, but without any of the haughty bravado I'd come to associate with her.

My heart ached for Eric. I knew how much this hurt him. He'd spent the last six years cleaning up the reserve and trying to keep it that way. Now, here he was confronting it head on in his own home. It also explained her often runny nose and her erratic behaviour.

He sighed deeply, "Continue, Will."

"What happened after he gave you the money?"

"Since I was still wearing the dress, I promised to send it to him. Then he left."

"Did he say where he was going?"

"Yeah, to that stupid lecture." She cinched in the tie to her bathrobe, causing it to gape further, revealing a lacy pink nightie.

133

Will's gaze lingered, then he abruptly raised it to her face. "Did he say where he was going after the lecture?"

She shook her head and wiped her nose. "I figured he was going back to Ottawa." She cast a hesitant glance at her father. "He's decided to pick up the dress today."

Eric tensed, as Decontie leaned forward. "When?"

"I'm supposed to let him know when the coast is clear."

"Meaning?"

She took a deep breath. "When my dad was out of the house." She glanced back at Eric. "I'm so sorry, Dad."

He closed his eyes, as if not wanting to accept or forgive what his daughter had done. Teht'aa slumped even further into the chair.

"Call him," Will said. "We'll see whether you have better luck in locating him."

She picked up the phone and dialed a number she was obviously very familiar with. After a few seconds, she said, "Hi, George. This is Teht'aa." The policeman leaned forward in anticipation. "You can come any time. My dad's gone for the day." She hung up.

"Great, you found him."

She shook her head. "Nope, just his voice mail."

"No matter. It could be enough to bring him out of hiding, if that's what he's doing. If so, we'll be waiting. Now tell me about Robbie. You told the police in Montreal that the two of you were together the entire time after you left the vicinity of the Forensics Lab. Was he with you when you were talking to Dr. Schmidt?"

She hesitated.

"No more games, Teht'aa. We need to know the truth."

She sighed. "No, he wasn't. When Robbie and I were leaving the café, George took me aside while Robbie went to get his truck. But it was only for a couple of minutes."

"Did Robbie and Dr. Schmidt know each other?"

"No. Not as far as I know. When George and his latest fling came into the café for lunch, I introduced him."

"Did you know the woman?"

"No, just another sucker squaw."

"And what time did this take place?"

"I don't know. We'd just ordered lunch, but it was late. Don't think we got to the restaurant until around one thirty or so. So it might of been ten, fifteen minutes later."

Will made a note of it in his notepad. "Did you introduce him to Ed and Billie Payne?"

"Yeah."

"Did Dr. Schmidt and his friend leave the restaurant with you?"

"Don't think so. George went back inside. They were still eating."

"And the Paynes?"

"Like I already told the cops in Montreal, they stayed behind. Just me and Robbie left."

"And what time was this?"

"Three o'clock...or thereabouts."

"Can you be more accurate?"

"Not really, I don't have a watch." She paused. "Wait a minute. It was about quarter to three. I remember looking at a clock on the wall."

Decontie paused for several minutes while he filled several pages in his notebook with text. "Now that your memory has been jogged about Dr. Schmidt, perhaps it's jogged other things loose. Was Robbie with you the entire time between two forty-five and four thirty pm?"

She closed her eyes. A tear seeped from under a fringe of feather lashes. "No, not quite. I...I was making a score."

"You were buying cocaine?"

"Yes," she whispered, keeping her eyes clenched tight, as if afraid to watch the love bleeding from her father.

"And what did Robbie do?"

"I told him to wait, that I'd be back in about fifteen minutes."

"What time was this?"

"Maybe around three thirty."

"And was Robbie waiting for you when you returned?"

She breathed in deeply and let out a long slow breath. "No, he wasn't. His truck was gone. So I waited at the curb until he came back."

"How long?"

"About twenty, thirty minutes, maybe longer. Don't know for sure." She sighed. "I was enjoying my score."

Decontie nodded in understanding. "I guess you can't tell me what time he finally came back."

"Yes, I can. It was four thirty," she said with a sudden return of her confidence. "I'd just asked the clerk at a store for the time."

"I suppose this clerk will be able to vouch for your presence during the time you were waiting for Robbie and would corroborate the time of his return."

"Oh." She picked at her bathrobe tie. "Look, Robbie might've came back a bit later. I don't know for sure."

"And where did this take place?"

"Near Concordia University."

"Street name?" I could see Will was finally beginning to lose his patience.

"Was a side street. Think it was Bishop."

"Store name?"

"Dunno. Book store, I think."

"Montreal police should be able to find it easily enough and verify your story."

She raised beseeching eyes to the cop. "What's going to happen to Robbie?"

"Nothing yet, as long as we can firm up the times and place him away from the Forensic Laboratory at the time of the murder. I don't know Montreal all that well, but I think it places him about a fifteen-minute drive from the lab."

"But Robbie couldn't have killed the guy. No way. Besides, he's probably got an alibi for that time. Why don't you ask him?"

"I'd like to, but he hasn't come back from Montreal."

TWENTY-ONE

An hour later, I left Eric and Teht'aa in a Mexican standoff. Eric was trying to convince his daughter to go into rehab, while she was doing her best to persuade him, but more likely herself, that she wasn't an addict and didn't need to go. Since both were strong-headed, it was difficult to predict who would win. But my bets were on Eric, for I could see that Teht'aa really was regretting the debacle with the dress and would eventually give in, if for no other reason than to appease her guilt and please her father.

My truck bounced along the dirt road toward one of the back sections of Migiskan Village, to where Jid's aunt's bungalow hid under a canopy of maple. The boy had called, sounding distressed, to say he wanted to go back to my place. Apparently one of his cousins had come down with strep throat, and his aunt was blaming him.

The route took me past the treed property where Robbie lived with his father. Chief Decontie's official SUV and the SQ police cruiser were parked next to the single storey log house with its many lean-to additions. Since I didn't see Robbie's silver truck, I assumed he was still unaccounted for.

I slowed to watch the two cops and the detective walk away from the work area, where the outline of the Paynes' almost finished canoe stood out in stark relief. Sergeant Beauchamp carried several plastic bags, which appeared to contain some of Robbie's tools. As the three pairs of eyes turned in my direction,

I took my foot off the brake and onto the gas. I didn't want them stopping me to ask what tools, if any, were missing.

A forlorn Jid greeted me from his perch on the unpainted wooden stairs of his aunt's house. Sergei lay with his head in the boy's lap, almost as if sensing his buddy's loneliness. As the two of them ran towards my truck, his aunt, unsmiling, watched from behind the screen door.

"Sorry, Meg," she shouted, "but I can't have any more of my kids getting sick. So until the Ancient One is returned to the land, best he stay away, eh?"

I waved a half-hearted goodbye, figuring it was useless to try and convince her that Jid was probably no longer infectious. Chances were some other child had infected hers. Nor did I want to get into an argument over the disease-causing properties of the bones.

"Don't pay any attention to your aunt." I ruffled Jid's thick black hair. "She's just letting her love for you be blinded by her fear. When things simmer down, she'll realize her mistake. In the meantime, it's you and me, kid. We'll have a great time together, eh?"

His smile unleashed a few tightly-held tears.

I wrapped my arm around him. "Do you want to drive by your house and get some more of your things?"

"You bet, the rest of my Spiderman comics." He wiped the streaks from his face.

"But you must have twenty at my place. Aren't you getting tired of him?"

"No way. Spiderman's my fave." He gave the dog sharing his seat a playful punch and buried his face in the thick, curly fur.

The two front windows of Kòkomis's bungalow peered out from the coolness of the afternoon shade of the surrounding trees. The small, squat building reminded me of his grandmother, quiet and serene. Jid squirmed with excitement. He'd not been back since the day of his grandmother's death, a week ago. Although I knew this trip would be hard for him, I thought a visit to things familiar would help him heal. Before the truck had come to a complete stop, he and the dog were racing up the dirt walkway to the side door.

"Kòkomis," he shouted. "I'm—" He stopped with a sudden lurch. His shoulders dropped. His fists clenched. I wanted to run up and hold this all-but-abandoned boy in a protective hug, but I knew he had to face the reality of his grandmother's death by himself.

The dog, sensing his friend's distress, remained by his side. For several long minutes, Jid stood, his head bowed, almost as if he was in prayer. Then he braced his shoulders, raised his head and with solemn determination walked towards the empty house.

He hesitated for only a second before he opened the door which, like most doors on the reserve, was never locked. He stepped into the waiting void. I gave him several more minutes alone.

He was brushing the last tear away when I entered the muggy darkness of the main room. The air wasn't quite as musty as I would've expected after being closed up for seven days. Then I noticed a side window was partially open, which I must've forgotten to shut.

Jid ran to his room, one of the two small back bedrooms. While he collected his things, I sat at the table, where Kòkomis had spent many an hour making deerskin handicrafts. An unfinished moccasin lay next to her various containers of coloured beads, its partially completed beadwork as precise as all her other work. I used to marvel at her deftness, working entirely by touch. She only called on her grandson's eyes when selecting the colours for the designs.

I surveyed the long, narrow room that had served the many

needs of daily life, eating, cooking, working and sometimes sleeping, especially in the winter months when the small potbelly stove couldn't generate enough heat for the two bedrooms. Despite the room's stark poverty, it exuded a homey comfort.

I wondered what would happen to the house. Jid couldn't continue to live here on his own. Moving in with his aunt was the most obvious choice, but for the moment she wasn't willing, which was surprising in this community where children came first. And I was hardly an option. The band would never agree to his being raised by someone not of their heritage. Besides, kids weren't exactly my thing, at least not full-time.

My eyes lighted on an old Hudson's Bay blanket that lay unfolded at one end of the sagging sofa. Something else I'd forgotten to tidy up on our last visit. Then I saw the dirty dishes beside the sink and realized their implication at the same time as Jid came out of his room, saying, "Someone was reading my comics."

"Yes, I think someone was here, too. Any idea who it might be?"

"Probably my cousin Chuck. Him and my aunt got into a big fight yesterday. He didn't come home last night."

Yes, most likely the rebellious teenager. Still, my thoughts had initially fallen on someone else. Robbie. Knowing this house was empty, he might've decided it was safer to stay here than return to his own home, where the police would find him.

I decided to check with Kòkomis's lone neighbour across the road, but she proved unhelpful, only remembering seeing lights last night. However, she'd assumed it was Jid, so hadn't bothered to check it out.

"Heard 'em leave early this morning," she said. "Door banging woke me up."

"Did you see a truck or car?"

"Nope. Weren't nothing parked out front. I woulda noticed."

In all probability, Jid's cousin had been the overnight guest.

On our way back through the centre of the village, I stopped at the Migiskan General Store to stock up on milk and other equally healthy fare for a growing child and to add to my dwindling supply of thirst-quenching lemonade. With the nearest competition a good thirty-minute drive away, the store's potholed parking lot was invariably packed, not only with the vehicles of local residents but also those of nearby cottagers and visiting fishermen. Today was no exception. The usual hum of chatter greeted me as I opened the glass door, and as usual, rather than the narrow aisles being filled with intent buyers, everyone was crowded at the small coffee counter at the back of the revamped bungalow.

Like many rural stores, the original structure had been never meant to house a business. At some point in its history, the front room had been converted into a store, while the owner continued to live in the back rooms. As the years advanced, walls had been knocked out and more space converted, until the retail operation occupied the entire floor space. Now, the only indication that it had once been a residence was its bungalow-like exterior. Inside, it had the sterile box-shape of any store, except for the alcove built onto the back for the coffee counter. Needless to say, this had become a favoured collection point for gossip.

At this time of year, the store also had another reason for its popularity: air conditioning. It was one of few such spots in this land known more for its ice and snow than for its few short weeks of summer heat. Except this year, of course. And the year before last. And the year before last and so on... I hoped this wasn't setting a trend. I preferred my northern woods cool and aromatically moist, as they were supposed to be, not hot and crackling dry, as they were this year.

I felt the refreshing coolness wash over me as I stepped

through the door. Several hands waved at Jid and me from the counter, accompanied by a few shouts of "Hi."

Although I didn't feel much like mingling, it was part of the store's ritual. Usually, I quite enjoyed the few minutes gossiping about the latest goings-on while sipping the *de rigeur* cup of coffee. But today, after all that had happened in the last forty-eight hours, I didn't feel much like talking.

Sure enough, the first words spoken were, "Hear Will was talking to the chief's daughter."

I nodded noncommittally to the speaker with the bristling brush cut, Ben, one of Eric's councillors. "Milk, no sugar," I ordered, then turned to the waiting audience of six, which included a couple of the regulars. There was Frosty, a local trapper, so-called because he'd lost a finger to frostbite, and Marge, sad, no-kids Marge, as she was referred to by the community. After her husband had died, she'd made this afternoon visit one of the top priorities in her day.

"Yeah," I said. "The Chief spent about an hour or so with Teht'aa, but then left, satisfied." I left it at that.

"Hear Will's looking for Robbie," Ben continued.

"So I gather." I took a shallow sip of the hot coffee and asked Sally, the store manager's buxom teenage daughter, for two chocolate cream donuts. I passed the second one to Jid, who bit into it with gusto, then ran off to the comic section with the donut still in his mouth.

Trying not to betray my keen interest, I said, "I don't suppose any of you guys have seen him?"

Several heads were shaken, but Frosty piped up, "Thought I seen his truck last night. But weren't sure."

I sank my teeth into the donut and felt the explosion of cream inside my mouth. I was hoping someone else would ask the next question.

Good old Marge came to my rescue. "Where was that?"

"Near the old woodlot at the Wolf Lake turnoff."

This would place him in the vicinity of Jid's house. Maybe he *was* last night's visitor after all.

"Did ya tell Will?" Marge asked.

Frosty shook his silvered head. "Nope. Figure it's up to Will to find out for hisself. I ain't gonna squeal on the guy. Whatever he done, he done for good reason."

Several nods of agreement followed, while Marge said, "He'd better get those old bones buried soon. I hear Betty Whiteduck's come down with this here bad throat."

So Robbie's people believed him guilty too. But perhaps "guilty" wasn't the right word; that implied a crime. In their minds, they might not view the killing and theft as such. More like a necessary act.

I had a sudden thought. "You know, guys, the ancient remains were stolen two days ago. Don't you think if Robbie had taken them, he would've returned them to the land by now? But people are still getting sick. Maybe he didn't take them." A couple of people raised their heads in interest.

"Besides there are two other possible suspects." All eyes turned towards me. "Police are also looking for the other archeologist. He's gone missing, too."

"Yeah, but why kill someone if you already got the bones?" Frostie asked.

"Will told me that this Dr. Schmidt wasn't going to be allowed to study them any more. Knowing him, he'd be very upset by this, maybe upset enough to kill for them."

"Yeah, maybe," replied Frosty. "You said there was some-body else."

"Teht'aa's old boyfriend, Larry."

"I can see that guy killing someone," Bill chimed in, "but

144

he's Mohawk. What he want with Algonquin bones?"

"Maybe like you, he wants them reburied."

"Hardly. More likely he done it for money. Only thing gets that guy going." Bill slurped his coffee, then added, "Calls himself a warrior, hmpfh."

Bill did have a point. I supposed Larry could've stolen them in order to sell them. But was this a strong enough motive for murder?

"What'll happen to us now?" Marge cried. "If one of these guys got 'em, he's not gonna return 'em to Mother Earth. The spirits are gonna stay angry, and the sickness is gonna get worse."

Marge turned her watery eyes towards me. "Meg, you and me, we're friends. But you shoulda left those bones in the ground. Look at the grief they're givin' us now."

Eric had warned me about stirring up a hornets' nest. It looked as if I'd done that in spades.

Everyone continued to sip their coffee in silence, each lost in private thoughts.

After a few minutes, Ben said, "Bush sure dry, eh? Will's asked us to issue 'no fire' warnings."

"Sure is. I ain't never seen it this dry," Frosty added. "I hear tell Bear Lake Reserve up near Temiskaming is fightin' a big one. Sure hope it don't happen here. Could ruin our traplines."

Several grunts of acknowledgment, while Marge gazed at me over the rim of her coffee cup. She raised her eyebrows as if to say, "See, another reason for getting them bones buried."

I decided it was time to finish my shopping.

TWENTY-TWO

I found Jid sitting cross-legged on the store's linoleum floor beside the magazine rack, his attention riveted on the latest Spiderman comic.

"Time to go, guy," I said, casting my eyes over the rack. The choice was limited to mostly hunting and fishing magazines, and, of course the all-pervasive scandal sheets and movie mags. But one did catch my eye, *Windspeaker,* one of the major First Nations' voices. On the cover was a photo of Eric, chin to chin with a man I recognized to be Grand Chief of the Sonhatsi Mohawk.

As I reached for it, a sneering voice behind me said, "Keeping up on the latest dirt?"

I turned to find myself facing a Larry, his arms crossed and legs splayed out in bouncer stance. "What are you doing here?"

"Just paying my girlfriend a little visit."

"Girlfriend? I thought she'd thrown you out."

"You talkin' about Robbie?"

"Seems to me he's more an item in her life than you are."

"Teht'aa knows whose canoe to hitch a ride in. And it sure ain't with that piece of moose shit." He spat.

"Whatever you say, Larry." Since he was here in front of me, I said, "By the way, have you talked to the police yet?"

"What for?"

"About that argument you were having with Dr. Meilleur before he was killed."

"You're not going to hang that shit on me. No way."

"What were you arguing about?"

"None of your damn business."

"So you don't deny it."

"Look, Miz Snoop, I was with my buddies all afternoon. No way can the cops pin that killing on me."

"Okay," I said, not believing him for a moment. But I figured it best not to challenge him, just in case he had murdered Claude. I wouldn't want to be on his hit list and besides, this was something the police were better equipped to do.

I turned to the boy. "Come on, Jid, time to go."

He closed the treasured comic with a sigh and carefully put it back in the rack with the others.

In part because he hadn't asked, I said, "Bring that with you."

"It's okay. I already read it."

"No, please, I'd like to buy it for you."

"Gee, thanks." His grin spread from ear to ear.

As we headed out of the store, Larry called out, "Keep your nose outta where it don't belong. And you can tell the same to your boyfriend."

But I felt I had the last word when I saw Detective Frazer driving into the parking lot. I rolled down my truck window and shouted, "If you're looking for Larry Horn, he's inside." I drove off.

Still, I wondered what that threat to Eric was all about.

*   *   *

A couple of hours later, I was sitting with Jid on the screened porch eating a late lunch when I heard the soft purr of a car engine stop at the front of the house. Sergei erupted into his usual cacophony of barking. Knowing Eric's Jeep never sounded that smooth, we hurried around to the front to discover the Paynes extricating themselves from the shimmering mass of their Navigator. Jid let out a war whoop and ran towards them.

"Sure glad we found y'all." Billie clasped Jid against her breast and kissed him gently on the crown of his head. "Landsakes, child, what a time you've been having."

At first I thought she was referring to the boy, but when I saw her blue gaze directed towards me, I replied, "You can say that again. You just getting back from Montreal?"

Ed nodded. "Sure is a mighty pretty city. Just like New Orleans with that there Frenchie stuff." While his words suggested enthusiasm, his tone lacked the gusto I'd come to expect.

Billie's demeanour also seemed subdued, her eyes missing their usual twinkle. Instead of her standard cowboy attire of jeans and a bright western shirt, she was clothed in sedate grandmotherly knits.

"Is everything okay with you two?" I asked.

Both raised startled eyes towards me. "Yeah, sure," Billie quickly answered. "Why you asking?"

"You two don't seem to be your usual jolly selves."

Billie glanced at Ed, who replied, "My honey's been feeling a might poorly the last while. So we thought we'd have a few medical tests done while we were in Montreal. It's the reason we're late getting back."

"I'm very sorry to hear that. I hope it's nothing too serious."

"It's cancer, honey," Billie said bluntly. "Had a bout a few years back. Thought I had it licked, but the symptoms I've been feeling lately tell me it's come back."

"But I keep telling her not to get herself in a tizzy," Ed interjected. "It could be any number of things making her feel poorly. Let's just wait for these test results. More than likely it's something that can be easily cured."

But I could see in his eyes that he didn't really believe his brave words. "Jid and I were just having a sandwich. Why don't you two join us?"

"That's mighty kind of you," Billie said, mustering up her brightness. "We already ate, but sure could do with some ice tea."

By the time I returned to the porch with three tall glasses of iced tea and a tumbler of lemonade for Jid, the three of them were immersed in a heated card game.

With a faint twinkle in his eye, his worry pushed aside for the moment, Ed placed some cards on a pile in the middle of the table. "Two fours."

Jid raised an eyebrow, then cried out. "Cheat!"

Ed laughed and overturned the cards. Sandwiched in between the two fours was a five. "Guess you caught me, son." Ed collected the pile while Jid hooted with glee.

Billie turned to me. "We were mighty upset when we heard about the arrest. Such a sweet girl. Shame to think she'd do such a thing."

"You must be talking about Teht'aa, although 'sweet' would hardly be the word I'd use to describe her."

"I know things ain't going well between you and her, but just you wait. The both of you'll come around to seeing the goodness in the other." She patted my hand the way a grandmother would a stubborn grandchild. Did she think I was just as much at fault? Surely not?

Billie continued, "I know Teht'aa was upset about those old bones, but I sure never thought she'd kill that nice archeologist."

"I guess you haven't heard the latest. The police don't think she did it. She has an alibi. Robbie is currently their chief suspect. But Dr. Schmidt is also on their list. And I'm hoping they'll soon add Larry."

Billie glanced at her husband, then turned back to me, her

brow arched in worry. "But Robbie couldn't have done it. He was with us."

"Yes, but I understand he and Teht'aa left and joined up with you later."

Ed replied, "That's right. Robbie joined us at our hotel after dropping off Teht'aa. We were staying in one of those cute Frenchie places in the Old Town. He had another beer with us, then went back to get her. Way I see it, she's the one without the alibi."

"Seems she has one."

"Y'all know where she was?" Ed turned a quizzical glance towards me. "She was mighty secretive. Acting like the cat that swallowed the canary."

Since Teht'aa hadn't told them, I felt it wasn't my place to either. "Have you talked to the police yet?"

"Not yet. A message to call a Detective Frazer was waiting for us at the Camp."

"When you do, don't forget to mention what you just told me. It will help Robbie."

"Will do," Ed replied.

"But Ed, honey," Billie spoke up. "I think you got it wrong about Robbie. Sure he came back for another beer, but after he left to get Teht'aa, seems to me he was gone a mighty long time before he came back with her."

Ed scratched his head. "I don't rightly recollect. I was too busy watching those pretty French girls. Sure do like those sidewalk cafés." He smiled broadly as Billie shook her head.

"Do you know what time this was?" I asked.

Billie answered, "I'd say late afternoon. Think he left a little before four, probably five before he got back with Teht'aa."

My heart sank. I'd really wanted the murderer not to be Robbie. "I guess you'd better tell this to the police."

"Such a nice young man. Sure hate to do this to him. Likely

he's got a good explanation." Billie glanced over at her husband, then back at me. "But you know, Meg honey, he sure was acting kinda quiet. Now I know he's a man of few words, but he didn't say boo to us when he come back after dropping Teht'aa off. Just drank his beer, then upped and left. Something was sure bothering him, that much I can tell you."

I supposed he could've been worried about Teht'aa's drug habit. But then again, he could just as easily have been thinking about how to steal the bones from the lab.

The three of us sat quietly sipping our iced tea, each lost in our own private thoughts, while Jid played a game of solitaire, Sergei splayed out on the floor beside him. Another hummingbird war raged just outside the screen porch door. At one point the ruby throated male embedded his long beak in the mesh when he mistook the screen for free-flowing air. For a few anxious seconds, with wings whirring, he attempted to extricate himself with no success. Then with one final effort, the beak slipped out, and he vanished.

"Poor thing," Billie said, "but easy enough to do when you're not seeing things for what they are."

Too true, I thought.

Ed shifted in his wicker chair. "I suppose we'd all better be thinking about our canoe, in case Robbie can't finish it. Unfortunately, Billie's condition has caused us to move up our leaving date. We're expecting the test results next Tuesday. Might mean we're heading back to Texas Wednesday. Gives us a week. Meg, how much more work do y'all think is required?"

"All that remains is attaching the bark to the frame and sealing the seams. I think another day, day and a half at the most."

"Well, Billie, what do you think? Should we try that there boyfriend of Teht'aa's? He said he could build canoes. Mind you, Meg, didn't y'all say the police were interested in him too?"

I was right. Larry and Teht'aa had tried to take their business away from Robbie. "Yeah, they are, besides I'm not sure he's got the necessary skills. There's another canoe builder on the reserve, although he's not as good as Robbie."

"Ed, honey, I'd just as soon we sit tight for a few more days and see what happens to Robbie. If he can't do it, then why don't we use this man Meg's recommending?"

"Whatever you say, Billie. It's your canoe." Ed relaxed back into his chair.

Billie glanced at the magazine I'd tossed onto the porch table. "Your honey's a mighty fine man." She pointed to Eric's photo on the *Windspeaker* cover. "But he sure do look angry."

"That he does. I wonder why." I flipped through the pages of the magazine until Eric's scowl confronted me once again. Sitting beside him in the photo was an equally angry Grand Chief of the Sonhatsi Mohawk.

"Chiefs Resurrect Ancient Feud", blazed the article's headline. So this was the mess Eric was caught up in. I scanned the article and soon learned the worst.

Eric, a chief of a band of the Algonquin, one of the more peaceful First Nations, had decided to take on a grand chief of one of the more militant First Nations, the Mohawk of the Iroquois Confederacy. This, however, was not the first time these two nations had been in conflict.

In the seventeenth century, the two tribes had warred over the right to use the lucrative fur trading corridor of the Ottawa and St. Lawrence Rivers. The Algonquins lost and were forced to use the much longer and more treacherous northern river routes of the Ottawa River watershed, rivers like the DeMontigny, to get their furs to the trading post at Quebec City.

And now, three hundred years later, Eric had embroiled the two tribes in another confrontation related to commerce.

"It appears Eric, in true Eric fashion, has taken on yet another noble cause," I said, turning my attention back to Billie.

"And what might this cause be, child?"

"The article says he's spearheading a group of chiefs who want to get all First Nations chiefs to agree to stop relying on illegitimate means for generating income on their reserves."

"So why's this Grand Chief looking madder than a bucking bronco?" Ed asked, picking up the magazine.

"Although it doesn't say here, I know from Eric that this chief is one of the biggest offenders. Heads up something called the Sonhatsi, a militant group that advocates Mohawk sovereignty because they say the Iroquois were once sovereign allies with the British Crown and never agreed to any change in this status."

Buried within the article, I noticed the name of the lawyer representing them, Thomas Whiteduck, which helped to explain his reluctance to take Eric on as a client, although it seemed strange that Tommy would work for the Mohawks in this particular situation.

"Surely they're entitled to their own opinion, ain't they?" Billie asked.

"Not if it's really a front for illegal activities, because, you see, they don't believe Canadian or American laws apply to them."

"That does colour it some. So what they doing that's so bad?"

"Smuggling. They take advantage of the dual Canadian and American citizenship and tax-free status the Iroquois enjoy because the tribe straddles the St. Lawrence River, which as you know is the U.S.-Canada border. They smuggle in cheap tax-free cigarettes through the river side of the Sonhatsi Reserve. They then sell the cigarettes to distributors outside the reserve. Needless to say, they make a significant amount of money on the mark-up they charge."

"But ma'am, y'all talking about nothing but a little boot-legging," Ed said. "Ain't no harm in that."

"Maybe not, but cigarettes aren't the only thing they smuggle. Eric says that they also use this route to bring in drugs and guns into Canada and to smuggle illegal immigrants into the U.S."

"Now you're talking serious business." Ed shoved his Stetson to the back of his head. "In Texas, we got more than our fair share of illegal Mexs and other Latinos. So why don't the authorities stop them?"

"Because the Sonhatsi Warriors play the sovereignty card and refuse to allow local police onto the reserves. It's become a political hot potato that no government authority wants to get burned by."

"Well, honey, it sure sounds like your man's got a tough job on his hands."

"Yeah, just what he needs, in addition to all the other jobs that are filling his plate, like this DeMontigny Lady fiasco. I'm beginning to wish that I'd heeded his advice and left the damn bones in the ground."

TWENTY-THREE

As the afternoon sun beat a hot, baking path across parched Three Deer Point, we moved our wicker chairs further into the cooling recess of the verandah. Thinking the Paynes had only dropped by for a brief chat, I'd expected them to leave after finishing their first glass of ice tea. When they requested a refill, I thought they were just being their usual friendly Texan selves, but when Ed asked for a third glass while his eyes gazed wistfully at his wife's bowed head, I realized they really wanted to be distracted from their worry.

Knowing of their keen interest in the past, I brought out some of my great-aunt Agatha's old albums that contained photos from the early 1900s of Three Deer Point and the surrounding area, including several intriguing pictures of everyday life on the Migiskan Reserve. In fact, I could have sworn one nattily dressed gentleman wearing a rakishly-cocked felt hat and plus-fours was the spitting image of Eric. Amidst hoots of laughter, Jid agreed. It was most likely his grandfather or another close Odjik relative.

Although Billie showed interest in the ancient photos, Ed's eyes strayed, spending perhaps more time gazing at his wife than the album, his brow dented with concern. Finally, halfway through the second album, he stood up and suggested it was time they head back to their cabin at the Forgotten Bay Fishing Camp.

Her lips firm in reluctant agreement, Billie apologized for taking up so much of my time. "At times like this, it's a help to be with friends. Waiting ain't easy. I find that no matter how bad the test results, knowing is better than the worry of not knowing."

I put my arms around her and gave her a hug. "I'm rooting for you. And please, feel free to drop by any time."

I watched the two of them climb into their SUV, their usual exuberance still and muted. Billie gave me a last wan smile before she closed the massive door. I felt helpless.

And as I watched the back of the Lincoln disappear around the first bend of Three Deer Point's long twisting lane, I thought of another friend, who'd also endured this terrible wait for what is essentially a sentence, life or death. In her case it was death. Within a month she'd been dead, of pancreatic cancer. About the only good thing you could say about her tragic demise was it had been mercifully quick. If Billie were to have a similar sentence, I hoped it would be just as quick. No one should have to endure a slow lingering death attached to machines and intravenous pouches. Sergei nudged me for a pat, and as I bent down to hug him, I thought about how we are more merciful with our pets.

Through my haze of worry, I barely noticed Jid run up the steps into the house. "Phone. It's Eric."

I shook myself back to the blazing afternoon and went inside.

"What's wrong?" Eric asked, obviously hearing the note of sadness in my voice. I told him about Billie.

"I'm very sorry to hear that. They seem like good people. Look, I was about to suggest you and Jid come for dinner at the Fishing Camp. Why don't I ask the Paynes to join us?"

We agreed to meet in a couple of hours, which would give Jid and me enough time to have a long, cooling swim before we canoed down the bay to the Camp.

*   *   *

By the time the boy and I set out down the long arm of Forgotten Bay, the sun was sinking behind the fringe of trees lining the high cliffs of the western shore. Deciding to mark the occasion, I wore my new silk top and did feel delightfully feminine, while Jid had his new Stetson carefully placed in the bow in front of him. He was afraid to wear it, in case it got knocked into the water.

We paddled alongside the lower eastern shore, past the empty forest still ablaze with the setting sun, past the damaged birch that marked the boundary between my property and the reserve lands. Although the end of the bay was cast in darkness, I could easily make out the high profile of the timber building of the main lodge and the lower profiles of the five small log cabins that stretched along the shore toward the cliffs on the left.

Eric had built the three-room efficiencies a couple of years before, when he'd wanted to augment his regular hunting and fishing clientele with vacationing families. Billie and Ed were staying in the one furthest from the lodge.

The parking lot spread out on the opposite side of the main lodge. Although it was for the most part empty, I could make out the lean shapes of a couple of sedans and the bulky one of a pick-up near the bar entrance at the side, and the black mass of the Paynes' SUV at the far end.

The strident strains of Shania Twain, no doubt coming from the bar, could be clearly heard over the calm water. I resented her intrusion into the peace the setting sun had brought to the land. Someone else obviously thought likewise, for the music suddenly stopped.

Now the songs of evening rose around us. The wistful "O Canada, Canada" song of a lone white-throated sparrow. The spiralling flute of a hermit thrush. The dull plop of a jumping bass.

"Look, a bald eagle." Jid pointed to the large black shape of a bird floating towards us, its wingspan well over two metres.

As it drifted overhead, I could clearly see the white head and tail of an adult bird, a wonderful sight. Yet less than ten years ago, they were non-existent in this, their traditional habitat.

Today, with the end of DDT spraying and other killing pesticides, they were making a slow but steady comeback.

After Jid helped me haul the canoe onto the Camp's narrow beach, he ran towards the main entrance and vanished into the light beyond. Wanting to continue to savour the evening's solitude, I remained on the beach, looking across the darkening bay towards Three Deer Point. High on the distant point, the windows of my home blazed orange in the setting sun. Then one after another, they blinked off as the sun disappeared.

Unfortunately, sunset also brought out the worst this northern land had to offer; whining, ravenous mosquitoes. One landed on my arm. I slapped it, then another and another. My peace was destroyed. Time to retreat inside.

As I turned to leave, I noticed a man with light-coloured hair standing on some rocks at the far end of the beach, near the Payne's cabin. He appeared equally engrossed in the twilight scene. When he turned in my direction, I recognized with a jolt the owner of the blond hair.

"George, what are you doing here?"

At first I thought he hadn't heard me, then he turned towards me. "Meg Harris, is that you?" He began limping awkwardly over the rocks to where I stood.

Not sure if it was a good idea to be alone with him, I glanced hurriedly around and noticed a couple of fisherman within easy shouting distance, unloading their boat. "The police are looking for you, you know."

"What for? I've already talked to them." He slashed at the mosquitoes circling his head.

"They hadn't this morning."

"Well, I have now. They stopped my car and hauled me off to a police station. Christ, they treated me like a goddamn criminal. Even searched my car."

I scanned his face for confirmation of his guilt but saw only anger. "Well, your behaviour hasn't exactly been above suspicion. You did take off after your tête-à-tête with Teht'aa."

"Christ, so it was Teht'aa who gave the police the idea I'd vamoosed. Damn the stupid bitch."

So much for true love, I thought.

"All those pigs had to do was ask my goddamn office. Sherry knew where I was. The damn frogs can't even look beyond their fucking French pricks."

Although I knew he'd once been a football player, the extent of his locker room swearing took me quite by surprise. "Hey, no need to swear at me. I didn't do anything."

His eyes seemed to focus back on me. "Sorry, got carried away. I guess you can say I'm upset. Not so much with the police, but with my little buddy's death. Christ, I didn't even know he was dead until the police accused me of killing him."

"I'm surprised you didn't know. It was all over the national news. Besides, I thought news of his death would've spread like wildfire amongst your fellow archeologists." I felt a mosquito prick my bare leg. I slapped at it and missed.

"Like I told the police, the minute my lecture was over, I took off to a friend's farm near St. André d'Avellin. He lives off the grid, hates technology, no phone, no cell, no TV, no radio. Hell, he barely generates enough solar energy to run his fridge."

"So I guess you left Montreal before Claude was murdered."

"Christ, you accusing me too? What in the hell would I want to kill Claude for? We were going to do that paper together."

"Yeah, but I heard the Ministry was about to dump you. Rumour has it they didn't want their archeologists sharing the glory with a *maudit anglais.*"

"It's a lie. Claude and I had a signed agreement." He swatted a mosquito on his brow, leaving a track of blood and a dead bug.

"Yeah, but they had the bones."

His lips twisted into a wry smile. "'Had' is right."

Was cynicism the only reason for his smile? "What did you do with them?"

"Can't you get it through your thick skull? I didn't kill him," he retorted. Then, looking me straight in the eye, he said, "Maybe you should be asking your Algonquin buddies who killed him."

Not liking where this was heading, I countered his attack. "You still haven't answered my original question. What are you doing here? It's two hundred and seventy kilometres from Montreal and a hundred and fifty from your home in Ottawa."

His demeanour suddenly shifted to a more sheepish stance. "Sorry, I got a little carried away. I didn't mean to get angry at you. I'm afraid Claude's death has completely thrown me for a loop. Christ, these bugs are bad."

He waved his hands around his head while I waited for his answer.

Finally, he took a deep breath and said, "Look, you know how damned important those remains are." His tone had become that of a pleading supplicant. It didn't suit him. "It may be another eleven thousand years before another find of such magnitude is discovered. We can't let these precious bones escape into oblivion."

As much as I sympathized with his dilemma, I realized Claude's death had changed things for me. The fate of the Ancient One didn't justify the taking of a man's life. "Still doesn't answer my question. Why are you here?"

"I was vi—" He clamped his mouth shut and gave me a long sideways glance. Then he continued more forcefully, almost as if he'd made a decision. "I came here to talk to your boyfriend."

Before I could ask why, a voice from behind me said, "I'm Eric Odjick. What can I do for you?"

TWENTY-FOUR

Eric moved up beside me and held his hand out to the archeologist. "We haven't met, but I've heard lots about you."

The taller man hesitated a moment then shook the offered hand. "George Schmidt. I know your daughter."

"So I gather." I could almost feel the chill from the icy bite in Eric's voice. "Now tell me what business brings you, a spirit thief, as Teht'aa calls you, here to our people's reserve? And it better not be for that damn dress."

For a moment I could see that George was completely taken aback by the force of Eric's animosity, then he recovered. "I've come to negotiate."

"There is nothing to discuss. You're not having the dress. Just tell me how much you gave my daughter for it, and I'll write you a cheque." Eric crossed his arms and glared upward, refusing to be deterred by the difference in height. Bugs circled around both men. Eric chose to ignore them, while George slapped and smacked without success.

"For your information, your daughter approached me about the dress. Almost begged me to take it, so she could have her drug money."

I saw Eric cringe at these words.

"No, I want to negotiate on another matter, the DeMontigny Lady, or if you prefer, the Ancient One. I'm asking you to relinquish all claim; in return I'll say nothing."

"Nothing about what?"

George crossed his arms against his chest. "About what your daughter and lover boy were planning."

"You talking about Larry?"

"No, Robbie Kohoko," George said. "I overheard them planning to steal the bones."

The lodge's outdoor lights flashed on, lighting up the triumphant grin spreading across George's face.

"You're lying," Eric said. "She had the perfect opportunity to steal all the bones when you showed her them, and she didn't. So why would she plan to do it later?"

"Because I never took my eyes off her. Besides, she learned of a better opportunity when she overheard the boss lady telling Claude to leave for Quebec with the bones later in the afternoon, after all you guys had gone."

"Impossible," Eric spat out. "She doesn't speak a word of French, and there is no way that lab director would've been speaking English to another francophone."

But you, dear George, I thought, as an employee of a federal institution with years of French language training, knew exactly what was being said. There's only one way you would know what Teht'aa had overheard, and that was by listening in on the same conversation.

Then I realized something else. "George, didn't you just finish telling me that you didn't know the remains were being taken away?"

I caught the brief flash of startled acknowledgement before he firmed his lips in a smug smile. "You weren't listening. I didn't say that. I said—" The rest of his answer was abruptly cut off by the sudden sound of glass shattering.

"What the hell?" Eric exclaimed as he started running towards the source of the sound on the other side of the lodge. I followed close behind. A truck's engine roared into action. I turned the corner of the building in time to see taillights disappear down the road.

A small group of men were gathering around the Paynes' Lincoln Navigator. Broken glass glimmered behind it on the ground.

Across the parking lot, Ed was opening the door from the bar. "What's happening, boys?" he called out.

"Someone broke into your truck," a male voice answered.

"Hell and damnation," came Ed's long drawl as he started down the outside steps. He suddenly wavered and lost his balance, but managed to catch himself on the railing. For a moment, he clung to it as if trying to steady himself.

Worried he might have experienced a dizzy spell or other health problem, I called out, "You okay, Ed?"

"Pay no mind. My foot slipped, that's all."

He resumed his descent down the steps and arrived at the scene at the same time as Eric and me. I looked him over carefully to make sure he really was okay. However, a strong smell of alcohol told me a bit too much liquor was more likely the source of his stumble. I was surprised since he hadn't seemed like a heavy drinker.

Shards of glass clung to the frame of the Lincoln's back window. The rest of it glittered on several wrapped packages lying inside.

"Damnation," cursed Ed as he started to lift up the rear door.

Eric caught his arm. "Don't. Glass might fall on you. Just look through the opening to see if anything is missing."

"Can't see worth a damn," he muttered as his wide frame blocked out all available light. A flashlight suddenly shone through a side window.

"What all's happening, Ed honey," Billie called out. Her voice shook.

"Don't y'all worry yourself none, hon. Just someone taking a dislike to our vehicle." Ed continued his inspection. "Y'all left your Neiman Marcus bag in the cabin, didn't ya?"

"That's right," George suddenly said almost in my ear, making me jump. I'd forgotten about him.

"How would you know?" I asked.

For a second he appeared disconcerted as his eyes shot first to Billie then to Ed, then he said, "I was visiting them."

"That's right," Ed said. "This gentleman kindly agreed to sell us an ancient peace pipe to add to our collection."

"And it sure is a beauty. Y'all are welcome to come see it," Billie added, joining us.

"Better not be Algonquin," Eric said rather rudely, which startled me. He was usually more diplomatic. The stolen bones, the murder, his daughter and now this latest episode were beginning to have their affect.

"No, it ain't. It's Ojibway." Ed punctuated the sentence with a resounding slap at a bug. "Sounds like y'all a might worried we're buying it against the wishes of the rightful owners. But I assure you, son, we have a letter from the Chief of the Grassy Narrows Ojibway giving us the go-ahead."

Eric shook his head, as if in disgust. "Gordie must need the money pretty badly. But it's none of my business, so let's get back to your SUV. Has anything been taken?"

"Yeah, I think so," Ed replied. "Honey, y'all left that small black suitcase in here, didn't ya?"

She nodded her head.

"Well, it's gone. But that's the only thing missin', near as I can tell."

"Now why would someone want that old thing? Only filled with dirty clothes."

Eric scanned the group of four or five men that surrounded us. "Any of you see who did this?"

I noticed that George was no longer amongst the onlookers. He must've decided that since this incident had nothing to do with him, there was no need for him to stay.

"Nope, I was in the bar," said one man with an empty beer

glass in his hand. "Me too," said another.

I spied one of the two fishermen I'd seen earlier, one of the Camp's fishing guides. "Pete, you must've seen something, you would've had a good view from the dock."

The grin on his face vanished as he shoved his baseball cap further back on his head. "Nope. Was cleanin' out the boat when I heard the noise. Just saw some truck takin' off like a fish running from a hook."

"Did you recognize it?"

"Nope." He then glanced smugly around at the others, which only served to raise my suspicions.

"You sure? There can't be too many strange trucks driving around here."

Although he continued to stick to his negative answer, I was almost certain he knew the owner of the truck. No doubt someone from the reserve that he didn't want to get into trouble. I wondered if the others were also protecting the culprit.

Eric turned to Ed and Billie. "I've got someone calling the police. They should be here shortly. Meanwhile, let's get away from these bugs and wait in the bar."

"I wished y'all had told me you were going to call. We'd just as soon not involve the police," Ed said. "Sure hate to get a fellow in trouble, when all he did was break a window and help himself to an old suitcase with nothing much in it but dirty clothes."

"Have it your way, but you'll need a police report for your insurance claim."

"No need to bother the insurance folks. Besides, this'll be under my deductible. Don't know why I bother with the dang fool stuff." Ed swatted another mosquito. "But hell, I'm getting kind of tired of these bugs, I'll take you up on your suggestion for a drink. Could use one about now. Come on, honey bun. Think you could do with one too."

He wrapped his arm around his wife, and they slowly made for the bar entrance. We had almost reached the door when the darkness behind us exploded with the high-beam brilliance of a vehicle entering the parking lot.

"This'll be Decontie or one of his men," Eric said. "Ed, you go on inside. I'll tell Will we don't need him."

I went inside with the Paynes, where I found Jid completely absorbed in some awful reality TV show, which helped to explain why he hadn't joined the curious outside. Living in a house without electricity had given him little exposure to TV. Since moving in with me, I'd discovered that, when not outdoors playing with the dog, he could be found inside, lying in a similar stance on the floor, head resting on his hands, eyes glued to the screen.

Eric joined us after a while. In his hand, he carried a black suitcase. The fabric was scraped and torn.

"This the one?" he asked, holding it up to the Paynes.

Billie nodded. "Where'd y'all find it?"

"Larry Horn found it."

"Larry?" I said. "So that wasn't the police?"

"No. Said he found it on the road as he was driving in. Said clothes were scattered all over the road, so he gathered them up and put them back inside."

"Larry did this?" Since he wasn't exactly known for his Good Samaritan qualities, I wasn't sure I was hearing correctly.

"Yes, I had a tough time believing it too, and that wasn't all he had to say."

The screen door opened, and in stepped Larry himself. "That's right," he said. "Saw the guy who threw this out of his truck." He paused to give us all a broad grin. "It was that piece of moose shit Teht'aa's hanging out with."

TWENTY-FIVE

Although Larry wasn't exactly a credible witness, Eric felt he had to identify Robbie as a possible suspect when Sergeant Whiteduck arrived at the Fishing Camp a few minutes later. Even Ed concurred, despite his reluctance to add to the canoe builder's growing list of troubles.

Each new instance of Robbie's strange behaviour was only serving to add to his seeming guilt. But of what? Theft of the bones? Claude's murder? And what was the meaning of this latest act? Why would he want to rob a couple who'd been so kind to him? The only one who could tell us was Robbie. It was time for him to give his version of events.

Before Sergeant Whiteduck went after him, I suggested that if he failed to find the man at his own home, he might locate him at Jid's grandmother's place. I told the lanky cop about the unknown visitor who'd been staying at the empty house.

Partway through dinner in the lodge's pine-panelled dining room, Chief Decontie phoned. His men had apprehended Robbie at Kòkomis's bungalow, and he wanted Ed to come to the station to make a statement after dinner.

I tagged along as Eric drove the Texan to the police station. Jid opted to stay behind with Billie and the TV.

Finding a parking spot at the station proved a challenge. The limited space was taken up not only by the police department's three SUVs and a sedan, but also by a number of other vehicles, from dusty sub-compacts to dustier half-ton pick-ups. Several men were congregated at the front door of the one-storey red brick building. We didn't have to wait long for the explanation.

As we approached, Pete, the guide from the Fishing Camp, called out, "Eric, you gonna let 'em take Robbie to Montreal?"

"I was worried about this," Eric muttered under his breath, but before I could ask why, he continued in a louder voice, "Why you asking, Pete?"

"They'll hang him." Pete, still dressed in his fishing shorts and sleeveless T-shirt, stepped towards us. His arm muscles glistened in the brilliant sodium light as he blocked our way into the station. The other men crowded around us. I saw Sergeant Whiteduck's lean height watching from inside the glass door.

"Not likely. We don't have capital punishment in Canada."

"Hell, Chief, you know what I mean."

"Probably do. But best if you explain it to me, so I can understand properly."

"He was only takin' what rightly belongs to our people." Pete moved in closer, as if to emphasize his point. The scent of alcohol on his breath made me feel uneasy.

In response, Sergeant Whiteduck stepped out onto the front concrete stoop and called out. "Everything okay, Chief Odjik?"

"Yup. We're just having a little chat," Eric yelled back, then returned to the fishing guide. "But what if he killed a man to get it? Do you think that's okay?"

"Depends on the circumstances, don't it? Ain't there some kinda law about the right to defend what belongs to you?"

"I'm not sure, Pete. I think we'll have to let a court of law determine that."

"Yeah, but that's what's got us worried. We figure Robbie won't get no fair trial with them Frenchies in Montreal. He needs to be tried by his own people."

"I tell you what, Pete. Why don't I go inside and have a word with Chief Decontie to see what his plans are, okay?"

"Sure, Chief." He backed out of our way, as did the other men.

As I passed through them, I could smell the strong odour of sweat and stale beer.

Once inside the solid walls of the police station, I felt the tension ease from my body. "Surely, they weren't going to stop us from coming inside?"

"Let's just say I didn't want to test it," Eric said, then turning to Decontie, he asked, "Have Pete and the others been here long?"

The police chief was leaning into the counter, his ample belly jammed against the edge. As usual, his navy blue uniform bore a slightly dishevelled appearance, including a missing pocket button. He'd been perusing an official looking document and now passed it back to Corporal Matoush on the other side of the counter.

This new recruit, with his cropped black hair and his perfectly pressed uniform, was a recent graduate from the Police College in Saskatchewan. Eric and Decontie had wanted to beef up the qualifications of the reserve's five-man police force, so they'd made a point of seeking out natives with university degrees in addition to the appropriate police college training. Although Matoush was James Bay Cree, he seemed to have had no trouble being accepted by the Algonquin community.

With the document in hand, the corporal returned to his desk and picked up the phone. Although his words were indistinct, they had a French cadence to them.

From the open box on the counter, Decontie grabbed a greasy bannock, the bushman's version of a donut, without the hole, and turned to Eric. "They've been here ever since we brought Robbie in. In fact, another truckload of men drove up just before you arrived."

I looked around for Robbie, but failing to see his wiry form, I assumed he'd been taken to one of the two cells in the back.

"Shit, I don't like it," Eric said.

"Neither do I. The sooner we transport Robbie to Montreal, the better."

"So you do plan to take him there."

"Yes. Corporal Matoush is just finalizing the arrangements now."

"Anyway you could keep him here?"

"With that crowd collecting outside? Forget it. Besides, the crimes he's charged with happened off-reserve in Montreal, way outside my jurisdiction."

"But the break-in of the Paynes' SUV was on the reserve. Can't you keep him for questioning on that?"

"Not much to question him about. He admitted his guilt, although he refuses to say what he was after."

"Gotta be Billie's diamonds," Ed said, suddenly coming to life. To this point, he'd been acting more like a bystander, following Eric's lead, a role that seemed contrary to his usual take-charge Texan ebullience.

"The charm bracelet I gave her for our fiftieth wedding anniversary," he continued. "Noticed Robbie giving it the once-over the other day. Sure lucky we had it in the cabin and not in the Lincoln."

I narrowed my eyes. Robbie going after jewellery didn't make sense. "Why would Robbie want to steal jewellery? He leads a simple life. Expensive items like diamonds have no part in it, nor does the kind of money they could bring."

Chief Decontie answered, "I tend to agree, but he might've been thinking of fleeing to B.C., where his cousin lives. He'd need money for that. But whatever the reason, he's not saying."

I accepted his explanation for the moment. There seemed no other plausible reason for Robbie's strange act.

"I tell you, though," Decontie continued in his raspy smoker's voice. "He sure didn't want to get caught. My men earned every dollar of their pay trying to get him handcuffed and into the cruiser."

As if on cue, a male voice began shouting repeatedly from the cell area, "Let me outta here!" to the accompaniment of clanging bars.

"He's been carrying on like that since we put him in the cell. Like I said, the sooner I get him out of here, the better."

"Surely that can't be Robbie?" I said, surprised by yet another example of unusual behaviour. "He's so mild-mannered. I've never heard him raise his voice, no matter how justified."

Decontie shrugged. "It happens. Especially when you get someone like Robbie, who's lived in the bush most of his life. They go a little crazy when they're locked up."

Poor guy, I thought. What was going to happen if it turned out he really was guilty of Dr. Meilleur's murder?

While Ed gave his statement to Sergeant Whiteduck at a nearby desk, Eric disappeared into a side office with the police chief, leaving me to twiddle my thumbs at the front counter. Although tempted to sample some bannock (I had acquired a taste for the puffy deep-fried flour, water and lard mixture), an image of arteries clogged with fat dissuaded me. Instead, I watched the growing crowd through the front window.

Another carload of men, plus some women, had joined them. A crowd of fifteen or so people were now milling around Pete, who seemed to have taken on the role of leader. I knew little about Pete Smith other than that he had worked for Eric as a guide for the past three years and was popular with the guests. Before that, he'd lived off-reserve in Ottawa.

A familiar black truck advanced through the group, forcing them to step aside, and parked in the only remaining free space, the disabled spot. Out stepped Larry, warrior tattoo, greasy rat's tail and all. After giving the people a thumbs-up, he entered the police station.

"Fancy seeing you here," I said. The fact that he had so

boldly come to the police station told me that his alibi for the time of Claude's death must've stuck.

He sneered, "Just doing my civic duty." He sauntered up to the counter and hollered "Anyone here?" despite the fact that Corporal Matoush was sitting at his desk, tapping away at his computer. Both Sergeant Whiteduck and Ed had vanished.

Clearly annoyed, Matoush started to get up, but the sergeant pushed open the door from the cells and yelled, "Cut out the noise!" causing Robbie to resume his shouting. With a slam of the door, Whiteduck vanished back into the cell area, while Matoush continued with his typing.

Larry pounded on the counter. "Hey you! I thought you wanted my statement so you can convict the creep."

Matoush looked up. "Sergeant Whiteduck will be with you in a moment. Please have a seat, sir." I guessed manners came with the university degree.

From my seat beside the window, I waited to see how Larry would respond to this unaccustomed politeness. For once he seemed speechless, and with a yeah-whatever shrug to show he was still in control, he sat down beside me, leaving me with something of a dilemma. I had no desire to carry on a conversation, but there was no other place I could wait.

I needn't have worried. He seemed more interested in slapping his keys against his thigh than conversing. Within a couple of minutes, the door to the police chief's office opened, and Eric appeared. A second later, Ed emerged from the bathroom.

"Ready to go?" Eric asked.

Since I'd last looked out the window, Pete had amassed more disgruntled Robbie supporters. They completely blocked the way to Eric's Jeep. "What about the guys outside?"

"No problem," he replied with a certain amount of bravado. "I've come up with a solution that'll keep them happy."

With Pete in the lead, the group converged as the three of us stepped out the door.

"Chief, they gonna take him to Montreal?" Pete asked.

Before answering, Eric squeezed my hand tightly, which suggested he wasn't feeling quite as confident as his outward nonchalance conveyed. I squeezed back my support.

"Listen, everyone, I want you to know that I'll make sure he gets a fair trial."

"Yeah, only if it's done on the reserve," Pete spat.

"The trial has to take place in Montreal, where he committed the crimes. Nothing we can do to change that."

"Sure we can. We don't let 'em take him."

"Preventing him from leaving the reserve will only make things worse for him…and for us."

"We don't trust them fuckin' frogs," someone behind Pete yelled out.

A woman cried out, "They won't see past his red skin. They'll hang him for sure."

"The courts in Montreal are as fair as anywhere else in Canada. Besides, I've made sure that Robbie will be properly represented."

"Yeah, with some slick city lawyer who'll only be interesting in getting himself on TV," Pete sneered. "He won't give a damn about our people and our right to protect our heritage."

"I thought the same, so that's why I've retained one of our people, Tommy Whiteduck, as his lawyer."

I was surprised to hear Tommy's name. The young lawyer had been emphatic about not wanting to represent Teht'aa, citing conflict of interest, but perhaps that was because she was Eric's daughter and might have caused him problems as the lawyer representing the Mohawks in the mess Eric was involved in.

"Tommy will do what's best for Robbie and for our people," Eric continued.

I saw several heads nod in agreement. Although the night temperature was still stifling, a slight breeze was adding a cooling touch. The bugs, however, continued to swirl around the parking lot lights.

"So what do you say about calling it a night?" Eric continued. "It's late. Everyone's tired. Time to go home."

One or two voices said, "Yup," and several people began walking towards their vehicles, but Pete continued to block our path.

Out of the corner of my eye, I could see Decontie watching from inside the station. He'd probably decided that as long as it remained peaceful, it was better to let the band chief deal with the situation than the police.

"What can I do for you, Pete?" Eric asked.

"Look, Chief, I know you mean good, but Tommy has lived more time off-reserve than on it. How in the hell is he gonna be able to defend Robbie if he don't even know what it is to be Anishinabeg?"

I could feel Eric stiffen beside me. I knew what he was thinking. He, himself, had been accused of the same fault.

"As you know, Tommy's mother Marie was an elder. She would've passed on our teachings to her son. I can assure you, he knows what it is to be Anishinabeg. But Tommy has also recognized the potential gap in his knowledge, so he has asked for the assistance of Grandfather Albert. I don't think you can argue against our esteemed elder's right to be called the voice of our people."

The fishing guide acknowledged Eric's words but continued to block our way. Only a few men remained. The steeliness in their eyes suggested they would do whatever Pete asked them to do. He started to hammer his fist against his open palm. Eric tensed, readying himself for Pete's next action. Behind me, I could hear Ed's heavy breathing.

Suddenly the door behind us swished opened, followed by Larry's gruff voice. "Guys, you're blocking my way. Go find yourselves another spot to have a pow-wow."

It was enough to dilute the tension.

Pete began to step backwards slowly, as did his buddies. Without bothering to wait for an opening, Larry brushed past us and charged through. We followed close behind.

We clambered into the safety of Eric's Jeep. Before closing his door, Eric called out, "Pete, Chief Decontie is taking Robbie down to Montreal tomorrow morning. I don't want any interference. Like I said, I'll make sure he gets a fair trial in Montreal."

Pete's response was to slam his truck's door.

"Damn," Eric said as he jammed the Jeep into reverse.

TWENTY-SIX

I thought we'd at least have a peaceful night together at Three Deer Point before Eric would have to start dealing with whatever trouble Pete was going to cause in the morning, but the phone call from Decontie came two hours after we'd fallen asleep.

"Damn," said Eric after I passed him the phone. Sleepy-eyed Jid poked his head around the door and came in to snuggle against Sergei, lying on the old settee the dog had appropriated as his bed.

"And you did what we agreed on?" Eric continued.

While he listened to the police chief's lengthy reply, I snuggled closer, while keeping an ear open to find out what was happening.

"Good. Guess Pete's smarter than we give him credit for. Where's Robbie now? In his cell?"

The mention of Robbie started me guessing. And when Eric said, "As much as I hate to do it, I guess we'd better bring the provincial police into this in the morning," I'd pretty well reached my conclusion.

So when he hung up, I hazarded, "Despite what you told Pete about taking Robbie to Montreal in the morning, you and Will had actually decided to take him down tonight, hadn't you?"

"Yup, we figured it the best way to avoid trouble. But Pete outsmarted us. Already had blockades in place."

"Where?"

"On the main road, just before the boundary line between the band lands and your property."

Now it was my turn to swear. "Shit. They aren't going to damage my property, are they?" Although there were no nearby buildings, I still didn't like the idea of a bunch of troublemakers camping out in my woods.

"Nope. I think Pete is smart enough to know that any trouble he causes you would make things doubly worse for him. The SQ would have every legal right to arrest him and his men for trespassing. As it stands now, sympathy might be more on their side if the SQ arrest them on reserve land."

"So why bring the provincial police in?"

"Basically as a deterrent to prevent the confrontation from spreading beyond reserve borders. I'm hoping we won't need force."

"What do you plan to do then?"

"Decontie is going to try to take Robbie out again in the morning. We're hoping the light of day might bring reason to Pete and his men. That, and of course the confiscation of the two cases of beer Sergeant Whiteduck found in the back of Pete's truck." He chuckled. "But if they still won't let Robbie through, then I'll get some of the elders to help convince them."

"You know, there is another possible solution."

Eric raised his eyebrows.

"Bring him down the lake from the Fishing Camp to my dock. Your Jeep's already here. And my road joins the main road well out of sight from where the blockade must be. They'd never know."

"Maybe not at the time. But eventually they would, and I'd be afraid of the anger that would be directed against you. Besides, it's going to be difficult enough getting the band to accept you as my wife without giving them another reason not to."

For a second I continued to enjoy his warmth before I froze. Wife! I backed away from his touch and braced myself for the ages-old words that I knew would lead to disaster. Instead he said, "Is something wrong?"

Perhaps he hadn't realized what he'd said. "No…no not at all." Maybe if I said nothing, the dreaded word would sink back into the big black void from whence it had come.

"It's the word 'wife', isn't it? Sorry to spring it on you like this, but it just slipped out."

I tensed as his fingers played up and down my arm. "Meg, you know how much I love you."

I nodded dumbly, unable to return his words of love. Afraid of where they would lead.

Eric's searching grey eyes sought out my cowardly blue ones. I turned away. His fingers came to rest on the scar where the broken bone had pierced my skin. "Our relationship means a lot to me. I guess I'm hoping that someday we could make it more permanent."

In a panic, I leapt out of bed and sought the security of the boy sleeping beside his buddy. "Shsh…shh you'll wake up Jid. Let's talk about this later."

"Maybe we should talk about it now."

"Please, Eric, no."

"Are you saying you don't want to marry me?"

"Yes, I mean, no," I quickly blurted out. "Shit, I don't know what I mean. Let's not talk about it now."

"Is this your way of saying I'm not good enough?"

"Oh, Eric, how can you say that? Of course not. You're the only person that matters to me." I was the one who wasn't good enough.

"Then why don't you want to get married?"

Jid muttered something and shifted his position beside the

dog. His eyes, however, remained closed.

"Shsh…we're waking him up."

"Damn it. It's because of that bastard, isn't it?" he growled and jumped out of bed.

I clamped my hand over the scar Eric had just touched, the scar Gareth, my ex-husband, had caused when he'd thrown me against the kitchen counter and broken my arm.

"Why can't you forget the man? He's long out of your life." I rubbed the scar. The memory of the pain was still sharp. "I get it. You think I'll abuse you the same way that bastard did." By this time, the old hockey scar beneath his eye was glowing white, a clear sign of the extent of his anger.

"Eric, how can you say that? I know you're not that kind of man."

He pulled on his jeans, grabbed his T-shirt and headed out the bedroom door.

"Where are you going?" I called over the noise of his footsteps pounding down the stairs.

"I've got things to do," he yelled back from the downstairs hall.

"At three in the morning?"

The slamming of the front door was my answer.

I remained frozen at the top of the stairs, too stunned to run after him. Too stunned to cry. One moment we were a loving couple—the next moment… I didn't want to think about it. Why was I so afraid to tell Eric the truth.? But I really didn't need to ask myself the question. I already knew the answer.

I thought back to the ceremony performed more than twenty years ago, when, with no forethought, I had promised to obey my lawful wedded husband. Gareth, however, had heeded those words and had exacted every ounce of that promise until I was nothing but a bowing, scraping female with no will of my own. Alcohol, lemon vodka in particular, had become my only escape.

I jumped at the soft touch of a hand on my arm and looked down to see Jid's beseeching eyes staring up at me. At his side stood Sergei, casting the same sorrowful brown eyes in my direction.

"Please," Jid said,"don't cry."

My fingers reached up to my face and felt moisture. I hadn't realized I was crying.

TWENTY-SEVEN

When I stepped down from my truck, I caught the sound of easy laughter coming from around the bend.

"Someone's sure having fun," Jid said, as he walked beside me. I'd parked the truck about a hundred meters and out of sight from where I presumed the blockade had been set up on the main road.

"Yeah, it's probably Pete with some friends."

Although I'd assumed Chief Decontie would try to move Robbie first thing this morning, I didn't think it would be before the day shift came on at eight o'clock. It was a little after that hour now.

While the morning air still hung heavy with overnight coolness, the sun piercing the gaps in the trees promised a quick return to the heat. And the acrid smell of smoke told me the forest fires continued to burn in the north.

"Sounds like they're havin' a pow-wow." The boy's voice had taken on a note of hopeful glee.

So much for the confiscation of beer. Obviously, they'd found more. On the other hand, it also meant that Chief Decontie had not yet tried to go through the blockade, otherwise the laughter would be less carefree. As we tramped along the rutted gravel road, past withered foliage ghost-like from layers of summer dust, the laughter grew louder and more raucous. At one point I thought I caught the strains of Pete's voice issuing instructions.

"Wow," Jid said as we rounded the corner. "Just like Oka." As he quickened his pace, I placed a firm hand on his shoulder to restrain him. Maybe this hadn't been such a good idea.

About thirty metres in front of us spread a line of vehicles from the dense bush on one side of the road to a granite outcropping on the other. A freshly washed Dodge pick-up had been parked lengthwise in the middle of the road. A couple of others had been placed, headlights facing towards us, to plug in the gaps. Two very muddy ATVs were rammed into the ditches at either end to ensure that not even a bicycle could squeeze through.

The laughter stopped as Jid and I hove into view. The boy reached for my hand. "We won't go any further, okay?" I said, stopping. Jid gripped harder.

"Hey, Pete," called out a man with a familiar brush-cut and a weathered face, but one I couldn't put a name to. He lounged on a lawn chair perched in the back of the new truck. A rifle rested across his knees. "Here's the big man's fancy woman."

At his words, my heart twisted. I'd spent the remainder of the night cursing myself for being such a coward. As the rising sun hit my bedroom window, I'd called Eric, wanting to apologize, to try to explain, but had got only voice mail, at his home and his office. I'd hoped I would see him here.

Pete's baseball-capped head appeared above the cab of one of the front facing pick-ups that I now recognized to be his. He upended a beer bottle and drained it. In the other hand, he raised a rifle. "Payin' a little visit to loverboy, eh? Ya can't today."

I ignored his comment and searched instead for the tree markers that identified the boundary between my land and the reserve. Although it was difficult to be certain from this distance if the blockade was on the wrong side of the red-slashed tree, I decided to challenge him anyway. "I hope you're not on my property, Pete. If so, I'll have to ask you to move your trucks."

Pete laughed. "Ya think I'm that dumb? I know my rights. And I know this road is a right-of-way for all us Migiskan Anishinabeg."

"If you step one foot on my property, I'll have you charged with trespassing," I countered.

"You do that, lady, and we'll slap a land claim on you." Then, with a shake of his rifle in my direction, he resumed his seat on the back of his truck.

His words sent a momentary jolt of fear through my veins. Many a landowner whose property lay next to a reserve had found himself tied up for years in court over claims the land rightly belonged to the band. Although the deed to Three Deer Point dated back to 1891, when my great-grandpa Joe had won the property in a poker game, I wasn't about to test Pete's threat.

"Hey, kid," the man with the brush-cut shouted. "You should be on this side of the barricade."

Jid started to loosen his grip, but I squeezed tighter. "No, it's not a good idea."

"But they're my people."

"I know, but what these men are trying to do isn't right, and it might get dangerous." As if to support my point, Pete fired his rifle into the air, accompanied by a war whoop. Several other men joined him.

Jid wrenched his hand free and faced me. "I gotta be with them. Kòkomis told me I should follow the ways of our people."

"And so you should, but I don't think your Kòkomis would want you to break the law." I explained the situation with Robbie and what Pete was attempting to do.

"But Robbie's my friend. I gotta help him."

"He's my friend too, and the best way of helping him is to let him get a fair trial in Montreal."

"But that will be with white men, won't it?" His once trusting eyes had taken on a questioning distrust.

As I tried to come up with an appropriate reply, my attention was distracted by sudden honking and shouting coming from the other side of the blockade.

"Let me through this instant," yelled a voice I recognized with surprise to be George Schmidt's. "It's urgent. I need to get to Ottawa."

So George hadn't left the reserve, after all. I wondered why.

I turned back to the boy in time to see him racing towards the barricade. "No, Jid! Don't!"

But his pace didn't falter. He grasped the hands of the guy in the back of the new truck and was swept up onto the barricade. He raised his fingers in a victory sign as he beamed back at me.

I started to yell at him to get off the truck but realized it would be useless. A greater barrier than the blockade now separated us. I had become the enemy.

I should never have brought him. I should've known this could happen. Instead my thoughts had been too focussed on Eric. If he got hurt…or worse…I shoved it from my mind. I didn't want to think of the possibility.

"If you don't let me through, I'll ram your truck," shouted George.

"Go ahead," answered Pete. "Cause more damage to your fancy car than my old wreck."

He raised his rifle and pointed it at what looked to be the top of George's blond head. "I suggest you get back into your car and get the hell outta here. It's gonna get real hot here real soon."

Did his "real soon" mean Decontie was on his way?

I heard the crunch of gravel behind me and turned around to see a couple of SQ cruisers slowly coming to a stop in the middle of the road. Their flashing red and blue lights magnified the sense of urgency.

I immediately recognized the slim boyishness of Sergeant Beauchamp as he stepped out of the closest vehicle. Strapped into his bulletproof vest, he strode towards me with his hand within easy reach of his opened holster. "Madame Harris," he said in French, "I ask that you move out of the way. The situation may become dangerous."

"There is a little boy, a friend of mine, on that truck, who needs to be protected." I pointed to Jid, the smile now gone from his face. His wraith-like body was sandwiched between the bulk of two men who'd joined him. One of them was Larry. The other was Pete.

The blond policeman advanced towards the waiting men. Although their rifles remained at rest, I could sense their edginess.

When he was about ten metres from the barricade, Pete shouted in English, "That's as far as it goes, copper." He raised his rifle slowly. Beauchamp stopped.

"Madame, you must get out of the way." One of the other cops motioned for me to get behind the safety of the police cruisers. Two other vehicles had joined them. Their occupants, with guns pointed, squatted behind the solid metal frames.

Beauchamp, holding his empty hands up to show he came in peace, shouted in English, "I ask you to permit the boy to go to a safe place. A small child should not be involved."

"Sure he should," answered Pete. "Boy's gotta right to protect his heritage, same as everyone else."

"You want to have the responsibility for his death?"

"Only one killin' him would be you, copper."

I could see the fear creep across the boy's face and sense his indecision. I shouted, "Jid, it's okay. You've shown Robbie you support him. Now you can get out of the truck and go where it's safe."

He smiled wanly at me, then glanced up at Pete.

"I'd say we got ourselves a hostage. He's gonna stay right here with me." Pete wrapped the arm which held the rifle around the boy.

"Let the boy go," the cop shouted.

I held my breath as Pete continued to hang onto Jid, whose face was stark with fear.

"Hey, cop!" George's upper body suddenly appeared above the side of the truck, but was immediately shoved down by Larry, who joined him on the ground. A burst of swearing between the two men could be heard above the voices of other blockaders.

My eyes turned back to Jid. He was gone! Pete stood defiantly alone in the back of the truck.

"Where's Jid?" I yelled.

"None of your damn business, white woman."

"What have you done with him?"

"Hey cop! Over here!" George, waving his arms, limped up to the ATV blocking the left-hand ditch. "Can you get me out of here? I'm Dr. Schmidt, Director of Archeology at the National Museum of Canada. I have an important meeting to get to."

Ignoring the archeologist, Sergeant Beauchamp called out to Pete. "We want to know if the boy is safe."

"The kid's fine," George shouted back. "Now you gonna get me out of here?"

"Like the spirit thief says, the kid's okay. You think I'm dumb enough to do something to a hostage? No way. Now back off, copper." Pete waved his rifle at the policeman.

The cops around me gripped their guns.

Sergeant Beauchamp backed up several metres then stopped.

Pete yelled again, "The spirit thief can go. But his car stays."

"*Monsieur le docteur,* you must come on this side of the barrier. We will get your car later," the sergeant shouted.

As George hesitated, Larry yelled out, "If ya go, Georgieboy, I get to keep your car. Always wanted a Beemer."

BMW? Last car I'd seen George driving was a Honda Civic. The fossil business must be good.

Without saying another word, the archeologist disappeared behind the blockade, to be immediately replaced by the man with the brush-cut and beer-belly.

From behind the barrier, Eric's amplified voice suddenly rang out, "Pete, Robbie's father and some of the other elders are here with me. We want to talk peacefully over smudge. In the meantime, you can tell your men to put their rifles down."

My heart skipped at the sound of his voice. Would I see him?

Pete, with his rifle still firmly clenched, twisted his head around to where Eric must be standing.

"Sergeant Beauchamp, can you hear me?" Eric's voice continued.

"Oui, monsieur."

"I'd appreciate if you asked your men to put their guns away too. We need to resolve this in a peaceful manner."

"Agreed, but I need to be assured that the boy is safe."

"Not sure what boy you're talking about."

"It's Jid, Eric," I shouted. "Pete knows where he is."

I heard an exclamation of anger, then Eric replied, "Sergeant Beauchamp, I give you my assurance that no harm will come to the boy."

I hoped so, but I had my doubts that Pete would readily hand over his "hostage" to a man who would be trying to put an end to his blockade.

The police sergeant slowly raised his hands from his holster. He ordered his men to do likewise.

But judging by the reluctance with which some of the

officers put their guns down, they didn't think it was such a good idea. Still, within a few minutes, all were standing in front of the cruisers with their guns back in their holsters, their empty hands held out within easy view of the people manning the blockade.

Pete, however, remained unconvinced. Larry, now standing beside him, displayed the same stubborn stance.

"Pete," Eric said, "I thought you wanted to follow the ways of our people. Resolving conflict peacefully over smudge is the way of our people. Using arms is the white man's way."

Touché, Eric, I thought to myself. If any argument would convince Pete, that one should.

While I could see Pete begin to waver, it looked as if Larry was going to remain stolidly defiant. Finally Pete put his rifle down, and with a nod of his head, he motioned his men to do the same. Larry was the last to lay down his rifle, and only after an angry remark from the man standing next to him.

TWENTY-EIGHT

"Madame, this land belongs to you, *non?*"Sergeant Beauchamp asked, pointing to the forest on either side of the road. "I would like your permission to go on it in order to observe the negotiation."

"But to get close enough, you'll have to go onto reserve land. What happens if they catch you?"

He shrugged in true Gallic fashion. "It is my business not to get caught."

"I'm going with you."

"No, it is too dangerous."

"I don't care. I have to make sure Jid is safe."

"I can do that, madame."

"No, it's my fault he's there. I won't be satisfied until I see for myself." And if it were possible to remove him, I would, but I didn't dare tell this to the sergeant. "Besides, I know of a place that will take us close to the road without anyone being able to see us."

With another shrug, Beauchamp acquiesced and followed me into the spruce forest that covered a steep hill. Within minutes, we'd scrambled over the top of a granite outcropping and, keeping well out of sight of the men below, crossed into Migiskan lands and hidden ourselves behind a large boulder with a view through the trees to the road below.

The faint smell of burning sweetgrass told me the peace talks had begun. But all we could see from this angle was a Migiskan Police suv, parked about twelve metres below. Sergeant

Whiteduck leaned against the front door, obscuring most of the police force's stylized Fish Hook symbol. He was no doubt guarding Robbie, who must be inside, if the sound of the vehicle's running engine was anything to go by. With the windows tightly shut, air conditioning would be required to prevent anyone inside from succumbing to the growing heat.

On the other side of the cruiser stood another guard, whose black peaked cap and shoulders I could just make out through the leaves. But since that was all I could see, I couldn't tell if the guard was Corporal Matoush or one of the other two cops with the Migiskan police detachment.

"Do you see the boy?" I whispered.

"Not yet, but they've probably taken him further away from the blockade," the sergeant replied. "I'm sure he's all right."

At that point, a couple of blockaders moved into view a few metres to the right of the police car. At least I assumed they were blockaders, judging by the sudden alertness in Sergeant Whiteduck's stance. He pushed himself away from the door and approached them.

"That's as far as you go, Ted." Whiteduck's deep voice resonated upward through the trees.

"Ah, Sam, we just want to have a few words with our brother, Robbie. It won't hurt none."

"You ain't brothers, Ted. Back off. Besides, not even family can talk to him now."

"We're brothers in our struggle against the white man's oppression. You could be our brother, too. Just let us talk to him."

The sergeant's hand hovered over his closed holster. "If you don't back off, I'll arrest you for attempting to help a prisoner escape."

"You're nothing but a fuckin' apple," Ted shot back in disgust.

Before the policeman could answer, Pete's hoarse voice rang

out from somewhere to the right of us. "Ted, Bill, get the hell out of there!"

The men and the cop continued to face each other like gunslingers of old, then the two blockaders slowly backed away and disappeared under the foliage.

That insult must've hurt, I thought as I watched Sergeant Whiteduck stride back to his station beside the SUV. It could not be easy upholding laws set by a culture that had done its best to eliminate your own.

The smell of smudge told me where I'd find Eric, but it didn't tell me where Jid was. Perhaps Pete still had him.

Motioning Beauchamp to follow, I picked my way along the steep slope toward where I thought Pete's voice had come from. The smell of smudge grew stronger, as did the murmur of chanting.

I stopped when I caught sight of a group of people sitting in a small circle about fifteen metres below, at the side of the dirt road. I felt a momentary twinge as I recognized Eric's thick ponytail and his grandfather's embroidered deerskin vest. He was sitting cross-legged, facing in my direction, his head bent as if in prayer. In his left hand he held a brown speckled eagle feather, no doubt to show that he was also sitting in this circle in his capacity as an elder.

And beside him, sitting equally quiet, was the slim body of Jid, his fear now replaced by a demeanour that suggested he was feeling very honoured to be allowed to sit in on such a momentous occasion.

On the other side of Eric sat Police Chief Decontie. Beads of sweat on his brow glistened in the mid-morning sun. His tightly buttoned jacket strained with the pressure of his paunch as he leaned awkwardly forward, with his elbows resting uncomfortably on his upraised crossed legs.

With his back to me, Pete sat across from them on the opposite side of the circle. He still wore his fishing clothes from the day before. Although he seemed to be trying to project an air of indifference, the jiggling of his crossed legs suggested otherwise. Beside him sat the man with the brush-cut who'd pulled Jid up and onto the back of the pick-up.

Between these two sets of antagonists sat two other elders, a man about Eric's age and an older, grey-haired woman. Both wore ordinary clothes. The only indications they were more than simple band members were the large eagle feathers inserted into ornate leather holders that each held.

Grandfather Albert sat on the other side between the police chief and Pete. He wore his usual beaded headband over his wispy grey hair and his worn buckskin vest over a white T-shirt. In front of him lay the regalia of his medicine bundle spread out on the wolf skin. As he chanted, he fanned the smoke rising from the large shell with his black and white feather.

"What is the old man doing?" Beauchamp whispered as he sat down beside me.

"He is preparing the sacred smudge. He also happens to be the father of the accused."

"*Sacrifice! Le père.* I don't believe this man will permit his son to go to Montreal."

"Since the old man is definitely no friend of ours, I'm inclined to agree. But Eric knows what he's doing, so he must feel that Robbie's father will be objective."

Beauchamp shook his head as if to say, "I'll believe it when I see it."

Still chanting, Kohoko slowly rose and made his way around the circle with the burning smudge, stopping in front of each participant for ritual cleansing.

"*Mon Dieu, qu'est-ce que c'est que ça?*" Beauchamp pointed to a long, slender object that lay on the wolf skin next to where the old man had been sitting. "I have seen such things only in cowboy movies. In French we call it *un calumet de la paix.*"

"Peace pipe. Last time I saw one of those was in a museum. I wonder if he's actually going to use it."

When the old man resumed his seat on the ground, he ignored the reed-like pipe, with its carved stone bowl. Instead he spoke in what sounded like Algonquin, although his voice was so low, it was difficult to tell.

"Sacrifice!" the policeman swore again, which voiced my sentiments exactly. If they continued in Algonquin, we wouldn't be able to follow the progress of the talks.

But Pete came to our rescue, for he snarled, "Speak English, Mishòmis. Bob here don't speak the lingo."

You probably don't either, I thought, and you're afraid to admit it, since you're supposed to be arguing on the side of the traditional ways.

Unfortunately for the sergeant and me, the old man's soft, wavering voice made it impossible in any case to understand his words.

I decided to slide down the rocks to a closer spot with enough underbrush to keep me hidden from the people below, but I accidentally dislodged a small stone, which in turn dislodged others, sending a dribble bouncing to the ground below. One hit Pete squarely on the head. He turned. I ducked, but not before seeing Eric's startled eyes staring into mine.

"It was a squirrel, Pete." Eric's deep voice rang out loud and clear. As if to support him, one chattered shrilly on a branch above me.

I waited another couple of minutes before daring to raise my head above my screen of baby spruce.

Eric continued to stare in my direction then jerked his head as if trying to tell me to get out of there. But as I watched his amazement turn to outrage when Sergeant Beauchamp slid into his line of sight. I realized the full magnitude of our trespassing. If we were discovered, we could jeopardize Eric's negotiations.

We had to leave, but the way back was precarious. Easy enough to slide down this steep slope. Much harder to climb back up without being heard or seen. Sergeant Beauchamp mouthed "no" when he saw me looking upward. I nodded in agreement and crouched down further behind the spindly spruce that now seemed sparser than when I'd arrived.

TWENTY-NINE

As the mid-morning heat strangled the last of the night's coolness, Grandfather Albert droned on. He was kicking off the negotiation with a long, monotonous discourse in such a low voice that I could only guess what he was saying. From the few words I heard distinctly, he was reminding the others about the importance of their Anishinabeg heritage. Once or twice Eric tried to interrupt him in an attempt to speed him up and was summarily dismissed. Since I didn't believe a father could remain completely unbiased, I assumed the old man was laying the groundwork for keeping his son on the reserve.

Although the clump of young spruce effectively blocked any view I might have had of the entire circle, by moving my head from side to side I could catch glimpses of the participants through gaps in the boughs. Outwardly, Eric appeared to be listening respectfully to Grandfather's long monologue. But I knew from the tenseness of his jaw and the ramrod straightness with which he held his feather that he was beginning to lose patience with the old man.

On the other hand, the police chief's face, glowing with sweat, fully reflected his impatience. Clearly uncomfortable, the overweight man was constantly shifting his cross-legged position on the hard ground. He started undoing a couple of the top buttons of his heavy serge jacket, then a few more until finally he removed it all together, revealing his sweat-stained blue shirt.

Pete was showing his irritation too by the jiggling of his legs. The only people who seemed to be at ease with the slowness of the process were the other two elders. They sat like a couple of serene buddhas, occasionally fanning themselves with their feathers and nodding in agreement whenever Kohoko must've made a key point.

As the minutes ticked into thirty, the hard rock I was sitting on seemed to get harder. My back ached. When my right foot finally went to sleep, I shifted as best I could without making myself known to the group below. Within minutes, I felt the numbing tingle of lost circulation in my left foot. I shifted again. Sergeant Beauchamp's relaxed stance suggested he was faring better than I. As far as I could tell, he hadn't shifted his position since he'd crouched behind his own tree cover. I put it down to a body far fitter than mine.

Finally, Grandfather Albert stopped talking and pointed at Eric, who thankfully spoke in a louder voice. He kept his impatience in check, making no attempt to speed up the pace as he too spoke of the ancestors. His approach appeared to be meeting Kohoko's approval, for the old man nodded and grunted as Eric talked about the need to follow the ancient ways.

"Our teachings tell us to respect the world around us, to live not only in harmony with nature but also with the other peoples that inhabit our land." Eric flicked his eagle feather as if to emphasize the point. "In fact, the Creator placed the four peoples of the world on the four directions of the circle of life to show us the balance of harmony we must maintain."

This statement brought not only a loud grunt from the shaman, but also vigorous nods from the other two elders.

"They tell us that if we do not maintain this balance, we will wander around aimlessly, become ineffective, and in so doing will be destroyed."

More nods and grunts, and a sudden alertness in Pete. Maybe he'd guessed where his chief was going with this line of argument. I hadn't.

"Just as we respect the ways of the beaver, the deer, the eagle and all other creatures of Mother Earth, so must we respect, no matter how difficult, the ways of other peoples in order to maintain this balance."

Eric paused at this point and slowly gazed at each member of the circle. Pete's twitching stopped when Eric's glance reached him. For a moment I thought the fishing guide was going to say something, but he didn't. Eric's eyes then passed onto Kohoko, who remained likewise immobile, but I sensed it didn't come from a shaman's inner calmness, but from a father's anticipation.

Eric continued, "And these ways include their laws."

"Bullshit!" yelled Pete.

Grandfather Albert held his feather up for silence at the same time as he attempted to straighten his hunched back. I suspected that he was preparing himself for a rebuttal.

"Robbie has been charged with murdering a man, a man who belongs to a different people, a people that has been both our enemy…" Eric paused, "and our friend."

"Friend?" Pete spat on the ground. "Now you're showing your true colours, you fuckin' apple."

I reeled as the slap of that insult jolted Eric.

"Silence!" Kohoko commanded with an unexpected strength. "Angry Scar Man speaks. Your turn next."

By using Eric's Algonquin name, he was reminding Pete of Eric's solid Algonquin roots. Maybe I was misreading him— maybe he was on Eric's side.

To get a better view of Eric, I shifted to a ledge of rock at the fringes of my spruce blind. Eric's posture still suggested calm control. "These people are asking that Robbie be tried according to their laws for a crime that was committed on their land. To maintain the harmony of the circle of life, our teachings tell us, we must—"

Suddenly the rock ledge gave way, and I found myself sliding downwards. I grabbed at a tree in desperation. The branch broke. I grasped at a protruding tree root and only succeeded in wrenching my arm. I gave up and put myself in the hands of the gods as I slid on my backside over the rough stony soil, bounced over rocks and tree roots and landed amidst a cascade of falling debris, almost on top of Pete.

For a long, breath-stopping second, his face registered only confused dismay, then it twisted in rage. He leapt up and shrieked. "Spy! A goddamn spy!"

In his haste to cross the circle to Eric, he strode over the medicine man's regalia, sending several objects flying, including the peace pipe, which sent the old man scrambling to retrieve them.

"Traitor!" he shouted at Eric. "You planted your fancy woman so she could report back to your white friends." He spat these lasts words out with a ferocity that made me fear for Eric. It was just as well that the man didn't have a gun in his hands.

As Eric stared at me in disbelief, I cringed with the enormity at what I'd done.

"You've got it wrong. Eric had nothing to do with this," I cried.

Pete pivoted around. "Shut up, you white bitch! You're nothing but trouble. Hold her, Bob."

A vise grip clamped onto my arm. I struggled to break free but froze when I suddenly noticed that a number of blockaders had surrounded us with pointed rifles.

Then I saw Jid. Although he was standing next to the female elder, his distress suggested he might run to me at any moment.

I frantically shook my head at him. The last thing I wanted was the boy to be caught up in this mess. The woman seemed to think likewise, for she brought him tightly to her side.

At this point, the police chief intervened. "Stay calm, everyone. A most unfortunate incident. I'm sure Ms Harris didn't mean any harm."

"No, I didn't," I interjected. "I was worried about Jid. I wanted to make sure he was okay."

"He's got nothing to do with you, white bitch," hissed Pete, a rifle now firmly gripped in his hand. "So keep the hell away from him."

My fear suddenly changed to outrage. "Don't you white bitch me. After his grandmother died, I was the only one prepared to look after the boy. None of your precious people offered. They were too concerned about saving their own skins from the ancestor's curse, as if such a thing exists."

But I knew as I said these last words that I'd gone too far. Grandfather Albert pushed himself up to his full gnarled height and said, "Woman, you not of our people. You not understand our ways. Go. And no come back." Using his ancient peace pipe, he pointed in the direction of my land.

I looked helplessly around at the unsmiling, unblinking faces; fury projecting from many, benign sympathy from others. He was right. I didn't belong here. I should forget about being friends with the Migiskan, forget about Eric.

I wrenched my arm free, cast a last look at Eric and turned to leave.

"No, she has every right to be here," he cried out. He strode across the circle to my side. "Do our teachings not tell us to respect the harmony of the circle of life, where all people are equal?"

"What right do you have to talk of our teachings?" Pete snarled. "You didn't learn from your grandfather's hearth. You didn't suffer through the bad times like the rest of us. You weren't even here. You have no right to bring up our teachings."

At that point, Jid broke free from the elder's clasp and ran to stand between Eric and me. He reached for both our hands.

Although Pete's hateful words must have rankled deep, Eric chose to ignore them. Instead he said, "What is happening here? You men talk of wanting to follow our people's ways, yet your words, your actions, say the opposite."

"No, listen to Pete, *nigwisis.*" Kohoko used the Algonquin word I knew meant "my son", an endearment often used for a younger man. "You are Anishinabeg. You are right to follow our ways. But listen. The balance is broken. This woman break it when she disturb the ancestors. Look at us. Our people get sick. Brother fight brother. They say my son kill a man. The Ancient One must go back to Mother Earth. Then will be okay. The spirits happy."

The top of a policeman's black cap suddenly appeared behind one of the blockaders. "Let me through. We got a bigger problem," Sergeant Whiteduck yelled. And the men opened a passage for him.

"Chief Decontie, we just gotta call from the Owl Lake Reserve. Fire's broken out close to their community. They need help."

The police chief wiped the sweat from his face. "Okay, guys, put down your guns. We've gotta help our people."

His words were greeted by suspicion. No one dropped their gun.

"Okay, this is what I'm gonna do. Sergeant Whiteduck is gonna return Robbie to the detachment, and I'm gonna promise we won't try to take him off the reserve while we're fighting this fire. In return, I want you to put down your guns and come help fight it."

"How do we know one of your lackeys won't try to sneak him outta here?" Pete shouted.

"You have my word as an Anishinabeg swearing on the grave of his ancestors."

Pete turned to the shaman as if asking for his opinion and received a silent nod from of the grey head. "Okay, but I want him placed in Grandfather Albert's care."

"You know I can't do that. But I can give Mishòmis free access to his son. That way he can see for himself that Robbie isn't going anywhere."

Another nod from the old man, and Pete agreed by lowering his gun. And the sense of pending doom vanished.

But my problems were far from over. As the men dispersed, I turned to Eric. "Please, I'm so sorry. I didn't mean for any of this to happen."

"Why couldn't you have just stayed put on the other side of the barricade?"

"I was too worried about Jid…and I was worried about you."

His stern expression didn't change. "You're lucky your cop friend didn't try to save you. That would've sent Pete ballistic and killed any hope of a resolution to this mess."

I scanned the slope above but failed to see any sign of the cop's presence. "I think he's gone."

"Good." Eric's unsmiling eyes continued to stare into mine.

I waited for him to say something. The silence grew like a gulf widening between us. I had to say something before it became unbridgeable.

"Eric, I'm sorry about last night. I didn't mean to react the way I did."

Other than a slight twitch in his left eye, his face remained impassive. "We'll talk when I get back from the fire." He turned, leaving me standing alone, agonizing over his ominous words. Suddenly I felt the comforting warmth of Jid's hand in my own.

"Come on, Auntie," he said, "let's go home."

THIRTY

More than fifty men, including Pete and his gang of militants, raced northward with Eric to try to prevent the forest fires from engulfing their Algonquin brethren at Owl Lake. The TV was reporting that while a couple of outlying homes had been destroyed, the fire was still more than three kilometres from the lakeside area, where the majority lived. As long as the winds remained light, the fire could be controlled. But should the wind increase, the chances of saving the community lessened considerably.

Video clips showed water bombers dumping their loads onto the burning trees, while the men on the ground chopped down trees to create a fire break around the village. I assumed that was where Eric was. At least, that was where I hoped he was, well beyond the danger of the inferno.

Although I'd half-hoped to hear some word from him, I hadn't really expected to. Chief Decontie, who'd remained behind, called to let me know that he was safe, as were the other men. The policeman, however, didn't know where Eric was in relation to the fire but assumed the inexperienced Migiskan would be best employed creating the firebreak. He went on to say that as a general rule, only men with actual experience or forest fire training were assigned to deal with the fire itself.

Still, I knew Eric. He liked to get into the thick of things. If they needed more manpower to help battle the fire directly, he'd be the first to put up his hand.

I gave Jid the important task of monitoring the status of the fire. Given the extreme dryness, there were many fires in the province, over ten thousand square kilometres worth. Several times a day, he would log on to a website that reported on the latest activity. Using pushpins, he would mark out the areas on a detailed map of Quebec that we'd hung on the timber wall in the den.

Most of the fires were more than six hundred kilometres to the north of us in the James Bay area. Their only effect on us was the smoke we'd been smelling on and off for the last week or so. But there were a handful much nearer, the closest being the Owl Lake fire about a hundred and sixty kilometres to the west.

While it seemed a safe enough distance, there was the possibility that a strong wind could scatter sparks eastward. Given the extreme dryness of the forest floor, it wouldn't take more than a spark to ignite a new fire, which in turn could send more sparks east until its fiery breath had leapfrogged to the trees staring across the lake at me. From there, it was just another spark hitchhiking on the wind.

I shuddered at the thought of my northern paradise turning to a charred ruin and prayed that the windless air of the heat wave would remain until the forest fires were out. Rain, of course, was the best solution, but according to the weather forecast, this was even less likely to happen.

As I stared at the map, I realized with dread that there was a familiar wilderness, which, if the Owl Lake fire were to spread, was in more immediate danger of being consumed by flames. Less than ten kilometres away lay the forested shores of the DeMontigny River, where a little more than a month ago, Eric and I had conquered the whitewater. Then my heart sank further. Even if the river were spared, I wasn't sure whether Eric and I would ever paddle down its fast-moving waters together again.

But he'd said we would talk after the fire, although I wasn't sure if I could tell him what I'd never wanted to reveal to anyone—except for that one time, when Gareth had asked me to marry him. And look what it had done to that marriage. But I knew I couldn't marry Eric without telling him. It was only right that he should know the kind of woman he would be marrying, but perhaps it wouldn't get that far. Perhaps I would be able to convince him that a relationship that had love as the only bond had more meaning than one bound by legalities.

Since the blockade, Jid and I had kept to ourselves. I'd made one quick foray to the General Store, but the cold hostility that had greeted me from people whom I considered friends had unnerved and pained me. I knew I'd been wrong to eavesdrop on the ceremony and told them so, but for the moment, no one was accepting my apology.

However, I did find it ironic that despite all the rhetoric about protecting Anishinabeg heritage, no one had lifted a finger to prevent one of their own from living with me. Nothing had changed. Their fear of the DeMontigny Lady's curse was greater than their sense of duty in taking care of a young orphaned boy, which was fine by me. I'd become very used to his happy, energetic presence and was growing to love him more each day. As for Jid, aside from his momentary rebellion at the blockade, he had expressed no desire to remain with his people.

For the past three days, I had tried to alleviate the anxious wait by frequent swims with Jid in the bathtub-warm water of Echo Lake and walks in the cooler evening air with the two buddies. This morning we were breaking our routine. We were going to catch ourselves a fish dinner. I would never be called an avid fisherman; in fact, I disliked the sport. I hated having to deal with wriggling live bait, and I found it boring, sitting motionless for hours in a boat waiting for some poor misguided fish to bite.

But the previous evening Jid had coerced me into going by promising that he would deal with the slimy worms and that he would keep me amused by telling jokes. Besides, this heat was creating still mornings as close to perfection as you can get on a lake.

This morning, however, there was a certain tension in the breathless air, a tension I couldn't quite identify, just something that made me feel uneasy. I'd even suggested to Jid that we wait till the next day, but he was adamant that this morning's calm was perfect for catching the big fish.

After loading my great-aunt's ancient cedar-strip canoe with the worms Jid had dug up from my garden and the fishing gear Eric kept at my place, we set out at sunrise. With me on the stern paddle and Jid in the bow, we slipped out of the shadow of the Three Deer Point cliff and onto the sunlit plane of flat water. So still was the water that every fleck of dust, every fly and moth that had landed overnight was still floating undisturbed on the water's surface tension. It seemed such a peaceful morning that I told myself I was silly to worry. Nothing was going to happen.

We headed towards the western end of the lake to the narrows behind Whispers Island, where Jid's uncle had told him the bass would be biting on mornings such as this. We were the only boat out on the lake, though as we paddled past the entrance to Forgotten Bay, I could see activity at the Camp docks down at the far end. With Pete and no doubt other guides gone to Owl Lake, I wondered how the Camp was managing.

The fish were biting as we slid into the shade behind the island. At least they were gobbling up the bugs floating on the water. When Jid whipped his fishing line into the water, they ignored it. I flung my line out too and let the canoe drift with the imperceptible current.

I jiggled my line in hopes of attracting a curious fish. Nothing. Not even a nudge. I reeled it in and flung it back out again. Nothing. But whenever the canoe floated over a patch of sun, I could see fish among the rocks below.

"Why aren't they biting?" My impatience was taking over.

"Shsh…sh." Jid gently pulled on his line, reeled it in, then expertly sent it flying back out over the water.

"We're not supposed to make any noise," he whispered. "Uncle says the fish gotta get used to us. Then they bite."

"But I thought you were going to tell me some jokes."

"Later. Now we gotta pretend we're a lily pad." His brown eyes twinkled as he laughed. "A very big lily pad. Uncle says fish like to hide under them."

I reluctantly reeled my line in again and tried to send it out as far as Jid's but only succeeded in snagging it on an overhanging branch. Not bothering to suppress his giggles, he cut the line, attached a new sinker and a hook with its requisite worm, and cast it for me with a "this is how it's done" glint in his eye. He then managed to pass the rod back to me without so much as a wobble of the canoe.

The canoe continued its aimless drift over the rocky depths. An occasional nudge from a paddle kept it in the waning shade of the island's high granite shore. I sensed a nibble or two, but when I pulled the line, I felt only the weightlessness of the worm. Jid, however, began to have some success. He reeled in a couple of bass, but declaring them too small, he threw them back in.

I tensed at the sound of an approaching motorboat bouncing off the far shore, then relaxed as it faded behind the island. I didn't want our solitude disturbed.

My rod suddenly bent with the weight of a real fish. I strained and groaned with the effort of reeling in the fighter, inch by inch. Given the battle he was waging, I figured it had to be some behemoth from the deep, weighing at least fifty pounds. Expecting something the size of a small shark, I was amazed to see how insignificant it appeared in the net Jid used to land it. But when he held up the flailing fish, it was a perfectly respectable bass. Even the boy agreed and slipped it into our catch bucket.

The struggle had pushed the canoe almost to the southern end of the island. Although the sun was now rising over its high cliffs, Jid thought we should stay close to the depths that plunged beneath their granite edge. According to his uncle, as the sun heats up the water, the bass go deeper, and he was right. Jid had no sooner sent his line catapulting into the water than his rod arced with the weight of a big one.

I tried to hold the canoe steady as he struggled to bring it in. If we'd been in a motorboat, I would've helped him. But in the canoe, I didn't dare move from my stern position, otherwise we'd both end up in the water with the fish. With his knees locked under the gunnels, his back and arms strained with the effort of reeling in the fighting fish.

At one point, my focus was momentarily distracted by the sound of a motorboat, but it was immediately taken up with trying to keep the canoe from tipping as the fish dipped and jived through the water. Jid was tiring fast. I inched myself carefully forward to try to take up some of the strain.

Suddenly the roar of an engine burst around the corner, and the next thing I knew, I was fighting my way to the surface of the lake.

THIRTY-ONE

When my head bobbed above the water, my eyes fell on the canoe floating hull side up, its side split by the impact. I searched frantically for Jid. Worried he was caught under the canoe, I dove and to my horror saw, wedged under the hull, first his orange lifejacket, then his lifeless limbs and finally his head, face down. I strained to lift the canoe off him and only succeeded in pushing myself further under the water.

I burst through the surface, yelling for help to whomever had rammed us. I gulped down another breath, dove back to the boy, grabbed his lifejacket and jerked him deeper into the water and out from under the canoe. I immediately turned his face to the air when we popped back up. Arms reached down and lifted him up. A near-invisible fishing line trailed after him.

"It's okay, lady, we got him," a male voice said.

"Is he alive?" I squeaked between gasps for air. Terrified of the answer, I grabbed onto the side of the boat and tried to raise myself up so I could see Jid.

"Better not do that, lady. You might tip us. Matt here's working on your boy."

Before I let go, I caught a glimpse of a bald head bending over Jid's head with chin upraised in the classic CPR mouth-to-mouth breathing stance.

I hoped he knew what he was doing. Although I hadn't used the lifesaving technique in over twenty years, I would never forget the time I'd saved an elderly woman from drowning while summer lifeguarding during my university days. I lifted myself partially over the boat's side. "Let me do it. I'm trained."

The boat rocked. Jid's lifeless head slipped off the man's lap, and he lost his rhythm. Shit. I slipped back into the water, but not before realizing I'd seen blood on the boy's face.

"Look lady, if you want your boy alive, just stay off the boat, okay?" snarled the other man, then in a more sympathetic tone said, "He's in good hands. Matt's a doctor. In fact, we both are."

"There's blood. How badly is he hurt?"

"Hard to tell. Won't know until Matt gets him breathing." From the stern the kindly, suntanned face of a man in his late fifties peered down at me. A worn Tilley hat bristling with fishing lures hid most of his grey hair. "Look, I'm awfully sorry about this. Never thought anyone else would be out on the lake this early."

"We'll talk about it later," I said, my anger for the moment suppressed by worry.

I listened to the deep intake of breath and the measured expirations of the bald man, and I tried to hear an answering breath from Jid. "Look, shouldn't we be taking him to the Fishing Camp, where we can call for an ambulance?"

Normally the fact that this area was too isolated for cell phone coverage didn't bother me. Today it did. It could save a life…

"Once we get him breathing," came the answer. "How about yourself? Are you okay? It looks as if you have a cut on your face."

As he said these last words, I felt for the first time the tingle of pain on my forehead. It hurt more when I touched it. Blood mingled with the water on my fingers. Despite the warmth of the sun, I could feel myself beginning to shake. "Yeah, I'm fine," I said. "Just get the boy breathing."

Matt's loud inhalations and exhalations continued.

"If he's getting tired, I can take over," I said.

"No need to worry about Matt. He's like the Energizer Bunny. He just keeps going and going."

Matt's deep breathing continued as my anxiety increased exponentially. I'd done it again. If Jid were to die…

I should've paid more attention. I should've been on the lookout for other boats. What was I going to tell Eric, his relatives, his people? Please, if there are any gods up there, please don't let Jid die, I prayed.

As if in answer to my silent entreaty, I heard a coughing sputter, followed by a short intake of breath.

Several interminable seconds later, the fishing hat doctor said, "Good, he's breathing on his own."

At last. And I said a silent prayer to Jid's Kije Manidu.

"I'll help you into the boat now, and we'll ramp up this fifteen horse and get us to the Camp."

For once, I wished Eric had put drug-runner sized engines on his boats and not the putt-putters he insisted were the only size needed for fishing.

When I clambered over the side, my euphoria was immediately dampened. "What's wrong with him? He's not moving."

I'd expected to be greeted by a weak but smiling Jid. Instead I saw his thin body lying stretched out on the boat's aluminum bottom with his head towards the bow and his legs tucked under the middle seat. The doctors had wrapped towels and clothing around him to keep him warm and to cushion him from the cold metal. Although I could see his chest rise and fall with his breath, there was no other movement. His eyes were closed. His forehead bulged with a bandage, no doubt from the medical bag by the bald doctor's feet.

"Looks like he has a concussion," said Matt, who I could now see was a compact, wiry man about the same age as the other doctor. His skin had the pinkish glow of too much sun. He sat in the bow with Jid's head stabilized between his feet. "He has significant swelling and a deep cut on his forehead, probably from hitting the side of the canoe. Once we get him onto land, I'll be able take a closer look at it."

"We can take him to the reserve's Health Centre. They should have everything you need."

Matt nodded. "You look like you could do with a check-up too. Here, take this."

He threw me another towel, which I wrapped about my trembling shoulders. I sat on the middle seat holding Jid's legs between mine to keep them from being disturbed by the boat's chugging through the water. I ignored the blood dripping from my forehead onto the white Fishing Camp towel covering his legs.

As we raced past the Three Deer Point cliffs, I glanced up at my cottage. If only I had heeded my premonition and not given in to his entreaties, we'd be safely up there in the screen porch with Sergei, enjoying our breakfast.

His face looked so drawn and still, his breathing so shallow.

When the bald doctor bent down to check Jid's pulse, I noticed for the first time the whiff of a very familiar smell. Alcohol! I scanned the boat for its source and found the top of a clear liquor bottle sticking out of the fishing gear wedged under the doctor's seat. These damn doctors had been drinking. At seven o'clock in the morning! No wonder they'd rammed us.

But I shoved my rising anger back down. First things first. These two were the closest doctors, the only ones in the thirty-five kilometre distance between here and Somerset. I had to make sure Jid was okay first. Then I'd blast them.

As we neared the Camp dock, I started shouting above the drone of the engine for someone to get a truck, to let the nurse at the Health Centre know that we'd be coming in with an injured boy.

A woman, braids flying, raced toward one of the pick-ups in the parking lot, while several other people ran toward us. The boat dribbled along the side of the dock as the fishing hat doctor killed the engine. Hands grabbed ropes and pulled us in. Other hands reached down to lift Jid from my arms. They settled him gently on the rough dock planking, where Matt examined him with a stethoscope. We waited in silence.

Finally Matt looked up. "Well, his pulse is normal, breathing normal. No sign of any internal bleeding. Just need to get him to that Health Centre of yours."

Someone placed the Camp's collapsible stretcher on the ground, and others lifted the still form onto it.

I felt a comforting arm around my shoulders. "Don't you worry none, child," Billie said. "He's gonna be fine, nice, healthy boy like that."

Clutching Jid's limp hand, I walked beside him to the black looming shape of a familiar SUV.

"We all thought this here truck'd be more comfortable for the boy," Ed said as they placed him on the plush carpeting lining the back of the Lincoln.

I wedged myself in beside him, but not before asking Ed to have someone call Decontie to make sure one of his men examined the doctors' boat before anything was removed from it.

I remember little of that short drive to the Health Centre other than the blur of trees as Ed drove the Lincoln as fast as he dared on the rutted gravel roads, and the limpness of Jid's body as it jostled with the bumps.

Judith, one of the Centre's two registered nurses, and Pauline, a nursing assistant, were waiting by the front door with a stretcher. Matt jumped out of the front seat of Ed's car and barked some orders. The still unconscious boy was carefully lifted onto the stretcher and wheeled through the Centre's open doors.

Before I had a chance to begin my anxious wait with Ed and Billie in the waiting room, the fishing hat doctor arrived and told me to remove my wet clothes, put on a gown and lie down on the table in an examining room. After the usual poking and prodding, blood pressure, temperature readings and three stitches to the cut on my forehead, he declared me fit.

"I can't say again how sorry I am that this happened," he said. "And of course I'll pay full restitution for your canoe and any gear you lost."

"Why don't we let the police decide where we go from here?"

"What do you mean? It was an accident, pure and simple."

"Maybe not if it involved alcohol." Even now I could still smell it on his breath, and I sure hoped it hadn't impaired his medical ability or his friend's.

His face turned a brilliant shade of red. "What? You think we were drinking at this hour of the morning?"

"I saw your bottle."

"Look it was just a little nip to get rid of the morning chill. But if it'll make you happy, I'll take a breathalizer test."

As if someone had been listening in, a knock sounded on the door and Pauline poked her head around to say Sergeant Whiteduck wanted to see the doctor.

Although my clothes were still damp, I didn't fancy sitting around in a hospital gown, so I put them back on. I resumed my seat in the waiting room on a hard plastic chair, between the Paynes.

"Any word yet on Jid?"

"Not yet, child," Billie answered, taking my hand in her frail one while Ed put his firm arm around my shoulders. Their comforting touch was almost too much as I tried to shove back the tears that were rising unbidden.

Across from us sat Jid's aunt, the one who'd refused to take him in out of fear of the DeMontigny Lady's curse, and his uncle, the fishing sage. I greeted both of them and told them how sorry I was about the accident.

Both responded with clenched lips and grim nods. Neither spoke nor gave any hint of the casual friendliness that had touched our previous conversations. I felt as if I'd returned to the icy barrier of wait-and-see distrust that had greeted me in my initial dealings with the Migiskan community not long after becoming their neighbour more than four years before.

"Ed and I've been talking," Billie continued. "We all think it might be opportune to bring in Grandfather Albert."

Annoyed with the way the old man had treated me, I replied without thinking, "What's he going to do for Jid other than mumble a bunch of hocus-pocus?"

I knew I'd gone too far the moment I finished. The outrage on the faces of Jid's aunt and uncle confirmed it.

Even Billie's face expressed shocked dismay. "Now, Meg, I know y'all didn't mean those hurting words. You're not yourself at the moment, what with your worry over Jid and all."

"You're right, I'm sorry. I didn't mean it."

But I could tell from the unyielding stance of Jid's relatives that they didn't believe me. Nor should they. They knew as well as I that words spoken in the heat of the moment were all to often the unfettered beliefs of the speaker. And in this case it was all too true. That was my real opinion of the old man. I couldn't pretend, so there was no point in apologizing any more.

"I can understand, child," Billie continued, "why y'all might not be wanting to believe in this fine man, you being so healthy 'n all. But Grandfather Albert has a real power within him for healing. I've felt its power myself."

It took me a moment to understand what she was referring to, then it hit me. She'd been seeking his healing powers to help her with her cancer.

The door to Jid's examination room suddenly sprang open, and Matt stepped out. Directing worried eyes towards me, he said. "Ma'am, could you step into the room, please. I'd like to talk to you about your son."

Jid's aunt suddenly stood up. "She ain't his mother. In fact, she ain't even kin. I am. Anything you got to say about Jid, you say to me."

Matt raised his eyebrows.

Numb with worry, I said, "She's right, but I've been looking after him. I have as much of a right to know how he's doing."

"He's still in a coma. X-rays reveal a skull fracture and some brain swelling that needs to be taken care of. We can't do it here, so we're going to send him to the hospital in Somerset. The ambulance should be here shortly."

"What do ya mean, take care of?" Jid's aunt asked. "Ya gonna open his skull?"

"That's for the doctors in Somerset to decide. Could be the swelling will go down on its own with the proper medication. And if not, they might need to do some surgery. But not to worry, he's young and healthy."

"How is he otherwise?" I asked.

"His breathing is good, and he appears to have no other ill effects from the near-drowning."

"May I see him?"

The doctor held the door open. But before I could step through, his aunt, followed closely by her husband, brushed passed me and they took up position on either side of his bed, leaving me the bottom from which to view his limp body. So small, so pale, so unbelievably still, the only sign of life the steady rise and fall of his chest and the slow regular drip of the intravenous.

I prayed that he would wake up and become once more the lively little boy I'd come to love as if he were my own. My prayers were cut short by the paramedics whisking their stretcher into the room. Within seconds, the boy had been tucked into the back of the ambulance and the doors closed. My final view of him was the paramedic bending over him to attach wires to a monitor while his aunt sat beside him holding his hand.

It was only as the ambulance was pulling away that I realized I hadn't said goodbye.

THIRTY-TWO

It was time to return her, and it looked as if I was the one who had to do it.

That was the conclusion I was reaching while I sat with the Paynes in the waiting room of the Somerset Hospital, anxiously awaiting word of Jid. After the ambulance had raced off with his aunt by his side, Ed had offered to take me to the hospital. I'd agreed, knowing I was in no condition to drive, but upon arrival, we were told only family could be with the boy, so we waited uneasy hours in the sterile waiting room. At one point his aunt and uncle came out to wait while the doctors operated on their nephew.

"It's all your fault," his aunt said angrily, taking a seat as far away as possible in the crowded room. "You should've left those bones in the ground."

I pretended her words didn't bother me, but they did. She was right. I was to blame. As always. I shouldn't have taken Jid fishing. And...I shouldn't have disturbed the Ancient One.

Against all rational thought, I was beginning to believe the irrational. I had caused the spirits' anger. They'd even tried to warn me of pending danger this morning, but I'd chosen to ignore them...as I'd been doing all along. Look at all the calamities that had occurred since I had found the bones.

First, Jid had come down with strep throat, then the disease had spread to other band members, ending with the tragic death of his grandmother. Then the Migiskan had started quarrelling with the authorities over rightful ownership of the remains, which had culminated in the theft of the bones themselves and the murder of the archeologist responsible for them.

A normally mild-mannered man stood accused of being both the killer and the thief, while his community was fighting bitterly amongst themselves over whether his crimes were in fact crimes.

Then there was the revelation of Teht'aa's drug problem and the return of Billie's cancer... and the rift between Eric and me.

After this morning's accident, which had struck like a bolt of lightning sent from the gods, I couldn't pretend any longer that this was all coincidence. Something else was going on, and maybe, just maybe, it was because the gods were angry. Grandfather Albert had threatened dire results if the Ancient One wasn't returned to Mother Earth. I was beginning to believe he was right and that Jid's fluke accident this morning meant that the remains were still unburied.

Because I was the one who had disturbed her, I felt I was the one who should return her to where she belonged. When I did, I hoped the spirits would be appeased, and Jid would survive the accident with nothing more than a sore head. I no longer cared about the bones' scientific value. Saving a child's life was more important.

Although Jid's operation had gone well, the doctors would continue to keep him in an induced coma until satisfied the swelling had gone down. This could take several days. Since only his aunt and uncle were allowed into his room, I decided my waiting time could be put to better use by trying to return the Ancient One to where she'd lain hidden for over eleven thousand years beside the DeMontigny River.

My first task was to locate the remains. Although I still found it difficult to believe that Robbie would steal them, let alone kill for them, I could only assume that the police had sufficient evidence to charge him. Therefore I would have to find out from him where they were hidden. Not an easy task with him sitting in jail and me not allowed near him. There was, however, one person who had ready access. His father, Grandfather Albert.

Although I did not like the idea of asking for help from this stubborn old man, who deemed me his enemy, I felt this was one instance in which he would help me.

I'd also have to do this without George finding out, for if he were to learn that I was destroying his chance of obtaining the Clovis Chair, he would do whatever he could to stop me. But maybe his harsh handling by Pete's men at the blockade had been enough to send him back to Ottawa and keep him there.

My hopes, however, were soon dashed, for as I passed the Migiskan General Store on the way to the old man's house, my eyes fell on the tall, limping man with his bright blond hair. I would just have to stay well out of his way and make sure Grandfather Albert didn't tell anyone other than his son.

Although George could be here with another artifact for the Paynes, I also thought his continued presence could just as likely be a sign that the Ancient One was indeed somewhere close at hand. Believing Robbie had stolen the bones, he would no doubt assume they were here on the reserve and was probably doing his best to try to find them before they were lost to him forever.

As I drove past Robbie's workshop, I glanced at the Paynes' almost-finished canoe, standing forlornly on its table perch, and wondered if it would ever get completed. Even though I'd visited his workshop on numerous occasions, I'd never been inside the simple log house he shared with his father. It was one of the few original buildings left on the reserve. Most of the haphazard and ruggedly-built cabins erected in the reserve's early years had been replaced by government issue; your classic boring, vinyl-clad bungalow that more properly belonged in a treeless suburb than amongst the birch and pine of the reserve.

Like most First Nations reserves in Canada, all land and buildings were communally owned. The concept of private property did not exist. This was in keeping not only with traditional native ways but also government policy. It was the responsibility of the Band Council to determine who lived where. Although Grandfather Albert, as the band's esteemed elder, had been offered his choice of any of the shiny new houses, he'd insisted on staying in the home his forefathers had built when the reserve had been established in the mid 1800s.

Ancient it indeed looked standing in a shaft of late afternoon sun a short distance from Robbie's work yard. Tiny, single-paned windows. A corrugated tin roof, probably put on when metal had replaced cedar shake. Its tarnished surface was splattered with tar and a few gleaming squares where repairs had been made. It was doubtful a coat of paint had ever graced any of the wooden surfaces of the overlapping lean-to additions, now blackened by weather and age, but the round cedar logs looked as sturdy as the day they had been stacked one on top of the other to form the outer walls.

Albert Kohoko, his hunched height barely reaching past the mid-point of the frame, was standing in the cabin's opened door when I stopped my truck.

Bracing myself for a venomous onslaught, I put on my friendliest smile and said, "Hello, Grandfather Albert."

True to form, he growled, "You! What you want?"

I took a deep breath and said, "I have a proposition for you."

He hunched his shoulders as if to say, "So?"

Although it was unlikely anyone was nearby, I nevertheless said, "Can I come inside? It's something I want to keep just between the two of us."

I could feel the power of his piercing black eyes as they tried to penetrate my thoughts. Then, almost as if he had read them, he abruptly turned in the doorway and headed into the half-light of his home.

It took a few seconds for my eyes to adjust to the darkness of the small room, lit only by the tree-shaded daylight filtering in through two narrow windows. Although I'd expected the air to be hot and muggy, I was pleasantly surprised by a moist coolness. Perhaps there was something to be said for small windows and thick logs. Then I noticed the thick block of ice sprinkled with sawdust standing in a large metal pan in the middle of the room. The original air conditioning.

I didn't need to ask where the ice had come from. I remembered from my early visits to Three Deer Point, when my great-aunt had been very much alive, the big blocks of lake ice that had been cut during the winter. Aunt Aggie had stored them under layers of insulating sawdust in her ice shed dug deep into the ground. She'd used them in her ancient icebox, despite having electricity since the mid 1960s, and she'd used them just as Grandfather was doing, for air conditioning.

"You return our ancestor's bones to Mother Earth," the old man said, without waiting for my proposition.

"I want you to help me."

He nodded as if it were a given. "Tell me how you do this?"

"I plan to rent a float plane and fly the bones into the lake where I found them. I would like you to come with me to give them a proper burial."

"Good. I come."

I'd noticed that at no time did he ask where I was supposed to be getting the bones. I took this to mean that he already knew their current hiding place.

"I'm doing this for Jid."

He nodded as if he already knew.

"We need to do this as soon as possible. I'm looking at tomorrow, if I can charter a plane that quickly." I was going to try Boreal Airways, the same airline company Eric had used to fly us in to the start of our fateful canoe trip.

"Good." His wispy grey hair drifted with another nod of his head.

"I am assuming you will bring the bones with you." I waited for his response.

"When you ready, I ready," he said, without directly admitting anything. Nonetheless, I felt his answer confirmed my suspicions that he either had the Ancient One or knew where she was located.

"You tell no one, eh?" he continued.

"I agree we should have absolute secrecy with this. We don't want anyone stopping us or returning to the site after we've buried her."

"Good." He started walking towards the door, signalling the end of our conversation.

Before I stepped outside, he placed his arthritic hand on my arm and smiled. "You do this, you good lady. Kije Manidu be happy."

I smiled back, feeling for the first time since my modern ways had collided with his ancient wisdom that we'd finally opened the door to establishing a truce.

THIRTY-THREE

Unfortunately, the earliest Boreal Airways could fly Grandfather Albert and me to the DeMontigny River was in two days. Although I hated to wait another day, I had no choice. The only other airline servicing the river was completely booked for the next week, and the only road access was via unmapped logging roads, which I didn't dare try in case I got lost.

I reluctantly agreed to be at the Boreal Airways dock on the Ottawa River a little before dawn on Tuesday. The pilot cautioned me that he only had enough time to drop us off, not enough to wait for us to finish our business.

I didn't view this as a problem. I figured if Robbie was a skilled canoeist, his father no doubt was. Besides, it was a relatively easy one-day paddle with only a couple of Class I rapids and some swifts before the river emptied into the Ottawa. We could paddle our way out.

It also solved a problem that had been facing me since coming up with this solution; how to keep the pilot from learning about the burial and its exact location. This way, should he eventually learn of our real intention, we could pretend the Ancient One was buried elsewhere.

"Just as well you're puttin' in at this section of the river," the man said, after processing my credit card deposit. "That fire 'round Owl Lake has spread. Gettin' pretty close to some of the upper stretches. Too bad. Such gorgeous country."

This meant Eric was still very much involved in fighting this fire, which could explain why he hadn't yet called me. At least, that's what I tried to tell myself. Unfortunately, it also meant he was still in danger.

I called Decontie, who could only tell me that at last report, all the Migiskan men, including Eric, were still out in the bush somewhere near Owl Lake. Since no one had called to say otherwise, he assumed everyone was safe.

"But," he went on to say, "I know they had to evacuate some of the Owl Lake men who'd become trapped when a section of the fire jumped and came up behind them. Fortunately, they were able to make their way out along a shallow river. But some of the men did get badly burned, and of course they're all suffering from smoke inhalation."

"I'm sorry you told me this. Now I really will worry."

"You shouldn't. As far as I know, our men are still making the fire breaks around the community."

"But I'd heard the fire has spread beyond Owl Lake, so maybe more men are now needed to fight it."

"Chances are if the fire isn't threatening any built-up areas, they'll let it burn, hoping it'll be stopped by rain or some large lake or river."

"I gather it's headed towards the DeMontigny River, so maybe they've stopped fighting it."

"I'll give Owl Lake a call tomorrow and get back to you if I hear anything more on Eric."

I hung up, feeling somewhat relieved, but with it came another fear. It meant Eric might soon be coming home. Then he'd want to talk, and I hadn't made up my mind what to do. Tell him my dirty little secret, one better kept buried, and watch the same haughty coldness wash over him as had washed over Gareth? Or not tell him and live with the fear that he would eventually find out. Because he would. My mother would feel duty bound to tell her daughter's new husband what his new wife had done.

If only I could persuade him to keep our relationship as it was: no commitments, no strings attached, no need to involve relatives.

As I agonized over my quandary, I could feel the old urge creep over me, the urge to drown myself in alcohol. I even went into the kitchen and retrieved a bottle three-quarters full of wine left over from a dinner with Eric a few weeks ago. But when I poured it into a glass and smelled the vinegarish fumes, I told myself things weren't that bad, not yet.

When I called the hospital, I learned that Jid had taken a turn for the worse. He'd run into some breathing problems and was now on a ventilator. There was no point in my going to the hospital. He'd been moved to intensive care, where access was restricted. For the moment he was resting easy, and they would call if there was a change.

I gulped down the glass of wine. I then took it and the bottle to the porch.

The chilling hoot of an owl woke me sometime during the night as I sat slumped in Aunt Aggie's rocker. I shook my befuddled head at the sight of the empty bottle lying on the floor beside a trickle of dried wine. In the old days, it would've taken a full bottle of vodka to get me this drunk.

I stumbled off to bed.

*   *   *

Next morning, the phone's shrill ringing thrust me back into consciousness. My head pounded, and my tongue felt like it were wrapped in fleece. It was a feat just to form the simple word, "Hello."

"Meg, honey, that you?"

It took a moment for me to clear my head enough to say, "Yeah, Billie, it's me. You okay? You don't sound too good."

"Something terrible's happened."

Now I was awake. "Oh, dear. It's the cancer, isn't it? Your test results have confirmed that it's come back."

"Not yet, honey. I'm still crossing my fingers. Supposed to find out tomorrow. Afraid this is something else. I'd just as soon not talk about it over the phone. I hate to intrude on your kindness, but do y'all think you can pay us a visit?"

My clock indicated it was ten past nine. I really had slept in. "I just need to get dressed, have some breakfast, then I'll boat over. Say in a half hour. Is that okay?"

"Ain't you a saint. Ed and I'll be waiting in our cabin."

It was more like an hour before my motorboat was nudging the Fishing Camp dock. It had taken me longer to get myself going. I'd tried several times to reach the nursing station at the hospital, only to get a busy signal. Thinking a little nip would help not only quell my worry over Jid, but also get me going, I'd wasted many minutes searching for another bottle of forgotten wine, but I'd stopped when the memories flooded in, memories of sitting slumped at the breakfast table beside a partially empty vodka bottle with my mind more befuddled than when I'd wakened. I knew that no matter how bad things were, I didn't want to return to those days.

However, Billie must have detected the stale smell of last night's binge on my breath. As she hugged me in greeting, she said, "Bit early for that, ain't it, child?"

Embarrassed by her question, I said instead, "So what's the problem?"

I must've spoken a little too abruptly, for she replied, "Now child, y'all got too much on your mind. Best we don't bother you none with our troubles."

"Look, I'm sorry. I didn't mean to sound rude. Please, I want to help if I can."

"I know y'all worried about that poor boy. But he's gonna be fine. Nurse this morning said he had a good night."

"Good, you got through. Did she say whether he was still on the ventilator?"

"Landsakes, she made no mention of that. Just said he was resting easy."

"Well, at least he's no worse."

I sat in the armchair across from where she and Ed sat on the sofa. All the windows of the small sitting room were wide open to let what remained of the night's coolness drift in. Neither of them seemed their usual relaxed Texan selves. Maybe, despite what Billie had said, they had been given the test results and didn't want to share their bad news.

"You both look worried. Please, tell me what's bothering you."

The small woman gripped her husband's hand. The circles under her eyes seemed darker. "Now child, I know y'all gonna think badly on us. I know Ed and me did wrong. But we want to make it right."

These words left me confused.

"We took the Ancient One."

The shock of these words had me drawing only one conclusion. Its horror must've reflected on my face for she said, "Please, child, you must believe us. We had nothing to do with that poor man's death."

"But if you stole the remains, then you must've had something to do with it."

"We didn't steal them. Someone did it for us."

"Surely not Robbie?" I thought of George's allegation, which in this instance didn't make sense. Robbie would've stolen the bones for only one purpose, re-burial, and I doubted the Paynes would pay good money to see them disappear into the ground.

"No, Dr. Schmidt," Billie replied.

The bastard, I thought. Accusing Robbie of stealing them in order to point the finger away from himself. "Then he must've killed Claude."

"But he said he didn't do it."

"And you believed him?"

Ed squeezed his wife's hand, then turned towards me. "I know you must be thinking we're some kind of terrible people about now. But we want you to believe that if we'd known it would lead to a man dying, we never would've agreed to George's request."

Ed breathed in deeply, then continued. "He called us the day before the ceremony. George was worried the Indians were gonna win."

I'm afraid at this point my anger took over. "So you went to Montreal, sat in the ceremonial circle amongst your friends and pretended to support their cause, when in reality you knew that their heritage would soon become your own personal property. How could you?"

Billie cringed and turned away, but Ed replied in a low voice, "I know we did wrong, that's why we've come to you. Please hear us out."

"I thought you didn't know Dr. Schmidt before Teht'aa introduced you at the café. At least that's what she said. Or is this another one of your deceptions?"

Ed winced. "For some years now, we've been dealing with Dr. Schmidt's company, Fossil Finds, one of the best in the business at locating museum quality artifacts. But we all thought it best to pretend we were strangers. Didn't want people linking us to each other."

"So what exactly was the plan? George steals the remains for your collection, with the proviso that he has ready access to them?"

"Yeah, that's pretty much it in a nutshell. He also thought it'd be harder for the authorities to get them back if they were out of the country."

I could only shake my head at such boldness. While as recently as a day or so ago, I might've applauded this attempt to keep the ancient remains within the hands of the archeologists, I didn't any more.

Ed continued, "That there Mohawk friend of Teht'aa's was gonna take them across the border for us."

"You mean Larry?"

"Yeah, him. Hate to say it, Meg, but it was you that gave us the idea, when you talked about the Mohawk tribe that uses their reservation to smuggle goods across the border."

"Given his militant views, I'm surprised he agreed to it."

"It was the dollars talking, child," Billie answered apologetically. "We were gonna pay him a packet."

The Sonhatsi Grand Chief was just as militant about the rights of the First Nations people. I doubted he would let Larry take the remains through his reserve only to have them disappear into the hands of white men, unless... "I suppose you bought off the Grand Chief too."

Ed smiled sheepishly. "Larry said we had to grease the wheel. Said it would go towards providing new sports equipment for their school."

So much for protecting one's heritage when the almighty dollar beckons. Look at Teht'aa.

The three of us sat in uneasy silence, each locked in our own thoughts. I still couldn't believe how two such seemingly nice people could get involved in such a criminal scheme. But obviously they thought owning the ancient remains was more important than their friends or upholding any laws.

Billie suddenly spoke up. "George couldn't have killed that

Frenchman." Her voice carried a ring of relief. Clearly she'd been worrying about it. "Ed, honey, remember when we were at that café, George told us he already had the bones, said he'd left them in a secure place."

"That's right," Ed replied.

"But we know from the news the Frenchman was still alive at that time. In fact, if I recollect rightly, he was the man who came into the café just as we were leaving?"

"Yeah, but I remember that the little guy looked madder than a bronco with a hornet under its tail."

"What time did this happen?" I asked.

"I'd say shortly after three o'clock. The little guy was sure mad at George. Kept shouting some French words at him. Only one I remember sounded like 'vauler' or something like that."

"Could be *voleur*. It means thief. I'd say Claude had just discovered the bones were gone. Did you see what happened after that?"

"Afraid not. We all left to go to our hotel."

"Well, I'm prepared to wager that Claude threatened to go to the police. The only way George could stop him was to kill him. Unfortunately, there is a very big 'but'. He has an alibi. It's also doubtful he would have the kind of knife used to kill Claude. It was a crooked knife like the one Robbie used on your canoe."

Billie glanced quickly at Ed, then back to me. "But he might've. We were real fascinated by that there knife, so we asked George to get us an old one." Her face suddenly took on a stark paleness. "I'll never forgive myself if we were the cause of that poor man's death."

"I think you'd better tell the police everything you've just told me. They might want to dig a little deeper into whether he really was giving the lecture at the time he said he was."

Ed leaned forward. "We intend to, but not yet."

"I'm sorry, but if you won't, I will." I stood up to leave.

Ed held up his hand. "Miz Harris, I know it's a lot to ask of you, but please hear us out before you make up your mind."

How did I know this wasn't just a stall tactic? And how did I know they themselves hadn't had a hand in the murder? After all, having this extremely rare and valuable artifact in a collection would increase not only the collection's value exponentially, but also the prestige of the owners.

Still, for some reason, they'd called me in and volunteered the information. I hadn't sought it. Besides, the elderly couple slumped on the sofa before me showed all the signs of two people who were deeply regretting the killing they might've caused and none of the nervous bravado one would expect from a couple of determined collectors who would do anything to get what they sought.

"Okay, I'll listen, but be forewarned that I believe the only course of action is to inform the police." I resumed my seat.

Ed continued, "Like we been telling you, we wanted this here artifact for our collection, but after feeling it, looking at it, we changed our minds. That's right, eh, honey?"

"The skull has a power. I could feel it tingling in my hands." Billie cupped her frail, veined hands as if she were still holding it. Her face shone. "And it must've called Grandfather Albert, for he turned up on our doorstep yesterday. He said the Ancient One would help me."

So Kohoko knew the Paynes had the remains. Then why hadn't he used this information to free his son from police custody?

I'd no sooner asked myself the question than I knew the answer. The bones would be returned to the Quebec authorities without any assurance that they would be given to the Algonquin. Returning the remains to Mother Earth was more important than saving his son.

"Did he say how the bones could help you?"

"A wonderful man. Truly spiritual. He could feel the pain, the cancer in my poor body. Said these here bones, being so old and all, had special healing powers that only he knew how to release. Said his granddaddy had passed on the secret healing ceremony of ancient bones when he was a boy."

While I truly doubted a disease as life threatening as cancer could be cured by a ritual involving old bones, I couldn't help but feel the power of hope emanating from Billie. Perhaps that was more important. When hope collapsed, often the will to live did too.

"Did you agree?"

Billie nodded. "He was going to perform it this afternoon."

The timing fitted nicely. I'd begun to worry that I would have to move my plans to re-bury the Ancient One back a day or two to accommodate Billie.

Then I realized something. "Wait a minute, you said 'was'. Isn't he going to do it?"

"Can't. The Ancient One is gone."

THIRTY-FOUR

The remains have been stolen? Again?" I gasped, not certain I'd heard correctly.

Ed leaned back into the sofa. "We all figure it must've been while we were at dinner last night or breakfast this morning. Only time we were away from our cabin. Billie remembers seeing the Neiman Marcus bag they were in yesterday afternoon. When she checked this morning, after breakfast, the bag was gone."

"I don't suppose you've called the police?"

"We called you."

"Why me? The police are much better equipped to find the thief."

"We want you talk to the perpetrator. We think y'all might be able to convinced 'em to return the Ancient One so Grandfather Albert can perform the healing ceremony."

"You know who stole them," I said, more as a statement than a question.

"Your boyfriend's daughter, Teht'aa."

More shocking news. Was there going to be an end to it? "How do you know she's the thief?"

Billie answered, "Such a sweet girl. She'd taken to paying me visits these past days to see how I was faring. She knew about the medical tests."

"But that doesn't mean she stole the bones."

"When she visited yesterday afternoon, she accidentally dropped her glass of ice tea. It splashed onto the floor right near where the Neiman Marcus bag was hiding under this here sofa. She would've seen it when she cleaned up the mess."

"It still doesn't mean she stole the bag."

"This morning, after I discovered it was gone, I remembered seeing her through the window last night, while we all were having our dinner in the dining room. She was carrying a mighty big plastic bag, like one of them orange garbage bags, big enough to hide my Neiman Marcus bag."

"Okay, say she did take it. How would she know what was inside?"

"George could've told her. They used to be good friends. He saw me put the bones' special container into the bag when he delivered them to us the other day. In fact, he almost admitted he had when we told him about the theft."

"But why would she take them?"

"That had us stumped for a while," interjected Ed. "But we think her new boyfriend Robbie asked her to do it, so he could rebury them."

"Which his father also wanted to do," I countered. "Weren't you worried that Grandfather Albert would keep them after the ceremony?"

"That was our agreement," Ed replied. "We'd pretty much decided that some things are more important than science and having the best Native American collection in America. The medicine man was going to rebury them after our ceremony. In fact, he'd told us he'd already made arrangements."

Now it was my turn to reveal my role in their reburial. As I told her about my arrangement with Grandfather Albert and the charter flight scheduled for tomorrow morning, Billie kept smiling. At the end, she said, "See child, I knew there was good in you."

"If Teht'aa does have the bones, wouldn't she give them to Robbie's father so he could perform the healing ceremony?"

"We don't know. Could be she doesn't know about it. That's why we all want you to talk to her. Convince her to let us have them for this afternoon. Then she can have them back."

"But she'll never listen to me."

"We think she will, particularly if y'all tell her you've made plans to have the Ancient One reburied. Besides, we don't have anyone else to do it."

I agreed to talk to her, although without much hope of success. Still, I left the two of them looking a little brighter as I walked out of their cabin.

But I didn't need to go looking for Teht'aa. She was climbing into Eric's SUV as I reached the top of the stairs from my dock. Her father's red canoe was strapped on the top of the Jeep.

"Wait," I hollered, running towards the vehicle as it started down my drive.

The brake lights went on, and she jumped out. She wore the same body-hugging clothes she'd worn on our canoe trip. "You have to help me," she called out.

I stopped dead, while from inside the house Sergei barked. "You need my help? Why?"

"Larry's going to kill Robbie," she yelled back.

"Hey, wait a minute, slow down. How can Larry kill Robbie if he's in jail?"

"He's not," she said coming up to me. "I helped Robbie to escape last night."

Shit. How much more tangled could this mess get? "Let's go inside so I can let the dog out. Then I want you to tell me what's going on, starting with the theft of the bones from the Paynes."

This time hers was the face that expressed shock.

A few minutes later, with Sergei relieving himself outside, she confirmed what the Paynes and I had suspected. She'd stolen the Ancient One for Robbie after learning of its location from

George. Apparently the one-time boyfriend, still intent on recapturing her love, had bragged about his role in the theft, not realizing that rather than building himself up in her eyes, it only served to confirm her view of him as a spirit thief. Anyone with half a brain would've known what her reaction would be. George may have had a wall full of university credentials, but clearly common sense wasn't one of them.

Teht'aa confirmed that her motive for the theft was reburial.

"Is that why you helped Robbie escape? So he could return them to the DeMontigny River?"

"Yes. At first we thought his father was up to doing it, but Robbie was worried about his health. I guess Grandfather's not very strong, so Robbie insisted I get him out of jail."

"How did you do it?"

"Piece of cake." Her chuckle reminded me so much of her father that I felt a momentary twinge of anguish. "I've been taking meals to Robbie these past few days, and I've been in the habit of making enough for Sam Whiteduck, who's usually on guard in the evenings. He never suspected that I'd dumped some sleeping pills into last night's bear stew. All I had to do was wait a couple of hours later, go back and when Sam was out cold, steal his keys and let Robbie out."

I guessed she'd watched her share of "B" movies. "Weren't you worried about someone finding Sergeant Whiteduck before you returned?"

"So what if they did? Sam'd have a lot of explaining to do as to why he'd slept on the job, and I'd just try it again another night."

"So where is Robbie, or more importantly, the bones at this moment?"

"On their way to the DeMontigny River."

"But his father was supposed to perform a special healing ceremony for Billie this afternoon."

"I know. I feel bad about it, but when we learned that George found out about the theft, we decided we couldn't wait until tomorrow. We were worried he'd bring in the police and tell them that we'd stolen them from the lab. So Robbie and his dad took off early this morning."

"I thought you said Robbie didn't want his dad going."

"The old man insisted. Said the Ancient One needed a special burying ceremony to remove the spirits' anger."

"So why does Larry want to kill Robbie?"

"When he found out from George that the bones were gone, he got real mad. He's already bought himself a new truck with the money the Paynes were going to give him for taking them across the border. So he stole one of the Fishing Camp's canoes and took off after Robbie. George went with him."

I didn't bother to tell her that with the Paynes' latest change in plans, Larry wouldn't have seen his money anyway. "But they need planes to get there. And charters are booked."

"Robbie knows a logging trail near the start of the river. He was going to take it. Larry knows it too."

I reached for my phone.

"What are you doing?" cried out Teht'aa.

"Calling Decontie."

"No, don't. He'll stop Robbie and his father from burying the Ancient One."

"He's Anishinabeg too. I would think he'd want her returned to Mother Earth as much as you do."

"Hasn't acted that way so far."

"You mean with respect to Robbie. He's just doing his job."

"Yeah, and he'd be doing his job by returning the bones to that stuck-up lab director." She stood up to leave. "Look, I was hoping you'd come with me. But I can see you won't, so I'm going."

I placed the phone down. "Come with you where?"

"I've got to go after Robbie and his pa to warn them about Larry. Larry's got his rifle with him. He killed a man once in a drug fight. No reason why he wouldn't do it again."

I hesitated a moment, for I really didn't have any proof, just conjecture, but I finally said, "I think George is a murderer too. I think he killed that Quebec archeologist."

"No way!" Her face reflected her astonishment. "Impossible. He doesn't have the guts."

"Maybe he does." I told her about the meeting with Claude at the café and the crooked knife.

"But he was teaching a class when the guy got killed."

"Alibis can always be broken. Maybe the police didn't check his out thoroughly."

She nodded. "Yeah, I know he used to sometimes have grad students teach part of his class."

"So there, a possibility. Besides, wouldn't you rather it were George who'd killed the man than Robbie?"

"Yeah, maybe it was George, because I know Robbie couldn't have."

"All the more reason to call in the police. They'll be able to fly in and to stop Larry and George before anything happens."

"I knew I couldn't trust you," she said, heading for the front door. "You pretend you're sympathetic to our ways, but you're no different from all the other whites. You just want to make us like you."

THIRTY-FIVE

After she'd thrown down that gauntlet, I had no choice but to pick it up. I soon found myself bouncing through dense bush along a twisting, rutted gravel road in Eric's Grand Cherokee with Teht'aa at the wheel and my hastily packed dry bag in the back beside Eric's gear. Fortunately, I'd managed to get the Paynes to stay at Three Deer Point to look after Sergei. While Eric's daughter was out of the room, I'd called them back to tell them to bring in the police. Teht'aa might think she could handle a gun-wielding Larry or George, or worse, both. I knew we couldn't.

Although neither Teht'aa nor I were familiar with the road access to the DeMontigny River, she'd brought along the topographical map Eric had used on our canoe trip, which I realized with shock had been only a month and a half ago. Given all that had happened since, it felt like a lifetime ago.

I could see the red line of a logging road, the one Teht'aa said Robbie had taken. It was the only road, besides the one accessing the ZEC much further downstream, that came within striking distance of the river.

"What time did Robbie and his dad leave?" I asked.

"Around five this morning. Hang on." Teht'aa suddenly swerved around a back-end gobbling pot-hole, but she failed to avoid the next one. We bounced through it with a teeth-jarring crunch. "Guess my dad's fancy truck can take this stuff."

I held onto the dashboard as we bumped through another.

"We sure don't have to worry about our tax dollars being wasted on this road, do we?"

Teht'aa smiled, the first I'd seen since we'd left Three Deer Point a little over two hours ago. It was just after one thirty. I figured we were about a half hour drive from where this logging road intersected the river. But if the road conditions got any worse, it could take us longer.

"It probably took the Kohokos the same amount of time to get to the river, so that means they've been on it for about six hours. Do you know when Larry and George left?"

"One of waitresses saw them leaving the Fishing Camp just after breakfast, around nine o'clock."

"That puts them about four hours behind Robbie. And given Larry's lack of canoeing smarts, they'll probably fall further behind."

"That's what I'm counting on." Teht'aa chuckled. "What a creep. Talks the big talk about being a back-to-the-land Indian and can't even paddle like one."

"But Larry and George are still at least two hours ahead of us. I don't see how you expect us to reach Robbie first to warn him."

Teht'aa stared pointedly at me.

I felt an icy pit growing at the base of my stomach. "Surely you're not expecting my canoeing expertise to help get us past them?"

"Sure, why not? You did pretty good with Dad."

"But that means running many of the rapids I'd rather portage around."

"I grew up on the great rivers feeding into the MacKenzie River. I can do class IV rapids with my eyes closed. All you have to do is paddle when I tell you."

I glanced at her perfect profile. For once, the challenging jut of her jaw had disappeared. "If you can do this on your own, why do you need me?

"It's faster with two people, particularly with the portages around the worst of the rapids and the falls. You've been on the river. You know it. And…" her voice lost its biting edge, "Robbie told me about your wanting to help Grandfather return our ancestor to Mother Earth. I want to give you the chance to be there."

Well, wonders never ceased. Perhaps this was the beginning of the thaw. "Thanks. I appreciate it, and I'll try not to hold you back." Wouldn't this be the crowning touch? Eric's daughter and I finally become friends, just as he and I go our separate ways. But no, I wouldn't let that happen.

Teht'aa careened to a sudden stop in front of a fallen fir tree. We both jumped out and were immediately assaulted by the stench of burning wood.

"Shit," I said. "I forgot about the forest fires. Decontie said the Owl Lake fire was headed towards the river. We could find ourselves in the middle of it." Specks of grey dust floated in the air. Ashes! "Are you sure you want to go on?" I asked.

"We'll be okay. The river will protect us. Besides, this doesn't mean the fire's nearby. The wind can carry ash and smoke for many miles."

The brown dust covering Eric's Jeep was taking on a greyish tinge, as was the fallen, lichen-covered tree. Although the dead balsam spanned the entire road, we could see where other vehicles had crunched over and flattened its narrow topknot.

"Let's not hang around," I said, climbing back into the Jeep. "We're not only racing to catch up to Robbie, but we're also racing against this fire."

As the Jeep lurched up and over rocks, swerved around hairpin turns and bottomed sudden dips, I tried to read the topographical map. "You know, on our last trip it took us four days to get from the lake where the plane brought us in to the shore where I found the DeMontigny Lady. This road intersects about twenty kilometres upstream. Easily another full day of travel. So it could take us five days."

"We were lily-dipping. I figure we can do at least 40, 50K a day. Get us there in a couple of days."

I gulped. She really was intent on running most of those damn rapids.

"Besides," she continued, "I don't think Robbie is going that far. His dad mentioned something about not wanting to return her to where you found her. Since the spirit thieves know that spot, he's worried they'd come back to dig her up."

"Good point. Do you know where?"

She shook her head.

We swerved around another fallen tree lying partially on the road.

"Meg," Teht'aa said. "I've been thinking about what you said about George being the one who killed the Frenchman. You know, he's not the only one who had reason to kill the man."

"You mean other than Robbie?"

"Yeah. Larry."

"I've already thought of him, but he says he has an alibi for the time of the killing. Besides, with the bones gone, he no longer had a motive."

"It's got nothing to do with the Ancient One. Has to do with Oka."

At that point, the massive cab of a logging truck loomed around a curve. It occupied most of the road. Teht'aa jerked the steering wheel to the right and slammed on the brakes. The Jeep twisted and turned and slid over the loose gravel until it came to rest nose down in the ditch. A second later, the truck knocked the back end into the ditch.

We both scrambled out as I hollered, "What in the hell do you think you're doing?"

The driver likewise jumped down from the logging truck's cab and started gesticulating and yelling in an almost incomprehensible *joual*, the twangy vernacular of rural Quebec. I could just make out the words *"chemin privé"* meaning private road, which I supposed was true, but at this point, who cared?

Eric's SUV was firmly wedged into the deep ditch; its left back fender was smashed. The canoe balanced precariously over the windshield, where it had slid to a stop after the back strap had sprung loose. Fortunately, the belly strap had prevented it from completely toppling over, but the strap had loosened and was in danger of breaking. Teht'aa and I, with some grudging assistance from the trucker, removed the canoe. But what were we going to do now?

In exasperation, Teht'aa kicked the front tire. "We're done for. No cell phone coverage. And even if we could call, the nearest tow truck's probably a good couple hours away."

Without another word, the driver climbed back into the cab and began to ease his storey-and-a half load of logs past us.

"Hey!" I shouted running after him. "You can't leave us. We need help." Then realizing I'd spoken English, yelled the same message in French.

But he kept on going. I ran after him, waving my arms, shouting. The truck rounded a bend and disappeared behind a thick wall of trees.

Despondent, I turned back, but I'd no sooner reached Teht'aa, sitting likewise dejected at the side of the road, when the rumble of a truck's engine roared into life behind us. The driver had returned, minus his load.

Springing out of his cab, he managed to make us understand that he'd driven down to a wider part of the road, where he could park his load and turn around. He then unwound a long steel cable that was wrapped around the front bumper.

"Not the first time it happen, eh?" He laughed, revealing a mouth with more gaps than yellow teeth. His creased face looked as if it hadn't seen a razor in several days. He jammed his hand-rolled cigarette back into his mouth.

Within minutes, he had one end of the cable attached to the undercarriage of the Jeep and the other secured to a hook on the back end of the cab. He then climbed back into his truck. With as little effort as it had taken to get Eric's vehicle into the ditch, he dragged it out. Once all four wheels were firmly planted on the road, Teht'aa and I checked for damage. Apart from the fender bender, there was nothing more to raise Eric's blood pressure. More importantly, it was drivable.

While the driver helped us to secure the canoe back on the roof, I asked him if he'd seen any other trucks. But he shook his head, which meant that Larry and George had long since reached the river, and even now were riding its fast current towards Robbie and his father.

I then had a thought. "Is there another road that will get us to the river further downstream?"

He nodded his head vigorously and, gesturing up the road towards the left, said there was a road that would take us to where logs were stacked after cutting. I hastily retrieved the map, and he pointed out a spot about ten kilometers or so further downstream from where the road intersected the river.

"It don't go straight to the river," he said, "but there's a track, maybe a couple of hundred meters."

"Super. How far are we from it?"

"Maybe ten, maybe twenty minutes. Depend how fast you drive, eh?" Once more, his few remaining teeth were revealed in all their yellow glory.

Then he grew serious. "But, madame, I must tell you. Downriver is not safe. The fire comes. I think you better go back and make your canoe trip another day."

But Teht'aa's only response was to say, "Meg, if you don't want to come, go back with this guy."

After thanking the driver for his help—I didn't bother to remind him he'd been the cause in the first place—I climbed in beside her.

As we resumed our race to the river, I took up our conversation from where it had been so abruptly stopped by the accident. "Teht'aa, you said Larry had a motive for killing Claude. What was it?"

"Larry keeps talking about some spirit thief who got involved in the Oka crisis. Says the guy tried to act as a go-between for the police, because he understood our ways." She let out a coarse laugh. "Yeah, sure, just like George."

"Please, Teht'aa, some of us do genuinely want to be friends with no strings attached."

She gave me a long sideways glance, then shrugged. "Yeah, I suppose you're right. But this guy wasn't one of them. Seems he got to know the Warriors spearheading the blockade pretty well, but when it was all over, he fingered the guys to the cops. A couple of them got sent to jail."

"Yes, but wasn't that for killing a cop?"

"Yeah, I guess." Which I took to be a real concession on her part.

"But I don't see what this has to do with Claude or Larry."

"The spirit thief was supposed to be some really small guy, just like that Dr. Meilleur."

I supposed there couldn't be too many archeologists with Claude's small stature. "And Larry?"

"One of the guys jailed was Larry's cousin. He got killed inside."

It could explain the argument I saw between the two men. "Still doesn't mean Larry killed him."

"Larry told me if he ever came across the guy, he'd kill him."

THIRTY-SIX

Teht'aa and I stood on a granite ridge. Below us, a river of flying white stretched up to and beyond the next bend. I wasn't surprised. The many sets of paired lines on the map, marked with "RII" and "RIII" had warned me.

"I'm not sure which has me more scared," I said, "battling this stuff or meeting up with Larry and George, one of whom is likely Claude's killer."

"You're not going to freak out on me, are you?" Her eyes took on a steely coldness.

My spine stiffened as I rose to her challenge. "Nope. Of course not. Do you think Larry and George have already gone past?"

"Doubt it. Probably still upstream trying to rescue their canoe." Her smile brought the warmth back into her eyes.

"I'll look for the portage trail," I said. "Got to be one to get around this mess."

"No, we put in here." Teht'aa dropped her dry pack onto the ground. "Besides, the portage is probably on the other side of the river, where it's not as rocky."

I looked down at the froth several metres below my feet. "And where are we going to put in? The canoe will tip before we even get into it."

She pointed further upstream to the flat green of an eddy created by a jog in the river. The shoreline next to it was considerably less precipitous than where we were standing.

"Take my pack while I go back for the canoe," she said.

Before I had a chance to protest, she had already disappeared back into the foliage. I hoisted my pack onto my back and slung hers over my shoulder.

I hoped the remaining gear I'd seen in the back of the Jeep contained the items I'd forgotten in my haste, essentials like food, a tent and an axe. Maybe even a rifle, for if we did find ourselves face to face with Larry and George, it could prove very tricky indeed. A rifle would help to even the odds.

I crashed through the underbrush until I found an animal track heading in the right direction. It brought me to a low, damp dip in the land, where the calm water of the eddy stretched toward the racing white beyond. It looked even narrower at this angle. But I felt it was at least large enough for us to get enough way on before we crossed the eddy line into the rapids. Since it was unlikely Teht'aa could carry anything other than the canoe, I dropped the two packs on the ground and returned to the Jeep to get the rest of the gear.

Thirty minutes later, Teht'aa was seeking the Creator's blessing with a sprinkling of tobacco over the rushing river. Then I was pushing the bow of our loaded canoe into the eddy. Inside were crammed not only our packs but also Eric's tent and a small food barrel with an axe strapped onto the side. We'd secured all of it to the canoe, since as Teht'aa had said, if we did dump, we didn't have time to go after free-floating gear.

But there was no rifle. In her haste to pack, Teht'aa had completely overlooked the possibility of having to defend herself.

"Besides," she said, "they were both once in love with me. Probably still are. They wouldn't dare shoot us."

"I wouldn't be so cocky. What if Claude's killer realizes we suspect him?" Despite Larry's plausible motive, I still thought of George as the killer and hoped he was. If it were Larry, I knew he wouldn't hesitate to shoot us, but I thought George would. He didn't project the same instinct for raw violence.

But Teht'aa had brushed the threat off with a laugh. "We'll just have to stay well in front of him and get to Robbie first."

I leaned out over the canoe the way Eric had taught me and jabbed my paddle straight down into the boiling water as we crossed the eddy line. The canoe immediately veered downstream, and we were off. The river in front was a jumble of spitting white and upraised humps that barely masked the dark outline of the underlying rocks.

I saw no safe route of green through the turbulence, but Teht'aa must have seen a way. When she yelled out "Left!", I thrust my paddle into the water and pulled hard towards me. When she shouted "Right!", I reached across the bow, dug the paddle in and pulled. Miraculously, we wended our way through the roaring water without getting so much as a drop inside. I began to paddle with more confidence. I even managed to prevent a collision with a rock Teht'aa had not seen.

A few more brisk pulls and a sudden cross-bow pull, and we were plunging through the standing waves into the flat water below the rapids. I sighed with relief and made the "V" sign.

But when I turned back to the front, I gasped in horror. Black clouds filled the sky before us. Large flecks of ash, black and grey, fell around us, some containing the dying brightness of cinders. The fire! My worry over the rapids had completely erased it from my mind, and the spray had disguised its smoke, now seeping into my lungs. I coughed.

"Wet your bandana," Teht'aa shouted. "Tie it around your nose and mouth."

I also soaked my Tilley hat before placing it securely back on my head, threw water on my clothes, draped my shoulders and back with a wet towel, and covered the heavy vinyl of my dry pack with another one. Teht'aa did likewise. We were ready.

The rapids had taken us into a broader part of the river. Although the distant downstream shore was still crisply green, black clouds billowed from a height of land behind it. I could even make out intermittent flames amongst the swirls of spiralling smoke. Through my binoculars, the fire seemed to hover above the water, but I thought it was probably much further inland, a good kilometre or so. At least, I hoped it was.

Although I didn't expect to see Robbie and his father, I nonetheless scanned the water in front of us. Surprisingly, I did see movement, but when I focussed the lens, I saw the heads of five deer desperately swimming to the opposite shore. A little to the right, a mother black bear and her two cubs, also intent on escaping the fire. But there was no flash of paddles. Nor was there any sign of a canoe behind us. For the moment we were alone, but it would only be a matter of time before we encountered one of the other canoes, and although I hoped it would be Robbie and his father, it would more likely be George and Larry.

We picked up our pace.

The fire's heat intensified as we neared the outlet. Day was turning to night as thick black clouds blocked the sun above us. Ash and burning cinders fell around us, sizzling as they touched the water. One touched my bare skin. I plunged my arm into the water and splashed it on my body and into the canoe. The heat and smoke seared my nostrils as I rushed to re-soak my scarf.

"The fire looks to be closer than we thought," I said, trying to quell my rising fear.

The canoe slowed to a halt. I turned around.

"It's not too late to turn back," Teht'aa said. I detected nervousness in her voice. A red welt marred the smoothness of her forehead where an ember had landed. "We can paddle back to the rapids. Then make our way through the bush back to Dad's truck."

Eric's Jeep! I'd forgotten all about it. He wouldn't be exactly happy if the treasured SUV for which he'd gone into debt was consumed by the fire.

"What about Robbie and his father?"

"I hate to leave them, but I think this fire is getting too close."

"You said earlier that the river would protect us."

She nodded. Her earlier bravado had vanished.

"Did you have something in mind?" Another ember burned into my arm, so I plunged my arm into the water.

"I remember a story my dad told me about his grandfather, I guess that's my great-grandfather. Dad told me how Mishomis survived a forest fire by using the river. He was out tending his traplines when he got caught in a sudden firestorm. Apparently it jumped from one side of the river to the other. The only way out was down the river. So he jumped into the water with his canoe. Hung on to a rope and let the current take it and him downriver away from the fire."

"You think we could do this if we have to?"

She nodded again.

I supposed it was possible. Eric's canoe had flotation tanks, so even if it did tip over, it wouldn't sink. Our gear secured inside would add to the flotation. Eric had attached a cord around the outside of the canoe, so we would have something to hang onto. Immersed in the water, we'd be protected for the most part from the heat and falling embers, and the canoe might serve to provide some kind of a shield. The only difficulty could be breathing, but I thought since smoke rises, the best air was probably that closest to the water.

There was only one more difficulty I could think of. "The

map indicates a section of rapids just after we enter the narrows, but it doesn't indicate their degree of difficulty. Can you remember? Because if they are Class II or higher, it might not be a good idea to be hanging on to the canoe. It could smash us against the rocks."

"I think the first one is fairly difficult, maybe a II or III, but after that I think we're okay. Just small stuff."

"I suppose if we did encounter problems, we could always let go and float down on our own. We're bound to meet up with the canoe further downstream."

Teht'aa shrugged and said nothing further. Her reluctance to commit to either option meant she was leaving it up to me to make the final decision.

While I was turned around talking to her, a sudden flicker of movement far behind us caught my eye. It appeared at the mouth of the stretch of whitewater from which we'd just paddled. Through the binoculars I saw the intermittent flash of paddles and the bright yellow bow of a Fishing Camp canoe. We were now between the proverbial rock and a hard place.

"Larry and George have just arrived. I think I'd rather take my chances with the fire." I flicked an ember off my arm. "Besides, I know you'll be able to take on whatever this river or the fire throws at us"

She flashed a grateful smile, dug in her paddle, and we lunged forward.

THIRTY-SEVEN

My confidence rose as we rounded the point and slid along a swift into the river, which narrowed to little more than twenty metres. Although the expanse of water didn't seem wide enough to stop a raging fire, the trees towering above us on either shore were safely green, with no sign of fire other than a heavy dusting of ash. Despite an increase in the rain of sparks, I felt confident that the fire's danger was still a safe distance away. Nevertheless, given the number of embers landing on the parched ground, I wouldn't want to stay there for much longer.

The fire's threat was immediately replaced by another, the roar of rushing water from around a fast-approaching bend in the river. Before I had a chance to let my fear take over, we were sliding between two large boulders along a tongue of green water into the boiling froth. Teht'aa had thought it was a class II or III rapid. The number of visible rocks and the high spray from what Eric called a rooster tail convinced me it was at least a Class IV. But my training took over, and when Teht'aa shouted "Left!" I repeatedly pulled my paddle in with all my might, and when she yelled "Right!" I did the same on the other side of the canoe.

My heart almost stopped when a dead spruce lying partially across the river suddenly sprang into view.

"Strainer!" I shouted as I paddled frantically to avoid it.

Once caught in the grip of its branches, the river's current would never let us go. Teht'aa jerked us to the left, and we plunged past with only the scrape of a branch along the canoe's side as a reminder.

But the momentary relief of our near-miss was quickly shoved aside when I saw the inverted wave of what could only be a hole coming straight towards us.

"Right!" I shouted. At all costs, we had to avoid being sucked down by the circulating force of the water.

But Teht'aa had already read the water, and the canoe was veering away from the hole. A couple more swoops around submerged rocks, through several standing waves, and Teht'aa had us catching our breath in an eddy. The view upstream made the rapids seem more terrifying. Thankfully, there was no sign yet of George and Larry.

"We did it! Well done, Teht'aa," I crowed, bursting with the rush of success. I began bailing out the few inches of water that had splashed into the canoe.

"And congratulations to you, too." Teht'aa beamed. Her confidence had returned.

Once we finished bailing, we continued our journey down the river. It was flat, and the current was strong. We could've rested our paddles on the gunnels and let the river do the work, but we didn't. It was even more urgent that we get to Robbie and his father to warn them about the two men closing in behind us.

Soot and ash continued to rain down on us, though the number of sparking embers did seem to be increasing. Thick smoke swirled above our heads. The air hung heavy and hot, forcing us to continue breathing through our wet scarves. Although the heat felt like it was coming from an open oven door, it was bearable. The trees on either shore still remained blissfully ignorant of the inferno coming their way. Once or twice, I thought I heard the faint crackle of fire. I picked up my pace.

We passed more animals; some gathered at the shore, others forging their way across the river. They came in all shapes and sizes, from the smallest field mouse to the largest moose. Even though some viewed others as food, none was interested in dinner. They were too intent on one purpose, escaping the fire.

We rushed easily through the next set of rapids and bounced over the rock garden that followed. We paddled hard to keep up our speed while I tried to ignore the growing ache in my arms and shoulders. The canoe sliced through the flat water towards the next bend in the river. The air grew hotter, the smoke denser. Splashing water onto the coals landing in the canoe became a major occupation.

"Teht'aa, the fire is getting closer," I called out. "Perhaps it's time to do what your great-grandfather did and get into the water?"

"Let's hold off for the moment. I think I hear the sound of a rapid coming up."

She was right. As we headed towards the bend, the roar was growing by the second, and also another sound that sent an icy chill down my spine. The sizzle and crackle of burning wood. But the shore in front of us was still green, although the trees were bent over by the force of the wind, which I now noticed for the first time. A hot, searing wind. Suddenly the top of a pine tree burst into flame, then another.

Without thinking, both of us stopped paddling and watched as sparks erupted from the burning trees and showered the ground below. A clump of dried-out underbrush ignited, then another. The current of the river moved us silently forward toward what I knew we were going to face when we rounded the corner. An inferno.

"We've got to get as close as we can to the left shore," I screamed, digging my paddle in.

Teht'aa shifted the canoe's direction towards the shore that was still green, still untouched by nature's anger. Given this wind and the quantity of sparks flying across the narrowing expanse of water, I wasn't sure though how much longer it would remain safe.

Hugging the river's edge, we rounded the bend in time to see a solitary pine on our side of the river become a tower of flame. Below its granite perch stretched the bubbling froth and spray of a line of dangerous whitewater, where the river suddenly narrowed to less than ten metres.

Damn. The demon rapids. The ones I'd been hoping to portage around. Nailed to the trunk of the burning pine was a triangular sign designating a portage, its worn track clearly visible to the left of the tree.

Neither of us said a word. There was only one way to get out of there. Down those bloody rapids, and we couldn't do it swimming. Too dangerous. We'd be battered by the rocks.

We both frantically re-soaked our scarves, our clothes, hats, life jackets and towels and poured water into the bottom of the canoe. The burning top of a tree on the other side of the river snapped and splashed with a hiss of steam into the water.

I glanced back at Teht'aa. She nodded. We were off.

I willed myself not to look up as we churned through a rain of burning debris towards the growing line of white.

"Left!" I shouted as I identified the safe tongue of green.

We surged through it and into the mêlée. I don't remember much, so intent was I on paddling for my life. Rocks, waves, foaming water, more rocks and the wedged remains of a snag. A sudden plunge down a ledge. The canoe lurching to a halt. The desperate pushing to get us free. Air filled with spray and burning debris. It was only later I realized the spray had cooled the air so we could breathe and maybe saved us from being badly burned. Then the unexpected: a spruce, every jutting branch an inferno of flame, toppled over, directly in our path, but it didn't collapse into the river. With its roots still attached to the land, its branches became a blazing strainer that would ignite all that it snared.

We plunged our paddles into the water and jerked the canoe away from its grasping flames. Then I was in the water, with the current pushing me straight towards the tree. I could feel its intense heat on my face.

Unable to avoid it, I swam to where it looked as if the branches might not reach into the water. Praying to whatever gods were paying attention, I took a deep breath and dove as deep as my life jacket would allow. Something snagged, stopped me, then released. When my head popped back above the surface, the tree was ten metres behind, and I was desperately searching for Teht'aa.

THIRTY-EIGHT

The river propelled me in classic whitewater swimming style, head up, feet first, bum down, over the ups and downs of the rapids, which, thank god, were petering out. My hand still clung miraculously to the paddle. I was headed downstream toward what looked to be some rocky shallows in the middle of the river, where I would be able to stop and look upstream for Teht'aa. I didn't dare try to swim to either shore. Both were engulfed in smoke and flame.

Surprisingly, I felt safe. The water and the rocks gave me a sense of security. They would never burn, and the river had widened enough to prevent burning trees on either shore from toppling onto me.

I glanced around, looking for Teht'aa's brilliant blue life jacket, hoping she'd floated free like me. Instead, I saw, not eight meters away, the red of our canoe, hull side up, drifting downriver in tandem with me. Although I knew I should endeavour to secure it, I didn't have the strength to push myself through the current to reach it. I figured it would end up in some pool further downstream, where I too would end up. Besides, I needed what energy remained to rescue Teht'aa.

My feet bumped into the rocks of the shallows and brought me to a halt. I hauled myself up higher, out of the force of the current, and turned my gaze back upriver. The upper branches of the strainer still burned, but the fire had died out of the lower ones. Bracing myself for the worst, I tried to discern if there was anything trapped in their smouldering web, but thankfully saw only the glimmer of free-flowing water. Nor did I see Teht'aa wedged among the rocks or trapped on the burning shore.

I sighed with relief. That meant she'd floated free, and I would find her downstream. Then I had a terrifying thought. What if she'd become trapped in a hole, and even now was circulating round and round in its grip. Bracing myself with the paddle, I stood up and scanned the rapids, searching for the telltale back-flowing waves.

A shout made me turn around, and there she was, standing on another outcrop of rocks, frantically waving in my direction. Eric's red canoe was wedged beside her, which meant she'd likely been hanging on to its far side as the canoe had floated past me.

So glad were we to find each other safe that when I finally reached her, we wrapped our arms around each other and hugged tightly, an act that wouldn't have been possible twenty kilometres of river ago. But the fire was pressing. Its heat seared our skin, and smoke clogged our nostrils. A few quick words and we were back in the water, one on each side of the overturned canoe, drifting inexorably towards what fate had in store for us. Neither of us spared a thought to the yellow canoe closing in behind us.

The river had widened into a smooth, incessant flow of water, orange water, mirroring the fire around us. It took only the occasional kick to keep the canoe in the centre, well beyond the reach of the flames. Although embers continued to rain down upon us, frequent immersions kept their damage to a minimum. Despite the heavy smoke that hovered above our heads, we were able to breathe the coolness just above the water. Teht'aa's great-grandfather had been right. This was the only way to survive a burning river.

Finally a swift shunted us past the smouldering remains of a forest and out into the open blue of another lake. Mercifully, the distant shore glowed emerald in the setting sun below a sky of velvet blue. Safe at last.

But as our danger from the fire began to fade, another danger surfaced.

"We'd better get this boat flipped over," I shouted to Teht'aa on the other side of the canoe. "George and Larry can't be far behind."

Her answer was to turn the boat towards a smooth granite outcrop. Behind it rose the vibrant green of a living forest. The fire hadn't reached this shore and likely wouldn't, for the wind was blowing the igniting embers in the opposite direction.

I felt as if I were using every remaining ounce of energy as we kicked the canoe into the shallows, struggled to untie the gear and remove it before freeing the canoe from the suction of the water and righting it. For many long minutes afterwards, neither of us moved nor spoke as we lay exhausted on the hot rock sucking in the cool, clean air. My shoulders and arms ached. My behind and legs smarted from rock encounters, and my throat was sore from the smoke. And the burns hurt. Larry could've fired his rifle by my ear, and I wouldn't have flinched.

"We made it," I whispered to Teht'aa. My teeth chattered from the shock of the ordeal. "You know, I wasn't sure we'd get out of there alive."

"Me neither," she whispered back. Her teeth chattered also. We reached for each other's hands and squeezed tightly.

"Do you think the Kohokos made it through?" I asked.

"Yeah, I think so." Teht'aa sat up, her face no doubt a mirror of mine, flecked with burns and grey with fatigue, her eyes bloodshot from the smoke. "They would've gone through that section before the fire reached it."

"I wonder if they've buried the Ancient One by now?" I glanced at the thick black smoke billowing behind the far shore about a half a kilometre away. Fortunately, the wind was moving it away from us along with the fire.

"I sure hope so, but it doesn't matter. We've still got to get to them before Larry and George do. Larry'll shoot first and ask questions later."

"You're right, particularly since he has another reason for doing away with Robbie."

She turned a quizzical glance towards me.

"You. He's not exactly happy that you left him for Robbie."

She shrugged as if she didn't care, then struggled to get up. "Oh, am I sore."

"Me, too. I don't think I can move."

"But we can't stay here. We've got to get going. The fire won't stop Larry and George. In fact, at the speed the fire was going, it may have gone through by the time they reached that section. They could be here any minute."

Even though I knew she was right, I found it difficult to rouse myself. After surviving the fire, I felt I could survive anything, even Larry's rifle. Nonetheless, I did get up, and as I did so, I glanced back to where the river had spewed us out from the fire. Nothing remained of the once verdant forest but charred trunks, burning embers and smoke spirals.

Then I saw something that made my heart stop.

THIRTY-NINE

I don't think Larry and George made it." I pointed across the lake to the still smouldering shore.

"Jeez!" Teht'aa stared aghast at the overturned hull of a canoe, brilliant yellow against the black devastation. "We've got to go get them."

As much as I feared the two men, I agreed we couldn't leave them stranded, possibly injured, even dead in this burned-out land. With a renewed sense of urgency, I helped her shove our canoe back into the water. We left our gear behind, figuring we would need the room if we found the two men.

In the growing twilight, we streaked across the flat water toward the yellow hull. Behind it the charred husks of once-stately trees stood sentinel over the ruined forest. Wisps of smoke rose from the remaining hot spots, but otherwise the land was silent and dead. It smelled of burned wood and another unpleasant odour I couldn't put a name to.

I'd been hoping to catch sight of them on the shore by their canoe. Teht'aa called out their names as we approached, but no one was sitting or lying nearby.

As we drew nearer, I realized why. "The canoe's caved in on one side. Probably hit a rock. It means Larry and George are either back upstream or somewhere else on this shore."

"Let's go in anyway and check it out, in case…" she stopped.

But she didn't need to finish. I knew she was wondering whether one of them had become trapped and was lying dead underneath the damaged hull.

"What's that over there?" she suddenly cried out.

I looked to where her paddle pointed and saw a brown lump barely rising above the water's luminescent surface. Fearing the worst, we paddled cautiously towards it. Although it appeared to be made of some kind of fabric, it was difficult to determine if it belonged to clothing, and the fading light made it impossible to see into the water.

The mass had weight and bobbed with the pressure of my paddle, but it was impossible to tell if it was a body. I gingerly brought it to the side of the canoe.

And heaved a sigh of relief. "It's a pack. Larry's or George's."

"Not Larry's. He had a vinyl pack like ours, a red one. And I doubt George would be using one this ancient."

She was right. It appeared to be one of those heavy canvas Duluth packs, once popular with trippers.

Before I could voice my next fear, the answer came.

"Hey, Teht'aa, over here!" called out a hoarse voice.

Teht'aa spied the black outline of a man on the opposite shore before I did, not more than a hundred metres from where we'd been regaining our strength on the rock. He was standing in front of what appeared to be a living, breathing forest, while not thirty metres away, patches of orange glowed in the blackened ruin. He appeared to be leaning on something, as if he were hurt.

"Who's that?" she shouted. I caught a hint of wariness in her tone.

I held my breath, praying it would be George. I didn't want to face Larry out here in the wilds, completely alone, without a weapon, even if he were injured.

"Robbie," came the startling reply.

"What are you doing here?" Teht'aa's shock was clearly evident in her voice. "You're supposed to be downriver."

Ignoring her question, he called back, "If that's a pack out there, bring—" his sentence was cut off by a burst of coughing.

I hooked some rope around it and passed the end to Teht'aa to attach to the stern ring.

"You okay?" she called back. "Where's your dad?"

"Tell you when you get here." He collapsed to the ground and lay immobile.

"Robbie! Speak to me," Teht'aa cried out.

"His throat's probably been damaged by the smoke," I said to Teht'aa. "We shouldn't force him to talk any more."

"Let's get to him as quickly as we can. I'm worried," Teht'aa replied as she sprang the canoe forward.

Despite the drag of the pack behind us, we managed to traverse the few hundred metres of water in what seemed like seconds. As we came up to the shore, I could make out what looked like blood dripping from a long gash below his knee. Soot and burns covered his face, his body and his clothes. They spoke of the ordeal he'd been through, as did the singed hair and the hollows beneath his eyes.

Before we'd properly beached the canoe, Teht'aa jumped out and rushed over to her injured lover, leaving me to haul it up onto the shore.

"You're safe, you're safe," Teht'aa kept saying over and over again as she clung to him while tears streamed down her face. The depth of her love surprised me, since I'd thought Robbie was just another fling, like Larry and George. But I shouldn't have been surprised; after all, she'd braved a forest fire for him.

I gave them a few moments, but since Larry and George were uppermost in my mind, I finally interrupted. "We can't stay here much longer. Night is closing in, and we need to figure out what's happened to Larry and George, since that's their canoe over there. You haven't seen them, have you Robbie?"

Robbie shook his head and said in a painful whisper, "It's our canoe. Got it from the Fishing Camp." He coughed. "Why are Larry and George on the river?"

"Because they want the Ancient One," said Teht'aa.

"I guess you've already buried her, eh?" I said, hoping he had. It might remove the danger. But would it? One of them was a killer. How would he react when he learned his source of income or his fame was gone?

But Robbie remained silent, almost as if he hadn't heard my question, or he didn't want to tell me the answer. I didn't persist. He'd no doubt tell us when he was ready. Instead, I reluctantly asked another question, fearful of the response. "Where's your dad?"

"Upriver," he whispered.

I hesitated. "Is he alive?"

He shook his head sadly. Teht'aa's breath caught.

Although Grandfather Albert and I had never exactly been friends, I had never wished him ill. I paused for a few seconds out of respect before asking, "Do you want us to go back upriver for him?"

He shook his head.

"Well, it's going to be dark soon," I said. "I think we should get going. Besides, Larry and George could turn up at any moment."

I was surprised we hadn't seen them, given all the delays. Maybe they were caught up in their own problems from the fire? But even if they were, they would have to come this way eventually, and I didn't want to be here when they did.

Robbie groaned as Teht'aa and I raised him carefully to his feet. Then, with his arms draped over our shoulders, we half-carried him to our canoe, where we helped him sit down in the middle with as little pain as possible. The movement started the gash bleeding again. It looked deep and ragged, in need of immediate attention. I hoped Teht'aa had brought along a first aid kit. I hadn't.

For the first part of the paddle back to our gear, Robbie remained silent, but as we approached the shore, he spoke up. "Don't have to go back for Nòs. Is where he belongs…with Mother Earth." He coughed, then continued. "I chanted the prayers of the dead as his body burned. His spirit's at peace." He coughed again.

"Amen," Teht'aa whispered.

"Amen," I joined in, then said, "You can tell us what happened later. For the moment you need to give your voice a rest."

He remained quiet for the rest of the trip, apart from a few groans, as we helped him out of the canoe. He sank down on the rocky shore and immediately closed his eyes.

"He's not going anywhere tonight." Teht'aa voiced a concern I had as well. "I think we should stay here."

"I agree. We could do with some rest too." My momentary spark of energy was dying fast. "But what about Larry and George?"

"It'll soon be dark and luckily, no moon tonight. They won't see us if we hide the canoe and pitch camp further in the woods."

"I bet they're staying put too. Probably just as exhausted as we are. But we'll have to leave at dawn if we want to keep ahead of them."

"Or we could hide out here until they pass by. That way we'll know where they are, and we can stay well behind them," Teht'aa said.

"Sounds like a plan. Let's hide the canoe now, in case they do come. Then, if you don't mind, I'll look after Robbie's injuries while you find us a campsite."

"Fine by me. I don't know the first thing about first aid. And in case you didn't bring a kit with you, Dad's is in my pack."

Robbie didn't move or even open his eyes as I bathed his many burns with lake water. It was becoming increasingly difficult to see in the growing darkness, so I chanced using my headlamp to survey them. None appeared particularly bad. Those with raw skin I dressed as best I could with gauze.

When I cleansed his gash, he didn't even flinch, not even a groan—and it was deep. In the headlamp's glow, I could see muscle and bone. Bits of rock were imbedded in the surrounding tissue. He winced when I dabbed the area with hydrogen peroxide and applied anti-bacterial ointment. It needed stitches, but the first aid kit had only the basics. I did the best I could to close the gash by wrapping layers of gauze around his leg.

All the while I kept my ears open, listening for sounds that didn't belong, like the telltale sound of paddles knocking against canoe gunnels. The night was so still. I felt the distinctive sound would carry a great distance, even over the distant noise of the rapids. But apart from the occasional crashing sound of a tree falling on the burned land, the lake was quiet.

After giving him a couple of Tylenol, Teht'aa and I half-carried her boyfriend to a relatively flat section of rock she'd found hidden behind a thick cover of trees and partially cushioned by pine needles. After removing his still-damp clothing, we placed him on top of a therma-rest, with Teht'aa's open sleeping bag covering him. He was asleep almost before his head hit the ground.

"Do you think he'll be okay?" Teht'aa asked. The stark glow from my headlamp emphasized the lines of worry on her face.

"A good night's rest should do him good. But we're going to need to get him to a doctor as fast as we can to make sure infection doesn't set in. So let's hope—" A sudden crashing sound stopped me.

Had they found us?

"Jeez!" Teht'aa muttered.

She flicked off her headlamp, and I did likewise. Blinded by the sudden darkness, I didn't dare move. My heart pounded. I looked towards the sound and strained to see, but saw only pitch black. My old fear of the dark raised its ugly head. I groped for Teht'aa's hand and found it searching for mine. All I wanted to do was run, but Teht'aa's grip kept me grounded.

Above the beating of my heart, I could just make out the sound as it slowly crunched through the forest towards us. I felt so exposed. There was no place to hide, night, our only protection. Maybe they didn't know where we were. If we didn't make any noise, any movement, maybe they would go past.

The sound continued its relentless pace towards us. Then it stopped.

I stopped breathing, afraid the least sound of my breath would tell them where we were. Teht'aa did likewise. We waited.

The walking resumed. I let out my breath, carefully. The sound got closer. I could hear what sounded like someone panting.

Suddenly Robbie groaned. The sound stopped. Then I heard a strange grunting noise.

Teht'aa flicked on her headlamp. Not two canoe lengths from us stood one of the largest black bears I had ever seen.

I froze. Larry would've been better than this.

"Put on your light," Teht'aa whispered.

I did.

"And don't move."

I didn't dare.

The bear blinked in the combined brilliance, his nose raised as if sniffing us out.

Teht'aa began speaking softly in a language I realized wasn't Algonquin, but probably her native Dene.

The bear remained still, almost as if he were listening to her words. His fur didn't appear as black in the light as I thought it should be. It seemed to have a greyish, matte-like finish, which I realized was ash. A red welt near his nose showed where he'd been burned. Like us, he'd fled the flames. My fear changed to pity; he'd been burned out of his home.

He continued to listen to Teht'aa's soft voice, then he turned around and lumbered slowly away, beyond the range of our lights. It was then I noticed the other animals. A couple of rabbits huddled under a bush. A deer, lying down, its hindquarter singed. And at the outer reaches of my light, the saddest sight of all, a wolf licking the bad burns of a young cub.

They paid no attention to us, showed no fear. Nor did I feel any. We were kindred spirits, refugees from the fire.

It seemed so surreal that I couldn't help but wonder if the spirit of the Ancient One was watching over us.

FORTY

Sometime during the night, the animals slipped away. Their fear of us must've taken over once their fear of the fire had dissipated.

Utterly exhausted, I'd slept the sleep of the dead despite having had a slab of granite for a mattress. Teht'aa and I had drawn lots. I got the remaining sleeping bag, while she got the therma-rest. Knowing Robbie's sleeping gear would be sopping wet, we hadn't bothered to check his pack, nor did we bother to unpack the rest of our gear or even set up the tent. We were just too damn tired.

Having forgotten my watch, I had no idea of the time, but I assumed from the angle of the sun filtering through the trees that it was mid-morning. Teht'aa and Robbie were both sound asleep. While Robbie's sleep appeared peaceful, Teht'aa's wasn't. She twitched and turned and was more off the therma-rest than on. When I replaced the towels she'd used for covers with my sleeping bag, I noticed the telltale runny nose.

Of course. Not having had any coke since yesterday morning at the very latest, she must be feeling its withdrawal effects. Poor woman. I wondered if she'd brought any with her and hoped not. This enforced abstinence might help to wean her off the powerful drug. Still, I couldn't help but wonder if its effects would impair her ability to get the three of us safely off this river. I knew I couldn't do it on my own, particularly with an injured man.

I wondered if George and Larry had paddled by yet, but

since water leaves only a fleeting trace of a boat's passage, it would be impossible to tell unless I actually saw them. When I stepped gingerly out into the open to check, I was relieved to see only empty, undisturbed water. Unfortunately, I could only see part of the lake, so for all I knew, they could at this very moment be paddling down the lake towards me. I hastily retreated back into the trees, but not before checking that Eric's bright red canoe remained equally well-hidden in daylight.

I was hoping their desperation would've seen them starting early from wherever they'd spent the night, so that either they'd already have passed by or soon would, that is if they hadn't also run into trouble and were stranded somewhere upriver. If that were the case, our worries would be over. Still, I thought it would be prudent for us to remain hidden until at least noon.

While Robbie and Teht'aa continued to sleep, I cooked myself a hot breakfast of pancakes and bacon. I was starved, having had only enough energy last night to eat a bag of trail mix before falling asleep. When I finished, I decided to dry out the things in Robbie's pack.

Although the pack had been out of the water since last evening, it was still damp and oozed water when I lifted it up. It was heavy, no doubt from its water-logged contents. It would appear that the Kohokos had stuffed everything into this one large pack. If this was their only pack, they certainly travelled light, unlike us with our two dry packs, tent bag and food barrel.

On the top lay a large, badly dented aluminum pot, its underside blackened from use. It was crammed with zip-lock bags containing a few simple food items, like flour, tea and some chocolate bars. I saw no sign of a cooking stove, only a small axe jammed into the side of the pack, so I assumed they relied on an open fire for cooking, not like us with our latest in high-tech micro stoves.

Underneath were a couple of sopping Hudson Bay blanket rolls, with no therma-rests for comfort. They probably relied on what Mother Nature provided, such as spruce boughs or moss.

Clothing was likewise minimal, two sweaters for warmth, a rain jacket and a change of underwear. Unfortunately, Robbie would have to put on yesterday's clothing, which hopefully would be dry by the time he needed it. I shouldn't have expected more than this minimal amount of gear—after all, these two men had spent their lives living off the land.

But my heart stopped when I pulled out the very last item. I hadn't expected to see it: Billie's Neiman Marcus bag.

"So she's not buried yet," a voice suddenly said from the trees, which sent me into high alert.

"Teht'aa, don't scare me like that," I almost shouted.

I extracted a heavy metal container from the bag. "I'm surprised the pack didn't sink, with this extra weight."

"Too bad it didn't."

I had to agree.

Teht'aa crouched down beside me and opened the container. I couldn't ignore the thrill I felt at seeing the drab brown skull that had once been a living, breathing woman walking this land over eleven thousand years ago. "We'd better be careful. Larry and George could still be upriver. There's been no sign of them this morning."

"Jeez, we gotta get her buried." She sprang up onto her feet. "I'd better wake Robbie up."

"I'm awake," Robbie croaked, his voice obviously still affected by yesterday's smoke. "Nòs died before he could bury her. He told—" He broke into a spurt of coughing.

"Better save your voice," I said.

"Need water," he sputtered.

Teht'aa passed him a water bottle.

After taking several long drinks, he continued in a stronger voice. "Told me to bury her at a sacred place belonging to the ancestors."

"Is it far from here?" I asked.

"A ways."

"Are you able to travel?"

"Yeah, I'll be okay."

"I think we should wait another hour or so. I figure if we don't see Larry and George by then, we can assume either they've already gone by or they're stuck upriver."

"Likely upriver. No way Larry could've paddled that shit yesterday," Teht'aa said as she dumped some of Robbie's flour into his pot.

"Yes, but what about George? Maybe he's a skilled paddler?"

Teht'aa shrugged. "Never went tripping with him." She poured some water into the pot and began mixing the ingredients for bannock.

As she poured the batter into Eric's sizzling frying pan, I couldn't help but notice the slight tremor in her hands. I sure hoped her withdrawal symptoms wouldn't get any worse, but the sooner we got off this river the better.

FORTY-ONE

A n hour later, we set out. I'd redressed Robbie's wound, which still looked angry and red. I hoped the Ancient One's burial wouldn't take long. Robbie needed to get to a doctor before infection set in.

Although we all agreed the chances of the two men appearing this late in the day were minimal, I couldn't help but feel exposed as the canoe pushed out into the middle of the lake. Despite the aches in my shoulders and arms, I found myself paddling with a determined stroke. The lake was as empty as it had been all morning.

With the wind blowing the smell of the fire away from us, I could pretend it had never happened. Only when I turned around did I see its blackened aftermath. Far in the distance, clouds billowed above the land it was currently destroying. I wondered how many more square kilometres of forest would be ruined before the fire finally went out.

Robbie sat sandwiched amongst the packs, while Teht'aa and I resumed our usual seats in the stern and bow. Yesterday's experience had molded us into a mean paddling machine. With minimal effort, we sliced our way toward the spot where the river became a river again.

As we sped over the flat water, I asked the question I'd been wanting to ask since finding the injured man. "Are you up to telling us what happened?" To the rhythm of our paddles, Robbie told us his tale.

"We put in around ten or so. There was smoke, but we figured the fire was a long ways away, so Nòs and I loaded up and headed off. We ripped through the first set of rapids. Nòs used to be one hell of a paddler. Could take on any river. He brought Yanks up here to hunt and fish. Knew this river like the back of his hand."

Robbie coughed and took a drink of water, then continued, "But when we got to the next set, I noticed him getting tired, so I told him to sit tight while I took us through. At the bottom we stopped at the portage to give him a rest. I could tell something was up. He didn't look good. Breathing wasn't good either. So I said, 'Why don't we bury the Ancient One here and make our way back to the truck?'

"But he said no. He wanted to go where Kije Manidu had left his mark. So we climbed back in. It was then I noticed the black smoke comin' from downriver. It sure scared the hell out of me, I tell ya. I knew we was gonna head right into it. So I asked Nòs again about turning back, but he said no.

"Jeez, he was stubborn." With his voice trembling from emotion, Robbie paused to regain his composure.

Our silence merged with the early afternoon stillness as we paddled down the river. We passed a cow moose, knee-high in the water, munching on marsh grass, with her suckling young calf. A casual lifting of the mother's head was the only sign that our passage was noted.

"See, the spirits aren't angry any more." Robbie's voice almost seemed to smile. "They know the Ancient One is returning to Mother Earth."

But I couldn't accept their peace offering. We were still a long way from safety. I glanced nervously behind to make sure there was no yellow canoe behind us and also to check to see how Teht'aa was bearing up. Apart from her runny nose, which she ignored, she showed no other signs of withdrawal. Her paddling was as strong as ever.

Robbie sat silent for a few more minutes, then continued his tale. "A coupla hours later, Nòs suddenly fell forward into the canoe. By this time it was just me paddlin'. Christ, I was scared, so I got him to shore as fast as I could and pulled him out. He was breathing, but sleepin' like. I cut down some spruce boughs, put his sleeping roll on top and laid him on it, and waited for him to wake up.

"I didn't know what to do. I couldn't leave him to get help, and I was scared to put him back into the canoe in case he had a seizure or something like that. He had one a couple of years back. Ended up in the hospital. Doctors said it was a stroke.

"Anyways, I waited, and I could see the smoke gettin' closer. Sparks and ash were flying all around. Finally I was afraid to wait any longer, so I laid him down in the canoe and tied him in, 'cause I knew more rapids were comin', and I was afraid he'd fall out. I guess I musta hurt him or somethin', 'cause he suddenly opened his eyes and said I had to promise that no matter what happened to him, I had to return the Ancient One to Mother Earth. And he told me where to go, where Memegwaysiwuk, the rock people once lived."

Of course. The perfect place. "I know where you mean," I said, checking the map for the portage near where Eric, Teht'aa, Larry and I had paid homage to the rock art of the ancients. "The place is about twenty kilometres downriver from here. We should be there by nightfall. But go on. I didn't mean to interrupt."

I heard him take a deep breath. "It wasn't too much longer after that that his whole body begins to shake, and he makes these funny gasping noises. Then all of a sudden, his back rises up, and he calls out to Kije Manidu. Then he falls back down and lies still. I could see his chest wasn't moving any more, so I knew he was dead." Robbie stopped, took another drink of water and remained quiet.

Both Teht'aa and I kept silent. We didn't want to intrude on his grief.

As we paddled along the narrow confines of the river, the current, combined with our determined paddling, sped us past a beach of round river stone that a city landscaper would die for, over several sets of easy rapids, past high granite cliffs fringed with red pine, past the large nest of a bald eagle embedded in a dead pine, over more rapids and past the high sandy ridge of an esker left behind by the last great glacier. It would have been deposited at about the same time that the Ancient One and her people began exploring this emerging land. Maybe she had even stepped onto its fine brown sand.

As much as I would've liked to stop for a late lunch, I figured we couldn't chance it, just in case George and Larry were really behind us. Still, I asked, "Robbie, how are you doing? Do you want to get out of the canoe for some lunch?"

"No way!" Teht'aa shouted. "We can't stop. Gotta bury the Ancient One."

Surprised at her seeming lack of concern for her boyfriend, I replied, "I think we should let Robbie make the decision. His injured leg might be hurting him."

"Yeah, sorry. Wasn't thinking. You wanna stop, Robbie?"

"Nope…I'm okay." But I could tell from the resigned tone in his voice that a brief stint out of the canoe might do him some good. From my bow position, I tried to turn the canoe towards shore, but felt resistance from the stern. "Teht'aa, please take us into shore. I want to change his dressing."

"Okay," she said brusquely as the canoe veered towards another beach made from round river stone. With little regard for Robbie or the canoe, she rammed it up onto the stones and jumped out. "We gotta be quick."

As we both helped her boyfriend out of the canoe, I couldn't help but wonder why she seemed so uncaring for a man she'd shown all the signs of loving.

The answer came when she said, "God, do I need a snort." She began tossing stones into the river. "Shit, why did I forget to bring some stuff?"

Robbie answered, "This'll be good for you, Teht'aa."

He winced as I pulled the dressing from his wound. It looked puffy and red, as if infection were starting to set in. I liberally applied more antiseptic ointment.

"Remember your promise to stop," Robbie said.

"Yeah, I know," she answered. "But shit, I feel like hell. I didn't know it was gonna be this bad."

"If I can stop drinking, you can stop snorting," he answered.

I turned to him. "You too?"

"Yeah, been off the booze five years."

"Three years for me."

We gave each other the kind of congratulatory smile that only former alcoholics can give each other, but it didn't help Teht'aa. She was just beginning to go down the long hard road of withdrawal. I just hoped she was able to remain sufficiently together until we got down this damn river.

After a quick bite, we were back on the water.

Robbie continued his story. "I figured Nòs would want to be buried in the traditional lands of our ancestors instead of the rez's Christian cemetery. I could hear the noise of a big rapid coming up, so I decided to bury him somewhere along the portage. But when I rounded the bend and saw the fire was closing in, I decided to let Mother Earth look after him.

"On the shore where the fire was headed, I made him a bed of spruce and put him on it. I put his regalia beside him. Though, to respect his memory, I kept one piece." He smiled wistfully as he extracted an almost transparent piece of quartz. "I chanted the prayers of the dead, sprinkled tobacco and waited beside him until it got too hot. I crossed the river to the portage. From a big rock, I watched Mother Earth take him. Now he's with the ancestors."

Robbie lapsed back into silence, while Teht'aa and I continued our relentless paddling. Teht'aa seemed less jittery for the moment. Perhaps the paddling had a calming effect. I figured we were still several hours away from the portage that would take us around the falls to the pool of water guarded by the Rock Spirits, and another day before we made it to the ZEC registration office and rescue. In the meantime, Teht'aa's symptoms would only get worse. I just hoped she would be able to hang in.

A little while later, she asked a question that had also been nagging me. "How did you get hurt?"

"That damn rapid. I shoulda knowed better. But I guess I was upset over Nòs's dying, so I wasn't payin' much attention. I slammed right into one of those damn rocks. Got stuck between it and the canoe. Thought I was a goner for sure. Didn't know I was hurt until I crawled up onto the shore. Musta passed out, 'cause I sure didn't hear you gals go by." He paused to take a drink of water.

A sudden loud, reverberating echo made the three of us look towards the sky downriver.

"Christ, what's that?" Robbie asked.

"Sounds like a helicopter to me," I answered. The thwumping was getting closer.

"Probably belongs to one of those logging companies," Robbie said.

"Or it could be the police."

"How'd they know I was here?"

"I told them, or at least I told Billie to call."

"Jeez, what did you do that for?" Teht'aa cried.

"I was worried we wouldn't be able to deal with Larry and George on our own," I answered.

"But they'll take Robbie back to jail," Teht'aa exclaimed.

The droning grew louder. At any moment the helicopter would appear over the tops of the trees.

"Let's get under those overhanging cedars," Teht'aa shouted. "I think the canoe'll just fit under."

I could make out the dark shape of the helicopter through gaps in the branches as it flew overhead. While I felt confident that its passengers wouldn't see us, I couldn't help but wonder if we weren't making a mistake. As much as I would like to think George and Larry were stranded behind us, they could've easily passed us during the night and even now be waiting somewhere downriver.

Still, the police would prevent us from burying the Ancient One, a thought which immediately brought back the image of a small boy struggling to remain alive. No. I had to do what I could to save Jid. We had to stay away from the police, so Robbie could bury the Ancient One. Besides, if we were lucky, the helicopter might even sight the two men and take them into custody.

Once the helicopter was safely beyond view, we continued our journey downriver, but this time we stayed close to shore. And lucky we were, for about a half hour later, just as we'd finished running another set of rapids, we had to make another dash for cover as the helicopter made its return trip downstream.

As its drone faded for the second time, I had another thought. What if they'd discovered Robbie's damaged canoe? They would assume he was dead or lying somewhere on the shore badly injured. As if in answer, an hour later a floatplane flew over. More cops heading to the lake to look for Robbie's remains. That should keep them occupied for a while and give us enough time to do what we were there to do.

The sun had long since left the river and was fading from the surrounding treetops when we reached the portage of the Rock People.

FORTY-TWO

Uncertain about what awaited us at the portage, we snuck up to it by hugging the near shore. About ten metres from the pull-out we stopped and searched for signs or sounds in the growing darkness that would tell us George and Larry were waiting.

After a few minutes, Teht'aa said, "I think it's okay."

Nonetheless, as we slowly approached, I kept my eyes and ears peeled, but there was nothing to suggest that the two men had recently hauled their gear and canoes over the rocky pull-out. Nor were fresh tracks evident in the mud just beyond.

"I don't think they've been here. Must still be upriver," I whispered. "But I'm not going to relax until we get this portage over and the Ancient One buried."

"Ditto," Teht'aa replied as she nudged the canoe onto the rocks. "This is a long one, and it's gonna take us at least three trips."

"How you feeling?"

"Like shit."

"Think we should spend the night here? You might feel better in the morning."

"No way. It's just gonna get worse," she snapped, then in a calmer tone asked, "Robbie, how you doing?"

It took a minute for him to answer, and when he did, I could tell from the grogginess in his voice that he'd been asleep. "Where are we? At the portage?"

"Think you're up to walking it?" I asked, while Teht'aa and I helped him out of the canoe. But when I saw him wince as he placed his weight on the injured leg, I knew that it would require both of us to help him over the rough trail. "I think it best you stay here, while we carry everything over first."

He grunted in acknowledgement as he slumped onto the ground, leaned back against the trunk of a stout cedar and closed his eyes. His breathing sounded laboured. God only knew how we were going to get him safely to the other side of what I remembered as being the most challenging portage on the river.

With my dry pack strapped on my back and my arms filled with as much as I could carry, I clambered up the steep incline of crumbling earth and tree roots that led away from the river. Teht'aa followed close behind. Once away from the river's lingering light, we were forced to use our headlamps. As the black forest pressed around us, my fear of the dark returned, so much so that I found myself starting every time my headlamp flashed on something not immediately identifiable. It invariably turned out to be an innocuous plant whose shape had been distorted by the light.

Finally I said, "Teht'aa, do you mind going in front?"

But as I struggled to keep up with her much faster pace, another worry took over. Maybe something would grab me from behind, like a bear. Every few minutes I would stop and nervously flash my headlamp on the back trail, only to find that when I resumed walking the gap between Teht'aa and me had widened. I knew I was being ridiculous, and I did all I could to shove my fear away as I hastened to catch up to her.

I was soon stopped by a wall of granite blocking the trail with no apparent path around it, until I noticed regular indentations in the rock leading up and over the giant boulder. Steps, probably cut by voyageurs over three hundred years ago. I scrambled up to the top in time to see Teht'aa disappearing around the next bend.

"Wait up," I called.

"Quit being so slow," she yelled back, but she waited until I reached her.

In the harsh light of my headlamp, her face appeared strained, her darting eyes intense but unseeing, her movements jerky. She turned without another word and sped off toward the end of the portage. I began to wonder if her speed wasn't her way of trying to deal with the withdrawal.

Some time later, the roar of the falls around which we were portaging began to rumble through the night. As we drew closer, the ground throbbed. I felt the damp coolness from its spray, then we began the descent towards the trail's end.

At one point, Teht'aa slipped on a wet rock and started to fall backwards, but I was able to catch her. Another time I tripped on a root and fell into her. We both landed like a couple of overladen sherpas on the hard, rocky ground. But apart from scrapes and bruises, we managed to right ourselves and resume our downward trek.

For a while the sound of the falls was muffled by the surrounding forest, but then it grew louder as the land started to level off. Between the trees I caught the intermittent glimmer of water. The portage was almost over. Thank goodness.

Suddenly a voice called out. "Well, well. Imagine meeting you ladies here."

I froze. As my headlamp lit up George's grin, I thought, Thank god Robbie isn't with us.

"How the hell did you get here?" Teht'aa shot back.

"Down the river. Same way you did," came Larry's voice from the other side of a camp fire. Its orange glow glinted off his rifle as he stepped around it. "Nice forest fire, eh?"

"Surprised you didn't get burned to a crisp," she shot back.

"Too damn smart. Waited until it passed by, then came through last night. But I see you weren't so smart." He pointed to the burn on his former girlfriend's forehead.

George cut in. "You must've been in front of us then. Where'd you spend the night? We didn't see your canoe."

Ignoring him, Teht'aa flung back, "Surprised you made it this far, Larry, or should I call you, the Gutless Wonder."

"You bitch!" He raised his hand to strike her.

But before he could, George grabbed his arm. "Forget it. Besides, she's right. If it weren't for me, you never would've made it through those rapids. I thought you Indians were masters of the river." He let out a guffaw.

Knowing Teht'aa wouldn't be able to let this insult to her people go unchallenged, I hastened to divert her before we found ourselves staring down the end of a rifle barrel. "Enough. We all agree we got this far safely. Now if you don't mind, Teht'aa and I have to go back to get the rest of our gear."

We needed to get back to Robbie to hide him before the two men remembered their reason for being on the river. And we needed to get away from that rifle. I didn't trust Larry's itchy finger.

But as I dropped my pack to the ground, George spoke up. "Not so fast, ladies. I'm assuming you're here for the same reason we are. Robbie and his old man. And I have a feeling you might be meeting them somewhere. Why else would you be here? Though, Meg, I am surprised to see you involved in the DeMontigny Lady's reburial."

In response, I adopted a nonchalance I didn't feel and remained silent.

He continued, "So come on, gals. Tell us where they are."

"We have no idea," we both shot back in unison.

Our voices must have expressed a little too much hysteria, for George just shook his head and said, "You expect me to believe that. You know where they are. Tell us."

Larry raised his rifle and pointed it directly at us.

I could see Teht'aa gearing up to fling another insult, so I intervened. "I'm surprised you didn't catch up to them. After all, you put into the water not long after they did."

"We've searched," George replied. "No sign of their trail. Even went further downriver, until we almost ran into two boatloads of cops waiting near the discovery site. So we high-tailed it back here."

"Yeah," Larry cut in. "Since Grandfather Albert couldn't bury her where you found her, I knew he'd be wanting another sacred place." I felt Teht'aa tense beside me as I girded myself for his next words. "Then I remembered the place your dad showed us."

I held my breath.

"The sacred place of Memegwaysiwuk, the Rock People." He pointed to the blackness behind him, to where I knew the granite outcrop with its sacred pictographs dropped into the river.

"Maybe you're wrong," I hastily suggested. "Since this is the traditional waterway of the Algonquin, there's got to be other sacred places."

"Yeah," Teht'aa added. "Maybe they've already buried her."

"But," George replied, "we would've seen their fresh tracks on the portages. And we haven't."

"Maybe they didn't portage," Teht'aa retorted.

"Over this chute?"

He had a point. "Once they buried her, they'd have no reason to continue along the river," I replied. "In fact, maybe the sacred land was further inland, and they hiked out afterwards."

"But we would've seen their canoe."

"Not if they hid it."

George and Larry glanced at each other. Maybe our bluff was working.

For several long silent seconds, we stared at each other, then George spoke up. "Maybe you're right."

I felt a glimmer of hope. "Look, I'm tired, it's been a long day, and we still have to get the rest of our gear over this portage. So if you've got nothing more to say, Teht'aa and I are going back." I turned to leave.

"Hey, not so fast," George said. "Larry and I'll come and help you. It's pretty rough getting a canoe up over that giant boulder."

FORTY-THREE

The closer we got to the start of the portage, the louder I talked and the more often I mentioned George or Larry's name in the hope that Robbie would hear. Teht'aa must've thought likewise, for her voice was also raised a decibel or two. George and Larry didn't seem to notice. They guffawed and joked as if the four of us were laughing it up at a bar. Their relaxed behaviour told me they had no inkling that the man they sought would shortly be in their sights.

Fortunately, Robbie must've heard our noise, for when we scrambled down the steep embankment to the river, he was gone. But the minute I realized he'd escaped, I frantically scanned the remaining gear, searching for the Duluth pack containing the Ancient One. I found it partially hidden by a clump of low cedar a few metres from the rest of our gear. Hoping neither of the two men had noticed, I whisked my headlamp away, in the direction of our canoe.

"Larry, could you take the canoe?" I asked. "And maybe George, you could carry our food barrel. Teht'aa and I will follow with the rest of our gear."

I was hoping to persuade them to leave first, with Teht'aa following close behind. This would give me a chance to find Robbie and warn him to wait until morning, when we should have the two men paddling back down the river. I also wanted to make sure he had enough stamina to survive the night on his own.

At least, that was the plan until fate intervened.

"Who the hell does this belong to?" George exclaimed, thumping his foot against the Duluth pack. "Sure doesn't belong to one of you."

I froze, not Teht'aa. "Of course it does," she shot back. "It belongs to my dad."

I quickly concurred. "That's right. An old pack of Eric's."

Larry eyed us suspiciously. "I don't remember seeing this on the last canoe trip."

"We didn't need it," Teht'aa blithely answered. "But Dad took his good pack to Owl Lake and left this old thing behind."

I was beginning to admire her quick wit.

"You ladies certainly do have a lot of gear," George pondered. "I think we should take a look at what's inside. Besides, didn't I see you dropping a dry pack back at the trail end?"

Before either of us could stop him, George was holding up a pair of men's boxer shorts. "And I guess you borrowed these from your father too."

"Okay, where are they?" Larry's flashlight scanned the woods around us while George began dumping the contents of the pack onto the ground.

"Hey, stop that. It's not your pack," Teht'aa cried out.

"Where is she?" George turned the pack upside down and shook it. Out tumbled the Neiman Marcus bag. My heart thudded. As one, Teht'aa and I leapt to grab it before George did, and lost.

Grinning, he held it upright, unsnapped the top and carefully reached inside. But instead of pulling out the bones' metal container, he pulled out the battered aluminum pot.

George spat on the ground. "Goddamn it, she's not here."

Although I was certain the container with the bones had vanished along with the injured man, I didn't dare shine my headlamp around in case it hadn't.

George shone his headlamp directly into my eyes. "What have you done with her?"

"I don't know what you're talking about."

"Cut that crap, Ms Harris. You know exactly who I mean, the DeMontigny Lady."

"Time you came clean, ya stupid bitches," Larry snarled and raised his rifle at Teht'aa and me. "Where's that piece of moose shit and his old man?"

I glanced at Teht'aa, who seemed to have shrunk, and said, "Okay, we did see them. Just put that gun down. It's making me nervous."

"Not till you tell us where they are."

Despite staring directly into the gun barrel, I lied. "Like I told you before. They headed off into the bush."

"Where?"

"Back upriver."

"Before or after the fire?"

"Before." Perhaps if I made the location far enough upstream, we would be able to rescue Robbie and make our escape downriver before they discovered the ruse.

"I don't believe you."

"Tough. It's the truth," I said with more courage than I felt.

"Then tell me how you managed to meet up with them, when we didn't?"

"Easy," Teht'aa jumped in, regaining her nerve. "They saw you coming and hid."

"Yeah, said your yellow canoe stuck out like a canary in winter," I added.

"So why do you have their pack?"

"Told us to take it," Teht'aa shot back. "Said that its weight would slow them down."

"And what about their canoe?"

My turn to come up with a plausible lie, which was partly true. "I'm not a good enough canoeist to solo whitewater, so we left it behind. Robbie said he would come back later to get it."

While George continued to shine his headlamp directly into my eyes, his silence and Larry's suggested that they were beginning to buy our story.

Finally, George said, "Nothing we can do about it tonight. We'll go back to our camp and return in the morning."

Super, I thought, they're taking the bait.

"We'll take your food barrel. Might come in handy," George continued. "But we'll leave your canoe behind. In the morning you're going to take us back upriver and show us where they went."

Yikes. How would we get out of this one?

The trek back took on a far more ominous tone. George removed our headlamps, rendering us all but blind in the pitch dark. Then, with him leading the way, we stumbled after, while Larry took up the rear, spurring us on with occasional prods of his rifle. I didn't dare make a sudden movement, in case it ignited his trigger finger, nor did I say a single word for fear his anger would set him off. His former girlfriend must've thought likewise, for she was similarly silent during our long hike back.

When we arrived at the granite outcrop that marked the end of the portage, I wasn't the least surprised when George insisted we stay in the full light of the camp fire. In fact, he added more wood to ensure it burned brightly. I must admit, thoughts of escape had crossed my mind. When Teht'aa had to go to the bathroom, Larry followed, while George guarded me.

The rustle of their departure was soon drowned by the noise of the falls, leaving George and me to wait in an uneasy silence. Then suddenly an angry shout erupted from Teht'aa.

George raced into the bush, with me running close behind. His headlamp lit up Teht'aa standing defiantly next to a pine, while Larry stood a few metres away with his hand held out towards her. In his palm lay a zip-lock bag filled with a white powder, which I immediately realized was cocaine. He ignored us.

"For the last time," Teht'aa said, "I don't want any."

"Yeah, but you need it. Look at your twitching. Just one little snort and everything'll be real nice, just like always."

"No!" Teht'aa stepped back behind the stout tree trunk as if she were using it as a barrier. Her eyes seemed to be starting out of her face as her mouth twitched.

Larry moved closer and dangled the bag. "Come on, babe, remember all those good times we had together."

At first she ignored it, then her hand slowly reached forward to grasp the bag; her resolve was gone.

"You bastard!" I shouted as I lunged for the bag.

But Teht'aa beat me. She swept it up and ran back into the clearing towards the fire. The three of us raced after her. But instead of stopping there, she continued running towards the water. With one mighty throw, she flung the bag into the river. Then she whirled around to face us. "It's gone. Do what you want with me, but I'm finished with coke or any other of your fancy drugs." As she said these last words, I realized Larry's role in their relationship. He'd been her supplier.

"Bitch!" Larry shouted gripping his rifle. He pointed it at her, held it steady then raised it and fired into the air. "I can't. I love you too much, Teht'aa." He flung the gun onto the ground, turned on his heels and walked back into the trees, leaving the three of us standing in stunned silence.

Teht'aa began to tremble, no doubt from the realization of how close she'd come to losing her life. I wrapped my arms around her as she convulsed into tears. But as I led her towards the fire, I felt another set of arms take over.

"It's okay, I've got her," whispered a male voice.

I looked over to see Robbie's anxious face.

George grabbed Larry's rifle and pointed it at Robbie. "Give it to me!" he demanded.

"Give you what?" Robbie replied calmly as he sheltered his girlfriend from the aimed gun.

"You know damn well, those damn bones."

Robbie remained silent.

"You've buried her, haven't you?" Teht'aa whispered. "Thanks to Kije Manidu."

George jammed the gun against Robbie's ribs. "Tell me where, or I'll shoot."

"Go ahead, shoot. But if you do, you'll never find out where the Ancient One is. And if you don't, who knows, I might tell you some day." Robbie grinned as he moved Larry's gun aside. But as quickly as the grin appeared, it vanished. "But I won't."

Holding the gun away, George smiled sheepishly. "Look I'm sorry, I didn't mean to point the gun at you. Just got a little carried away. If I promise that I'll return the bones to you for reburial after I've finished the analysis, will you tell me where she is?"

"George, you're an okay guy. You rescued our ancestor. I—"

Worried over what was coming next, I interrupted. Robbie had to know the worst. "You can't give the Ancient One to George. He's a murderer. He killed his colleague."

The two men stared at me. One man bore shocked amazement, the other resignation.

"No, he didn't," Robbie said.

"Of course he did. He killed him after Claude discovered he'd stolen the bones."

"No, it was me. I killed the man."

Now it was my turn to be shocked.

"It was an accident," Robbie said softly. "He nabbed me in the parking lot and accused me of taking them. I told him I didn't do it, but he didn't believe me. Kept shouting and hitting me. I hit back, but he wouldn't stop. Was sure one tough little bugger. Somehow he got a hold of the crooked knife in my pocket. Next thing he was on the ground, bleeding. I ran. Didn't know he was dead until the police picked up Teht'aa and me."

For a second my attention was distracted by what I thought was a strange sound mixed in with the roar of the falls, but then it vanished. "What were you doing at the lab?" I asked.

"I went back to steal the bones then changed my mind." He smiled weakly.

George didn't bother to hide his "so there" grin as he turned to me. "Why'd you think I did it?"

"Your precious Clovis Chair was more important to you than anything else. You couldn't afford to have Claude accuse you of the theft. That would've killed your chances for sure. As for your teaching alibi, I have a feeling once the police check it out, they will discover that a grad student had filled in for you. But most importantly you had a crooked knife."

"I see the Paynes have been talking. But what they didn't know is that I managed to convince my little buddy that Robbie had stolen the bones."

It explained Claude's accusation in the parking lot. "Seems to me you are equally guilty of Claude's murder."

George's gave me a nasty look before he turned his sights back on Robbie. "How about we strike a deal. If you let me have the bones, I'll tell the cops you were with me when my buddy died."

"Doesn't matter. I killed a man. I need to answer to his spirit, so I'll go to jail."

He cast his eyes to George, who didn't bother to hide his disgust. Next his gaze lingered on Teht'aa. With his dark eyes shining with love, he said, "I'm sorry."

Then he looked at Larry, who stood silently at the edge of

the fire's glow. "Sorry, about Teht'aa, man. Didn't mean to take her from you. Just happened."

Larry spat.

Robbie smiled at me. "What happens to the Ancient One is no longer up to me. It's in the hands of our people. They'll decide her fate. The place is known. And because peoples' ways can change, I left her in her metal case to keep her from rotting. Maybe some day our people will decide they can learn from her too. She'll be there waiting."

Only then did I realize that we were in the glare of a searchlight from a police helicopter hovering overhead.

FORTY-FOUR

I watched patches of late afternoon sun creep across the verandah flooring. Occasionally a gust would disturb the surrounding pines, causing the patches to swirl and scatter. It was hot, but not as hot as it had been, and it had rained.

It had been four days since the five of us had been taken off the river by the police, Robbie and George by SQ police helicopter to be arraigned for their crimes in Montreal and Teht'aa by car to the reserve, where she was to be charged for her involvement in Robbie's escape.

That left me with Larry. Even though he had pointed his rifle at us and had almost shot Teht'aa, he'd stopped himself, so none of us had thought to mention it to the police. Besides, he'd already paid the price for his bad behaviour. He'd lost Teht'aa for good. Fortunately, I didn't have to face him alone. Sergeant Beauchamp and another SQ cop stayed behind to help us with the gear and canoes. When we finally reached the ZEC Registration Office, Sam Whiteduck was waiting with a van and a canoe trailer to transport us back home.

Miraculously, it had started raining while we were loading up and continued to do so on the long, bumpy journey home. Larry and I spoke little, in part because I had nothing to say to him, but mostly because I was still trying to come to terms with all that had happened, in particular Robbie's confession. His killing of Claude just seemed too ill-fated.

When we arrived back at the reserve, Larry and I parted

without so much as a goodbye. I hoped I'd never see him again. No doubt he thought the same of me.

The day after I returned home, Will had Corporal Matoush drive me back to retrieve Eric's SUV, since Teht'aa was still in police custody. As we neared the area, I searched for signs of fire damage and saw none, although the smell of smoke hung heavy in the air. The fires were out, that much I knew. The morning news had reported that the previous day's downpour had doused them. Still, I wasn't sure if we'd be greeted by the burned-out wreck of Eric's Jeep. It had been a close call. But the car was intact, albeit covered in ash. The fire had passed by less than thirty metres away, almost as if the gods had stopped it at the last minute. And perhaps they had.

This day, just after lunch, Teht'aa had called. She was free. Tommy, whom I'd hired to defend Teht'aa, had struck a deal with Will Decontie. The police chief would drop the charges against Teht'aa on condition she participate in a healing circle.

"I want to do this," she said. "Drugs are ruining my life. I need to get off them. I want to heal my soul. I want to be whole for when Robbie gets out of jail."

I empathized with her and offered to do whatever I could to help her. Then she asked me a surprising question. "Meg, I know it's a lot to ask, but Dad called to say he wouldn't be home for another couple of days, something about helping Owl Lake to clean up. And well, I really don't want to stay on my own."

She paused while I digested the fact that Eric had called her, but not me.

"I know I've been a bitch, and I'm sorry. I want to make up for my bad behaviour. I was wondering if I could come stay with you, and we could start getting to know each other."

So I found myself sitting in Aunt Aggie's old rocker, waiting for the arrival of Eric's daughter with some eagerness, for our journey through the fire had shown me a Teht'aa with whom I'd like to become friends. I was trying not to think about Eric and the fact he hadn't called, not once. I didn't bother to come up with excuses. He hadn't phoned, because he no longer wanted anything to do with me. Plain and simple.

But on the brighter side, Jid was off the ventilator and awake. I wasn't sure when he'd begun to recover from the boating accident but got the impression he'd opened his eyes sometime during the night, in which Robbie was burying the Ancient One. Whether she had a hand in his recovery, I'll never know. But I'd like to think that maybe she had. Not everything needs to have a scientific explanation.

Yesterday, when I'd visited him in the hospital, he'd been all smiles, with every indication of a quick return to his rambunctious squirrel self. After his discharge, he'd be moving in with his aunt, but he lightened my heart by saying he couldn't wait to come visit his buddy Sergei. Maybe my house wouldn't be empty, after all.

I'd always found the rocking motion of the chair very soothing, the way Aunt Aggie no doubt once had. She used to spend hours gently rocking back and forth, watching the ever-changing lake view before her. I'd been sitting there for the past hour or so, sipping lemonade, listening to the sounds of silence and thinking and watching.

Several aluminum boats motored by, probably fishermen from the Fishing Camp. At the far end of the lake I spied one of their yellow canoes and wondered if it was the one Larry and George had used. I thought of that other canoe lying smashed on the burned-out shore.

Although my burns were healing nicely, images of swirling smoke, towering flames and a desiccated landscape still haunted me. I wondered if they haunted Teht'aa too. Perhaps this was her reason for not wanting to stay alone.

The sound of a car door closing brought me out of my reverie. Teht'aa had arrived. I got up to greet her, but judging by the barking, the dog had already beat me.

I turned the corner of the house, expecting to see Eric's freshly-washed Jeep. Instead I saw the Paynes' dusty Navigator with the finished birchbark canoe strapped on its roof and the elderly couple giving the dog bear hugs.

I hadn't spoken to either of them since my return, although I'd learned from Will that they had both been charged for possession of stolen property. I also wondered if they knew the results of Billie's cancer tests yet.

I approached them somewhat warily, for I couldn't help but blame them in part for what had happened. They must've felt a similar unease, for they broke away from patting the dog and watched me approach. Neither smiled, and both looked nervous.

Billie spoke first. I couldn't help but notice a certain aura of sadness surrounding her. "Meg, honey, I hope you don't mind our dropping in sudden-like. But we're leaving and didn't want to go without saying goodbye."

"Do you want to come in for some iced tea?"

"Sure would be nice, but we got to get on our way." She stopped as if not knowing how to proceed.

I was about to ask about the test results, when Ed spoke up, "We feel real bad about what happened, and we want to make it right. We know we done that poor boy wrong. If we hadn't agreed to George stealing the bones, Robbie never would've killed that man."

"But you didn't ask George to steal them. I think it likely he would've done it anyway. He's the one really responsible for Claude's death."

"And he's paying for it. I hear tell from our contacts that he's finished as an archeologist. His reputation is done. Even if he only goes to jail for a few years, no one'll hire him when he gets out.

"But that's no never mind. It's Robbie we're talking about. That poor boy never meant no harm. We've hired that lawyer friend of yours, Tom Whiteduck and one of the best defense lawyers in Quebec. We figure the two of them can get Robbie the best deal."

"I'm so glad to hear that. But what about yourselves? Will told me you've both been charged."

"That's right, honey," Billed answered. "And it's only fitting. We'll stay in jail for however long the good Lord sees fit."

"I doubt you'll have to go to jail. Given our justice system, I'm sure they'll view this as a first offence and let you off with community service or whatever they make people do. But please, I want—"

"Be that as it may," she cut in, "we'll find out when we come back for our sentencing. In the meantime, we've been given leave to go home and tidy up our affairs."

"That's why you're taking your canoe. Who did you get to finish it for you?"

"That guy y'all mentioned. But the canoe's not coming with us. We want you to keep it for us. We're going to sell it in a charity auction and give the money to the Migiskan. They've been so kind and friendly, and we've done nothing but cause them a mighty load of trouble. So I hope you can take care of it until it's sold."

"I'd be happy to. But please, I want to know about your cancer. Please tell me it hasn't returned."

Ed hugged Billie closely to his side. "'Fraid so, Meg. It's gone after her liver. Doctors here say not much can be done, but the University of Texas has a fancy cancer centre back in Houston. Maybe they have access to some experimental drugs you can't get up here."

"I'm so sorry." I embraced the tiny woman. She felt so frail and insignificant. "I'm sure the doctors down there will have something," I said trying to be hopeful, for without hope, there is nothing.

She remained a few moments longer in my arms, then broke free. "And I pray to the good Lord that you fix things up with your honey. He's a fine man. It'd be a shame to lose him."

"I don't want to lose him either. I'll do what I can," I said with less hope than I'd given her.

"There's another reason we want to get back home," Ed wrapped his arm once more around his wife. "As much as collecting has been our passion these past years, Billie and I realize it got away from us. We lost our way. So we're giving our collection away. Items we can't return to the rightful owners, we're going to give to the museums, Canadian and American, depending on which country they come from."

We chatted for a few minutes more before they left with promises to keep in touch. But as I watched the black Lincoln disappear through the trees, I couldn't help but feel that this would be the last time I would see either of them. Once Billie was gone, who knew how much longer Ed would last on his own.

As I climbed the verandah stairs, the phone started ringing. I ran to get it.

"Sorry, Meg, I won't be able to make it." Teht'aa's voice sounded happy. "Turns out Owl Lake didn't need my dad, so he's come home. But here, let me pass the phone to him. He wants to talk to you."

R.J. Harlick, an escapee from the high tech jungle, divides her time between her home in Ottawa and a log cabin in West Quebec. A lover of the outdoors, she can often be found roaming the surrounding forests or canoeing the waterways. Because of this love for the untamed wilds, she decided that she would bring its seductive allure alive in her writings.

The River Runs Orange is the third novel in the Meg Harris series, the sequel to *Death's Golden Whisper* and *Red Ice for a Shroud.*

More information on R.J. Harlick is available online at www.rjharlick.ca